Praise for

TESSA BAILEY

"Tessa disarms you with a laugh, heats things up past boiling, and then puts a squeeze inside your heart. The tenderness, vulnerability, and heat I am always guaranteed with a Tessa Bailey book are the reasons she is one of my all-time favorite authors."

—Sally Thorne, bestselling author of
The Hating Game

"Her voice feels as fresh and contemporary as a Netflix rom-com...Bailey writes banter and rom-com scenarios with aplomb, but for those who like their romance on the spicier side, she's also the Michelangelo of dirty talk."

—*Entertainment Weekly*

"Bailey crafts an entertainingly spicy tale, with humor and palpable sexual tension." —*Publishers Weekly*

"Tessa Bailey writes pure magic!"

—Alexis Daria, bestselling author of
You Had Me at Hola

"When you read a book by Bailey, there are two things you can always count on: sexy, rapid-fire dialogue, and scorching love scenes..." —*BookPage*

"[A] singular talent for writing romantic chemistry that is both sparkling sweet and explosively sexy...one of the genre's very best."

—Kate Clayborn, author of *Love at First*

Line of Duty
Protecting What's His
Protecting What's Theirs (novella)
His Risk to Take
Officer Off Limits
Asking for Trouble
Staking His Claim

Serve
Owned by Fate
Exposed by Fate
Driven by Fate

Beach Kingdom
Mouth to Mouth
Heat Stroke
Sink or Swim

Phenomenal Fate
Reborn Yesterday
This Time Tomorrow
Today Tomorrow and Always

Standalone Books
Unfixable
Baiting the Maid of Honor
The Major's Welcome Home
Captivated (with Eve Dangerfield)
Getaway Girl
Runaway Girl
Window Shopping
My Killer Vacation
Follow

TOO HARD TO
FORGET

TESSA BAILEY

FOREVER

NEW YORK   BOSTON

Forever
Hachette Book Group
1290 Avenue of the Americas, New York, NY 10104
read-forever.com
twitter.com/readforeverpub

Originally published by Forever in April 2017
First trade paperback edition: October 2022

Forever is an imprint of Grand Central Publishing. The Forever name and logo are trademarks of Hachette Book Group, Inc.

The publisher is not responsible for websites (or their content) that are not owned by the publisher.

The Hachette Speakers Bureau provides a wide range of authors for speaking events. To find out more, go to www.hachettespeakersbureau.com or call (866) 376-6591.

ISBNs: 978-1-4555-9418-4 (mass market), 978-1-4555-9419-1 (ebook),
        978-1-5387-4184-9 (trade paperback)

Printed in the United States of America

LSC-C

Printing 2, 2022

For Eagle

ACKNOWLEDGMENTS

Is it crazy that I want to acknowledge the characters most of all? They're the stars here and I've just been living in their world. I don't know why they decided I was worthy of having their stories whispered in my ear, but I love these Clarksons so damn much, it's crazy. I can't believe the third leg of their trip is already over, one more to go. With each book, I've felt a little part of myself heal along with the family, but I can't even tell you (specifically) what part of me was damaged in the first place. Only that I *needed* them and this road trip. So many family rifts out there, so many stubborn aunts and cousins and fathers who can't say what they're thinking. Daughters, too. I'm one of them. Maybe I'm saying my peace through the siblings.

In order to write this book—and every book—I received the help of a few wonderful, patient people. As always, my family comes first. Patrick and Mackenzie, you make this possible. I love you more than anything I could write here. Thank you for being mine. My editor at Forever Romance, Madeleine Colavita, this was our John Harbaugh book since the beginning and we totally did the man, the myth, the legend, justice! Thank you for your all star edits. My grandmother, Violet, whose real life siblings inspired these stories. I hope Peggy was every bit as wonderful as your sister, Peggy. Thank you for letting me have them for a while. Eagle at Aquila Editing (to whom this book is dedicated), for loving Peggy the best and being a fabulous beta, longtime reader, and friend. Thank you all so very much!

TOO HARD TO FORGET

PROLOGUE

Miriam Clarkson, January 13

Would it surprise you (whoever you are) to know that Peggy is the most complicated of my children? If she has fluttered into your orbit for a short amount of time, as her four fiancés have done (I liked the second guy well enough, but the rest were self-indulgent twats), your impression of her might include the following: pampered baby of the family, takes nothing seriously, shallow, out for a good time.

You would be . . . right.

But that's because you've only been allowed to see the top layer.

Look closer.

Peggy is a Rubik's Cube. Just when I think I've got one whole side fashioned into a solid red block, a white square twists into place and throws off everything. Where I could predict Aaron, Rita, and Belmont most of the time, Peggy would be the type to send me a selfie as she jumped from a plane, parachute strapped to her back.

After college, her unpredictable nature changed, however. It became more frantic. Less about having fun and more about...distracting herself from something with an adrenaline rush. I didn't try hard enough to find out what high she was chasing and then the appropriate window grew smaller and smaller. I worried she might find my concern forced or, worse, phony.

Fuck. This is getting pretty heavy, isn't it?

Bottom line: I sucked at momming. Thankfully, being mediocre in the parenting department didn't preclude me from seeing beneath the caramelized top layer of Peggy's crème brûlée. Someone took a fork and dragged it straight through the middle, leaving division among Peggy's already split personalities. Sweetness used to exist at the forefront, but now it battles for visibility among the other components, the hurt and confusion and self-doubt.

Peggy the bombshell. Peggy the liar. Peggy the mediator. Peggy the grief-stricken. The angel. The devil. The baby. The old soul.

You never know what you're going to get.

Especially now.

But look closer. She's not what you're expecting.

CHAPTER ONE

Once, when hanging a picture of Audrey Hepburn in her bedroom, Peggy had smashed her index finger with a hammer, leaving a permanent black spot beneath her fingernail shaped a little bit like George Washington's silhouette on the quarter. She put on a coat of nail polish every day—usually red—to hide it.

She stared in confusion now at the nails she'd covered in varnish only this morning, while waiting for food at the drive-through. How could it be chipped already? The metallic taste in her mouth suggested she'd chewed off the polish, but she would have remembered that, right? George's dark silhouette slowly turned his head and winked at her, so smug in his founding fatherness. *Oh man, I'm losing it.*

It was the sign that had gotten to her. *Welcome to Ohio.* They'd passed it a mile back and she'd been sparring with the urge to throw up ever since.

"Pull over, Bel." Peggy shot forward in her seat, giving

a series of taps on the back of her brother's headrest. "Can you just pull over?"

Belmont's eyes were steady on her in the rearview mirror, holding for a too-long handful of seconds, before he nodded, pulling the Suburban into the next rest stop. She tried to open the door before the vehicle even stopped rolling, but Belmont hit the lock button, as if predicting her move, earning the driver's seat a frustrated kick. As always, her brother took his sweet time locating a space, allowing a family of three to pass, before parking and shutting off the ignition.

At the absence of the ever-present engine rumble, their third and final traveling companion, Sage Alexander, stirred, her mouth opening wide on a yawn. Peggy watched Belmont and Sage exchange a "good morning, oh, center of my gravity" look, and that was all she could take.

Peggy pushed open the Suburban's back door, sucking in deep breaths through her nose as she traversed the littered patch of grass and asphalt toward the rest stop bathroom. The air around her was cold, damp, and charged, fragrant with the recent rain. Behind her, the sound of interstate traffic sounded so alien, she felt like a stranger in her own body in this unfamiliar place. People lived here year-round, going to jobs, taking their kids to school, shopping at the mall, and they would never even know she'd passed through. There was something both comforting and terrifying about that.

Before Peggy entered the beige, concrete structure, she glanced back at the Suburban to find Belmont and Peggy still staring at each other, neither of their mouths moving. Something awful and unwanted stabbed her in the chest. She didn't want to be this person. The resentful one who turned away from any sign of happiness in others. But how could she be anyone else? How?

In a matter of two weeks, she'd lost two siblings, Rita and Aaron, to love. And she was sure as shit on her way to losing a third in Belmont, if he ever woke up and smelled Sage's bacon. Being surrounded by so much magic was almost enough to make her believe a second chance at the real thing was possible for her.

It wasn't so far-fetched, was it? She had a college degree, great hair, and made damn good conversation. "Congratulations, you'd be the perfect trophy wife." She laughed under her breath. Love, or even the illusion of it, wouldn't be happening anytime soon, though. Not until she accomplished her mission in Cincinnati.

Facing the restroom once again, Peggy passed through the curved tunnel to find the bathroom empty. She came to a stop in front of the foggy mirror, her gaze landing on the string of engagement rings dangling around her neck. A little shimmy of her shoulders had the expensive baubles—symbols of her shame—clinking together with an eerie sound in the silent bathroom, layered with the plop of dripping water, the distant whoosh of traffic.

When the Clarkson siblings—and Sage, who'd arrived later—set out on this road trip from San Diego to New York, united in the responsibility to fulfill their mother Miriam's final wish of jumping into the Atlantic Ocean on New Year's Day, Peggy hadn't expected to reach Cincinnati so fast.

One more mile to campus and she would be sharing oxygen with Elliott Brooks. Coach Elliott Brooks. The man she'd let ruin her for all others.

This weekend, Peggy would be returning the favor.

Deep down inside her, something needed repairing. Rebounds hadn't worked. Facing her heartache only made it more real. Too much time had been wasted trying to patch up the gash herself, so she would be making Elliott's life hell. That's right. This chicken had come home to roost and she was extra crispy. After this weekend, she'd be walking away with the upper hand, as opposed to a bleeding heart. It was her last-ditch option. Her last chance to finally move on. Giving the coach a taste of his own medicine meant Peggy wouldn't have to swallow it anymore.

The sound of light footsteps signaled the approach of Peggy's best friend, and she quickly bent at the waist, then flipped her hair back, striking a pose just in time to greet Sage with an exaggerated wink in the mirror. "What were you dreaming about in that passenger seat, huh? Sex? Were you dreaming of a hairy mountain man stealing your virginity? Spill it, Alexander."

As expected, Sage sputtered, fingers knitting together at her throat. "No! I—a mountain man? I wouldn't even know what one l-looks like—"

"Sorry, I confused your dream with mine." Peggy pulled her blond curls into a messy bun, twirling the escapees around a digit. "But you were definitely moaning."

"Was I? Oh my—" In the mirror, she watched Sage square her shoulders. "You're just trying to distract me."

Peggy pasted a blasé smile on her face. "Why would I do that?"

"I wish I knew."

Outside, Belmont tapped the recognizable horn of the Suburban and they both jerked toward the door, but stopped before they could obey their mutual instinct to follow her older brother's bidding. "It's alumni weekend at the university, okay? That's all." Peggy leaned back against the sink and crossed her arms. "I'm just a little nervous about running into the old squad. You think the wedding planning business is brutal? Try impressing a dozen cheerleaders who expect to find any day now they're a long-lost princess."

Sage chuckled, a bloom spreading across her cheeks. "Oh. I would be nervous, too. If I was going to see old classmates. Everyone weighing their accomplishments against one another." A funny expression made Sage appear apprehensive, as though she were considering what her own reunion would be like. And didn't like what she imagined. She took a few steps, closing herself into a stall. "I'm glad you told me."

Peggy swallowed the ball of guilt in her throat. "Yeah."

* * *

Peggy couldn't pinpoint what drew her toward the tunnel. The football game was going to start in just fifteen minutes, and she was supposed to be leading the Bearcat cheerleading squad's warm-ups. But just like always, she was aware of his presence. On the field, pacing the sideline, terse instructions being delivered into his headset, while eagle eyes watched the team stretch and prepare. And in the same way she never failed to sense him nearby, his absence was having the opposite effect now. Instead of feeling hot and full, her stomach was cold and empty.

Pom-poms in hand, Peggy walked on the balls of her feet down the silent, airless hall leading to the football team's locker room. She had no authorization to be there but couldn't ignore the pull. She'd find him back there. The man who watched her as if she were the Promised Land one moment, hell the next.

Elliott Brooks. Head coach of the Bearcats. Two-time recipient of the Coach of the Year award. Uncompromising hard-ass known for demanding perfection not only from his team, but himself. Devout Catholic. They called him the Kingmaker, because so many of his players had gone on to be first round NFL draft picks. That man. The one who visited her bed nightly.

Well. In her dreams anyway. In real life, they'd never exchanged a single word. Their long, secretive glances were a language all their own, though. When cheerleading and football practices intersected, his burning coal eyes moved over her like a brush fire.

What are you looking at? *his gaze seemed to ask. But in the same glance, she could read the contradicting subtext.* Don't you *dare* look at anyone on this field but me.

Give me one good reason, *she would blink back, cocking a hip.*

And he would. Commanding the field with a whip crack command, stalking the sidelines like a predatory creature, seeing all, commenting only when strictly necessary. Those eyes would sneak back to her, though. Without fail. Their message would read, I'm a man among boys. There's your reason.

Or she'd imagined everything and the telepathic communication was in her head alone. A scary possibility…and one she couldn't bring herself to believe. Was it finally time to find out?

The crowd's excitement followed Peggy down the long tunnel, fading the closer she came to the locker room. That's when she heard the heavy, measured breaths. The forceful clearing of a man's throat.

His *throat.*

Before she could second-guess her sanity, Peggy stepped into the off-limits room, dropping her pom-poms and slamming back against the wall under the weight of his attention. It snapped against her skin like an open hand. God, he was gorgeous, even in his sudden fury. Hard bodied, golden from the sun, and righteously male, all stubbled and tall and full of might. The muscles of her abdomen squeezed—squeezed—along with her thighs as he stormed over, his words being directed at her for the very first time.

"What the hell do you think you're doing here?"

Don't lose your nerve now. Years. She'd been watching him for years. Since she'd entered the university as a freshman. Watched his triumphs from afar. And the horrible tragedy, still so recent. So fresh. "You should be on the field."

Elliott's crack of masculine laugher held no humor. "And you thought it was your job to come get me, cheerleader?"

So condescending. But accompanied by his raking glance down her thighs and belly...she couldn't help but be turned on by it. She loved him addressing her at all. Finally. "Yeah. I did. Everyone else is probably too scared of you."

Dark eyes narrowing, he stepped closer. So close, she almost whimpered, the fantasies having taken such a deep hold, her longing was on a hair-trigger. "Well, you were wrong. It's not your job. So pick up your sparkly bullshit and move out."

"They're called pom-poms and I'll leave when I'm good and ready." With an incredulous expression, Elliott started to move away, telling Peggy she needed to work fast. Toward what goal? She'd come with no plan. Had never expected to actually speak to this man in her life. "I've seen you watching me."

He froze, a muscle leaping in his cheek. "You were mistaken."

"No. I wasn't. I'm not." She wet her lips, gaining confi-

dence when his eyes followed the movement and she saw the hunger. The same hunger she'd watched grow, even while he begrudged it, over the course of the last few months. Since the tragedy. "You don't have to feel ashamed about it. Not now."

His fists planted on either side of her head with a bash, shaking the lockers, then his face hovered mere inches away. "What would you know about shame?"

Wetness rushed between Peggy's thighs as his apples and mint scent took hold of her throat like a giant metal hook. "I know the last six months were awful for you. They would be so hard for anyone. But especially you, because you carry everyone on your back. The whole school lives for Saturdays. If you'll win or lose." His brow furrowed, his scrutiny so intense, she wondered how her legs kept from giving out. They must have moved closer without realizing, because the tips of Peggy's breasts grazed Elliott's chest and he groaned. A harsh, guttural sound that might as well have been a symphony, it was so welcome to her ears.

"You..." His throat flexed. "You don't know anything about me, Peggy."

Her pulse went haywire. The wordless communication hadn't been imaginary. Those hard eyes really had been speaking to her. It was the way he said Peggy. As though he'd tested her name on his tongue a million times. "You know my name."

"I shouldn't," he grated, pressing closer, so she could feel he'd been affected below the belt. Very affected. "Damn you."

"You only mean that half the time. And I do know things about you. You have a different coaching style for each player based on their strengths and weaknesses. When they changed the coffee lids in the campus coffee shop, you kept *ripping off the extra little flap until finally you started drinking without the lid. Because you hate anything loose or unnecessary, don't you? I can tell your mood by the way you watch me on certain days, because I watch you, too,"* she whispered. *"Sometimes you're damning me. The rest of the time, you're wondering what I'd feel like—"*

"Stop."

"Or if I'd let you." A slow beat passed. "I would. I am. But not because you're the Kingmaker or some other ridiculous title. Maybe I'm not letting you at all. Maybe this is me begging." The B word liquefied her knees, as if they wanted to hit the ground and implore him in earnest. "You've been so strong and I—I want to feel that strength. Want you to feel mine. You're taking all the blame for what happened and—"

"Shut your mouth." His forehead ground against hers. "Shut your beautiful, ripe, little mouth."

Desire thickening in her blood like oil, Peggy removed one of the hands he'd fisted on the locker, lowering it to the space between her legs. His nostrils flared, hot exhales bathing her face, eyelids slamming to a close. But she didn't let his massive presence intimidate her. One by one, she smoothed open his curled fingers, then cupped Elliott's hand at the juncture of her thighs, encouraging him with a roll of her hips to mold the flesh beneath the built-in panties of her cheerleading skirt.

"It's okay to need this."

"No." His denial was a near-roar. "It's not."

Before the words had fully fled his mouth, Peggy went up on her toes and fused their lips together, pancake batter folding and folding in her stomach. His mouth was hard, his cheeks rough even though they were shaven. But the taste of apples and mint, and the grudging, restrained returning of the kiss, made him too addictive to stop. The battle inside him only went on a few seconds, until their tongues met, and then Peggy was plastered between his ruthlessly fit body and the lockers, his hand treating the private place between her thighs with nothing short of disrespect.

When he jerked aside the thin, red material and slipped a finger into her heat, shoving it deep with a grunt and a twist, Peggy flew across the bridge toward an orgasm, anticipating it in the tips of her toes, the downward pull in her belly.

"I can't do this," Elliott growled, before taking her mouth in another no-holds-barred wrestling of tongues and teeth. "I can't. You're too young—you're a student and I'm... Peggy, I haven't been thinking clearly."

Oh God, if he stopped, she would drop dead from disappointment. Her head spun, tummy clenching, lungs seizing with short, desperate breaths. But through it all, his obvious pain permeated, drawing them into the eye of the storm together. "This isn't wrong. Wanting me isn't wrong." Her hands shook between their bodies as she unfastened his tailored, black pants, lowering the zipper. The groan that left his mouth when she gripped his generous length and stroked would stay with her forever; it was so forceful and relieved and miserable, all at once. "Let go of what happened, just for a little while. We're the only ones here. Just you and me." She raised her left leg, hooking it around his hip, whispering, "I'm on the pill."

With a jagged breath, Elliott grabbed up Peggy's other leg, drawing it high around his waist as she guided his arousal toward her core. He entered her with a biting slam against the locker door, releasing the vilest of epithets into her ear. "Jesus Christ. This is what sin feels like," he rasped. "Wrong and right, at the same time. Life and death.

Blond, long-legged, and tight." A violent pounding of his erection into her already contracting flesh. "I should start saying my penance now, because it could take years to make up for the thoughts you've put in my head. And now I'm acting on them."

His hips moved faster, pinning Peggy's bottom to the locker, rattling it...rolling her eyes back in her head until the climax broke like a cresting wave, turning her thighs to conductors of vibration. "Oh...oh my God...please."

"Don't talk about God to me." His sweating forehead wedged into the cradle of her neck. "You're the reason I'm forsaking him."

"No," Peggy breathed, planting kisses on his mouth, his cheeks. "No one is perfect. Not all the time. Not even you." Her panting breaths were making her ribs ache, but his hardness moving in her body eclipsed any discomfort with bliss. So much bliss. "You don't have to be...faultless with me. Not right now."

Hard eyes lifted, snagging hers. "Which way do I have to be?"

The glimpse of vulnerability in Elliott—a man touted as Godlike in his genius and determination—raced through Peggy's veins like a drug. Had she really been the catalyst that drew out his undiscovered weakness? "Human."

As soon as she issued the word, she felt it spear him, could almost hear the effect it had. He was looking at her differently now, like she were a new discovery he'd made, but didn't fully understand. "You feel like ruin...but I can't stop. Can't stop." Coarse hands climbed up Peggy's thighs, wedging between her body and the locker to grip her backside. "Our father, who art in heaven..." The sound of wet flesh meeting began, as his pace increased. "Hallowed be thy name..."

CHAPTER TWO

Elliott Brooks hated banners.

Most of the time, he could accomplish tunnel vision, seeing nothing other than the green, manicured grass, the yellow practice jerseys, the white lines on his field. But the banners, they were so damn...colorful. They were a fishhook in his subconscious, trying to tug him back to the living and he resented it. Almost as much as the juvenile phrases splashed across the front.

Bearcats on the prrrrowl. Hell. He'd been looking at that damn banner flapping in the breeze since yesterday, when his entire focus needed to be on the practice taking place in front of him. They were matched up against Temple on Saturday and it would be the toughest game of the season. Unfortunately, their staunchest competition was rolling into town on alumni weekend.

Once a year, the University of Cincinnati invited gradu-ates back into the fold, making a big production of their glorious return and every ridiculous activity centered around his field, distracting his players. Goddamn Alumni Week. Hadn't four years on campus been enough? Some of them had graduated a matter of months ago, and already they needed reminding they were special? It was nothing but a pain in the ass. The marching band starting and stopping, instructions being called out—*Raise the banner! Now lower it!*—dancers twirling ribbons, cheerleaders chanting, newspaper reporters slinking around, somehow more tolerated than usual because of the almighty spirit of alumni week.

Elliott didn't have the spirit. He wanted everyone to clear the fuck out so he could worry about winning some football. Isn't that what everyone wanted from him? Victories? Another trophy for the front office?

Of course they did. At age thirty-eight, it was the one thing Elliott could be relied on to do successfully. Win games.

Across the field, a fresh group of smiling people appeared in the stands, wearing Bearcats sweatshirts, but clearly too old to be students. More alums looking to rekindle their memories, while he strove to forget his own.

Nonetheless, Elliott couldn't help himself. He scanned their faces, giving a jerky nod to no one in particular when he didn't recognize any of them. *She won't be here. She never comes. Stop looking for her.*

"Drill's over, Coach. You want to run the offense?"

Elliott cleared his throat way too loudly, thankful for the offensive coordinator's interruption. Damn, how long had his attention been off the field? Every year. Every year he did this to himself. "Our tight end is dragging ass completing his routes. Let's run every play in the book that gets him the ball until he wakes up."

"Ten-four."

Mentally running through the balance of what they

needed to cover before he called practice to a close, Elliott went back to consulting his clipboard. A chorus of squeals from the assembled cheerleaders—past and present—broke his concentration and he gritted his teeth, assuming another one of their long-lost members had returned from on high. Against his good judgment, he'd already checked that none of them were *her*. No need to look again and feel another damning swoop of disappointment.

It wasn't until he heard the voice that hell broke loose in his chest.

"All right. Who do I have to blow around here to get a decent toe touch?"

Elliott's grip on the clipboard went so tight, the heavy plastic cracked. He took several restoring breaths through his nose and mentally counted to ten, before lifting his head. Outwardly, his attention appeared to be on the cycling offense, but his gaze was cut to the side, where at least two dozen girls swarmed no other than Peggy Clarkson.

Lord, he shouldn't have looked. But then again, he'd never been able to keep his eyes off her, had he? He'd never had the problem before Peggy, or since. They were all students to Elliott, easily compartmentalized. Except for this one girl.

A woman now, he saw, and hell if she wasn't twice as incredible.

Our father, who art in heaven, hallowed be thy name...

The prayer went off like a shot in his mind, playing defense against the gorgeous image she presented standing in the area past the end zone in the patch of winter sunlight. She wore black tights...the thicker kind you couldn't see through. Leggings, he thought they might be called. Leather boots climbed up past her knees to wrap around thighs she'd once opened for him. Eagerly. They led to the firm temptation of her bottom, which he'd once asked her to keep covered in public, during a moment of weakness in the dark, while she took his thrusts. But the fitted, white long-sleeved shirt and furry black vest cut off at her thin waist, inviting everyone to look.

Just like him. Elliott was no longer making any attempt to hide his scrutiny of the new arrival. All the while, he polished the black rosary beads in his pocket, as if acknowledging the weaknesses of his flesh might excuse him for falling victim. A discreet throat clearing from his offensive coordinator told him his interest hadn't gone unnoticed, either. "You need something, Wayne?" Elliott demanded.

Wayne bent forward to prop both hands on his knees, wisely putting his attention back on practice. "Hey, no judgments here." The other man tipped his head toward the animated pack of cheerleaders and shot Elliott a look that bordered on apprehensive. "Even I remember *that* one, and I'm so far off the market, I don't even remember what it looks like."

That one. Peggy.

Of course Wayne remembered her. She was impossible to forget.

Didn't mean Elliott wouldn't continue to try. With a vengeance.

She's a married woman. He'd given away his chance. Thrown it right to the wind, and lamenting his decision now wasn't just pointless, it was masochistic.

Garnering his will, Elliott turned his back on Peggy's location and...immediately found someone fucking up his formation. Five someones, actually. This was why he resented distractions. They removed focus from the only two constants in his life: football and religion. He'd once allowed the balance to be upset between God and the sport, and as a result, a life had been lost. God's way of telling him his path in life was unchangeable. He'd been sent to this university to win football games and set an example, to guide good men to better futures, a responsibility entrusted to him by their parents.

And in between, he muddled his way through being a parent himself.

Elliott wouldn't allow himself time for anything else. He'd chosen football over his family, including his wife. Including his devoutly religious parents, who'd never understood his fascination with the sport. But three years ago, he'd found someone—the *only* someone—who'd been capable of tempting him away from his responsibilities. Away from his well-deserved guilt. Hope had flared so brightly, he could still remember feeling blinded. But he'd made his choice to live with the guilt. Away from her light.

A choice he refused to question or he risked insanity.

Elliott had made his bed, now he would lie in it. If he didn't win games, didn't bring home victories, his sacrificing of those who'd had the misfortune of coming into his life would be for nothing. Football had severed his one attempt at making a family, having a relationship with someone off the field, and it wouldn't happen again. Not in this lifetime.

* * *

Elliott had just blown the whistle to end practice when he felt Peggy approach at his back. Or rather, his players started shoving one another, throwing their chins in his direction like a pack of jackasses. Had he not put the fear of God into these men yet? Tomorrow's practice was going to be hell.

The hell of right now concerned him more, however. In a matter of seconds, he'd be in her presence again. Her. And there was a good reason for his team and fellow coaches to be staring with their mouths open while Peggy probably swayed up like a runway model. Not only was she a bombshell that always seemed poised to go off any second, but no one *ever* approached him.

Peggy had no such problem, apparently. In fact, before Elliott even turned around, he could sense her reveling in not giving a fuck, and panic slid into his blood like a sea monster. *She's gotten even braver.* Brave enough to divert his path again?

No. Not after all the work he'd done to lay the brickwork.

During those months of madness her senior year, she'd come to him at night. Or vice versa. When no one else was around. They'd be on each other before the sound of the knock even faded. Without restraint. No boundaries. Zero patience.

Being near her was too much of a danger to a man whose entire life was made up of rules. Rules that kept him from looking right or left. Straight ahead only.

Furthermore, someone had been smart enough to keep her.

Someone other than Elliott.

"*Head to the showers,*" he boomed too loudly, perversely pleased when everyone moved at once, without hesitating, like he'd conditioned them to do. "We'll be back here tomorrow, bright and early. Scrimmage against the B squad."

"Yes, Coach."

"Yes, Coach," came the amused feminine echo behind him. He thought the hour since Peggy arrived had given him time to prepare, but he was wrong. When he turned around, his gut screwed up like a fist. Fuck. Still the most beautiful woman he'd ever seen. It was more than just her blond pinup looks, though, wasn't it? Always had been. There was enough sharp wit in those dark gold eyes for a man to get lost. Like he'd almost done. And the wit was only a gateway to the compassion she'd spread over him like warm oil, enticing him to forgive himself. She was so *much*. Too much.

"Peggy," Elliott rasped, transferring his clipboard to the crook of his arm, so they could shake hands. A reflexive move. That was how he operated. Handshakes. Giving hugs and kissing cheeks weren't part of his day. But even the muscle memory couldn't make it feel natural. Not with her.

One of Peggy's eyebrows arched at his outstretched hand, but she recovered, twining their fingers together slowly. At the zing of static, the corner of her mouth jumped, like they'd traded a secret, and God help him, his cock thickened in his jeans. "Elliott," she murmured. "You look exactly the same."

He took his hand back out of necessity. "Three years isn't all that long."

"No, I guess not." For just a second, he thought her flirtatious smile turned forced, but it came back with such a glow, he figured it was his imagination. "It was long enough for them to put a giant statue of you at the entrance." Her teeth sank into that full lower lip and held, just enough to drive him a little insane. "I bet you hate it, don't you?"

"Yes." Damn. It didn't seem possible so much time had passed since they'd stood across from each other. Not when she could still call his bullshit a mile away, the way no one else ever had. "They could have waited until I was dead or retired."

"When it comes to you, I don't think those things are mutually exclusive." She hummed in her throat, her gaze tripping over his chest, lower. "Anyway, they already think you're God, so your immortality is a reasonable assumption." When she took a step closer, he almost dropped the clipboard. In favor of staving her off or yanking her closer? He had no idea. But she only lifted a finger, trailing the smooth pad across the seam of his lips. "The sculptor didn't get your mouth right, though. It's much more generous, isn't it?" Elliott snagged her wrist and her eyes lit with challenge. "Or maybe the sculptor just hasn't experienced it the way I have."

Lust and irritation joined forces in his blood, making it boil. "What the hell do you think you're doing here, Peggy?"

The seduction in her expression lost steam. "That's the first thing you ever said to me." She visibly shook herself, tugging her hand from his grip. "I'm here for alumni weekend. Obviously."

Still stuck on the former statement she'd made, it took him a moment to catch up. "You've never come before."

He counted three breaths from her mouth. "Noticed, did you?"

Time out. He would've called one if they were in the middle of a game and both sides were firing too hot, swinging on the unpredictable vines of momentum. In many ways, this confrontation so far had been a game. A testing of each other's strengths. Well, they were standing on *his* field. And on his field, he didn't deal well with surprises and unknowns. Time to put everything out in the open, even though he could feel acid rising in his throat. "Are you here with your husband?"

She froze so long, he wondered if she would answer him at all. "Um. No, he—he's back in California." A wrinkle appeared between her eyebrows. "I wasn't sure... I—I didn't know if you received the wedding invitation. You were moving houses when I left Cincinnati and—"

"My mail was forwarded," Elliott said, his voice low. "I got it."

Peggy backed away with an uneven nod. The currents running between them had changed so abruptly, but he couldn't decide on a reason. He'd admit to mentioning her husband as a way to throw up a necessary wall between them, but—

Elliott's phone rang.

He cursed, digging the device from his back pocket, frowning down at his daughter's name where it flashed on the screen. "Alice," he said to Peggy, without thinking. "She should be in theater rehearsal."

"You should answer it," Peggy said, still backing away from him. Way too quickly. "Maybe I'll see you around—"

"Hold on." He should have let her go. God knew he should have. But Elliott didn't walk away from an interaction without a final score on the board. "Just stay right there."

She tilted her head. "I'm not one of your players."

"Please," he growled.

When Peggy shrugged—and stayed put—Elliott answered the phone, teen angst meeting his ear in full stereo. "Dad, I have to change schools. My fucking life is over. You don't understand—"

"Watch your language. And you haven't given me a chance to understand."

A closemouthed shriek scraped down the line. One with which he was well acquainted. "Kim Steinberg broke her leg skiing this weekend and I'm the understudy for her character in *The Music Man* and I don't have the lines memorized. I faked my way through it because she's never even missed a day of school. Like, ever. Why would she want to stay home when she looks like that?" The sounds of papers being rustled came through the line. "Oh God, oh God. I took the bus home early so I wouldn't have to face drama practice. The fucking performance is in five days and I—I don't even know why I'm telling you this. You don't give a shit about my life."

Elliott watched Peggy's expression melt into soft sympathy, whether for him or Alice, he didn't know, but it was too reminiscent of those times he'd confided in her. A rarity for him, to say the least, and something he had no right to miss. "Five days seems more than sufficient to memorize the lines." He pressed the heel of his hand into his eye socket. "I have a few more hours here watching game film, but when I get home—"

"I never ask you for anything, Dad." Her breath snagged on the final word. "I just need help with this. Please. You don't understand."

Guilt battled against the never-ending pressure to win, win at all costs. "Alice," he said tightly. "We're playing Temple on Saturday—"

Peggy laid a hand on his arm. "I can go," she whispered, looking a little surprised at herself for making the offer. That made two of them.

"Hold on a second, Alice." Elliott covered the phone with his hand. Trying not to be obvious, he sucked in the sugar-sweet scent of Peggy. She'd swept it forward on her second approach, and it brought forth memories of her head thrown back on his pillow, her mouth laughing into his neck. "That's not necessary."

"It sounds pretty necessary." She took back her touch, fingers curling into her palm, and Elliott rejected the impulse to smooth them back out between his hands. "Maybe just tell her I'm from the school...a fellow faculty member."

Elliott couldn't hide his skepticism. "You still look more like a student."

She wet her lips in slow motion. "Noticed, did you?" Her low, seductive laugh made his boxer briefs feel two sizes too small. "I'm not meeting with my assigned alumni committee until tomorrow morning. My evening is free." No longer meeting his eyes, she shrugged. "And I know what it's like to lose your mother before you're ready, so I have that in common with Alice. She probably doesn't even know she needs the girl time."

Was that true? Before his wife's death, he and Alice had a relationship similar to the one he'd had with his parents. Functional. He'd been responsible, showing up to school events and teacher meetings when it counted, but never mastering the elusive closeness other fathers and daughters seemed to have. When he'd been with Peggy, right after Judith's passing, there'd been some progress. Peggy had forced him to open his eyes and see that Alice needed her father. He'd tried to maintain that uphill climb, but over time, they'd slipped back into how they'd been before. Functioning. If she needed something—especially girl time—he'd probably be the last to know.

"I'm sorry. I didn't know about your mother." He itched to reach out, run a thumb over the curve of her cheekbone. "I appreciate your offer, but I think we both know any kind of involvement with one another is a bad idea."

"*Involvement* is a pretty strong word." A smile teased her lips, but didn't reach her eyes. "You're worried for nothing."

"It's never nothing with you."

She held his gaze a long moment, before turning away. "Text me your address, Elliott. My number hasn't changed."

CHAPTER THREE

Peggy had spent three years working in retail as a personal shopper so she'd dealt with an abundance of attitudes, which she'd divided into three neat categories.

Number one: the tourist. The women who came in without a hot cent to spend, but couldn't quite hide their guilt over wasting her time. They did that upside-down smile, shoulder scrunch as they sent her running out into the store to pick up designer labels that would never make the cash register ding. But although they didn't help Peggy out in the commission department, they were her favorite, because they treated her like an equal and tried to set her up with their sons. Which Peggy never took them up on. Except for those five times.

Number two: the professionals. These women knew exactly what they wanted and didn't bother looking up from their phones while rattling off sizes and label preferences. Not fun appointments by any stretch of spandex, but the easiest, by far.

And then there was number three: the hell creatures. A retail worker's worst nightmare, these women took great satisfaction in making others bust their asses. They had no idea what they wanted, but they knew it wasn't *that* ugly thing. Peggy had spent many hours attempting to appease hell creatures, wondering why she was wasting her college degree fitting women for outfits in which to kill everyone's buzz at a party. Oh, she could *guess* the reason—if she were into psychological self-diagnosis. Which she was not.

Especially as she stood on Elliott's porch, still reeling over his assumption she'd spent the last three years married. And how she'd done nothing to correct him.

Not only had he sent her packing, but he'd lived through her wedding day without giving it a second thought. He really *hadn't* wanted something serious with her. The dreaded confirmation should have been enough to send her diving back into the Suburban and leaving Ohio in the dust, but instead, Elliott's lack of action had the opposite effect. Before she left this town, he was going to question his indifference. Regret it. That's why she was there. No getting caught in emotional rat traps.

Closing her eyes on a calming breath, she reached out to ring the doorbell. Noticing the black spot glaring back from beneath her fingernail, she tucked it into her fist and knocked instead.

When Alice Brooks opened the front door to Elliott's new house, it took Peggy less than ten seconds to categorize the preteen. However, Alice was in no way typical or expected; the Plinko disk, bouncing back and forth between two options, neither of which felt right. Huh. A tourist disguised as a hell creature. Peggy hadn't even been aware those existed.

Alice looked Peggy over from top to bottom, then hid

half her body behind the door frame. The move was self-conscious, especially when paired with a fifty-watt glare. "Who are you?"

"I'm Peggy. Didn't you father tell you I was coming?"

"Yes." She stared down at Peggy's boots. "You don't look like a teacher."

Peggy fluffed her hair. "Maybe my students just got lucky."

While the redhead examined her a second and third time, Peggy tried not to be obvious about doing the same. During the whirlwind of senior year, she'd only been to Elliott's home on two occasions. Both of those times, Alice had been staying with her aunt, so Peggy had only ever seen the young girl in pictures. Photographs on the fireplace mantle she'd managed to snatch a glance at while Elliott was in the bathroom or getting them drink refills in the kitchen.

At the beginning of her relationship with Elliott, the topic of Judith Brooks—Elliott's deceased wife—had been broached carefully. Over time, he confided just enough about their marriage for Peggy to understand they hadn't been close. The specifics of Judith's death, however, were as public as possible. One afternoon in winter, while Elliott was coaching football practice, Judith had slipped on a patch of ice on the driveway, hit her head, and gone into a deep coma. It lasted six months, the woman's health deteriorating, before Elliott had been forced to make the painful decision to take her off life support.

On the drive over, Peggy hadn't known what to expect, finally coming face-to-face with such a huge part of her ex-lover's life. As a college senior, she'd feared the possibility of being jealous over a child created with another woman. But Peggy was relieved as hell to feel nothing but sympathy for this young girl who'd spent the last four years without a mother. At least when Miriam passed, Peggy had been a self-sufficient adult (well, mostly) with siblings to lean on for support (just kidding).

Peggy put a warm smile on her face. "Are you going to ask me in, or should we run lines out here on the porch?"

Alice rolled her lips inward and stepped back, giving just enough room for Peggy to enter. Against her chest, she clutched a stapled bunch of papers, the words *The Music Man* in a bold, heavy font on the front. "Do you even know anything about this play?"

"Negative, Captain." Peggy set down her purse on the entry table with a flourish. "I am, however, quite an actress."

"You look like one. You look like Kim Steinberg," Alice grumbled, stomping farther into the house and giving Peggy no choice but to follow, trying as hard as possible not to stop and peruse family photographs along the way. No, she was too busy realizing she'd been categorized, same as she'd done to Alice.

Peggy took in the homey living room. It was huge, with oversized pieces of furniture to match. A low, square coffee table covered in the contents of a spilled Jansport backpack. Old wooden floors that probably creaked in the same pattern every time someone walked across them. The only thing missing was actual décor. No trinkets. No clutter. Clean and organized in a way that called to mind the man of the house. Putting those thoughts aside, Peggy focused on the forlorn-looking girl who continued to send her covert looks. "Who is Kim Steinberg?"

Alice flopped down onto the dark green leather couch. "She's a bitch," she said on a rush of air, then covered her face with both hands. "I don't know why I said that. She's actually nice to me, most of the time. It's just really hard to be nice back when she's so good at everything."

"I can see how that would be annoying."

"No, you can't," Alice spat, her soft nature from a moment earlier gone the way of the dodo. "I can't believe my dad sent you here. You're like a Barbie doll. It's like he wants me to feel shitty about myself."

"Look, I'm—" Way, way out of my depth. What had she been thinking? Offering to sweep in like a hero when she had no experience with young people, apart from the kids who sat in the waiting room coloring while she shopped for their mothers. Hoping for inspiration, Peggy scanned the room, landing on a copy of *Seventeen* Magazine, still halfway inside the backpack. On the cover, an overly tanned teenager who she didn't recognize smirked back. Bingo. If there was one thing Peggy knew, it was men. Around her neck, the foursome of engagement rings seemed to grow heavier. "Okay, so this bitch Kim is the female lead. Who's the guy?"

Alice was obviously trying to hide her smile over Peggy's use of the word *bitch* and failing. "What guy?"

"Come on. There's always a guy." She perched on the couch's arm. "You didn't memorize your lines, so—forgive me—I doubt you have a passion for acting. So. It's a dude."

"Justice Frick. He's the other lead, who I don't exactly have to kiss, but...there's like a nuzzle in the second act."

"Frick?" Peggy slipped down fully onto the couch. "That's his last name?"

"Yeah." Alice shook her head. "Slick Frick."

Peggy sucked in a breath through her nose. "Oh my God, that's awful."

"I know." Alice's smile was grudging, but she no longer appeared determined to disappear into the couch cushions. While the girl formulated her next move—her choices narrowed down to either letting Peggy help or kicking her ass out—Peggy studied Elliott's daughter through fresh eyes. Her shoulders were hunched, as if trying to hide herself, fingers picking at the hole in her jeans. A pang sharpened in her throat when an image of her sister popped up. The similarities between Alice and Rita were too there to ignore, and not for the first time since leaving her sister in New Mexico, the loss hit Peggy like a bus.

"Are you, like, crying, or what?" Alice squawked, surging to her feet.

"No." Peggy was horrified when her voice hitched. "Maybe a little."

"Why?"

"Everyone is just leaving me. You know?" The words burst out, like bees leaving a hive that had been smacked by a baseball bat. "Rita, Aaron. Miriam." Elliott. "They don't think I'm smart enough to have hurt feelings, because they're a bunch of assholes." She used the back of her hand to swipe away the annoying moisture leaking from her eyes. "They're not assholes. I don't know why I said that."

They both smiled at having issued nearly identical sentiments only moments apart. Alice left the room briefly and returned with a box of tissues, which she set down beside Peggy's thigh, before stepping back, dragging nervous hands over the sides of her jeans. "So. You really know how to make a situation about you, huh?"

Peggy's burst of laughter felt like a balloon popping inside her ribcage. "You're pretty funny, Alice." She gestured to the script, laying haphazardly on the coffee table. "Are we going to learn these lines or what? The clock is ticking."

Alice snapped the elastic hair band circling her wrist. "I hope you're a miracle worker."

"Miracle worker, I am not." Peggy stood and squared her

shoulders. "But if you're after a nuzzle from Slick Frick, we can get you there."

Alice's lips twitched. "Where did you come from?"

Again, the rings hanging against her collarbone seemed to heat.

Some say heaven, some say hell.

Peggy's smile faded when she remembered that by the time she left, Elliott would be firmly in one camp.

* * *

Elliott idled his truck to a stop in the garage, focusing on the green tennis ball that hung from the ceiling so he could pull in precisely two feet from the wall. Just enough space to walk from the driver's side to the kitchen entrance, but not so much that the automatic garage door wouldn't shut.

Once he'd switched off the ignition, he forced himself to wait, before climbing out of the driver's side. Maybe if he hesitated to go in the house, he would finally convince himself he hadn't rushed through the game films to get home. But the goddamn tug of anticipation in his gut at seeing the strange Suburban parked out front was undeniable. It was also manageable. Everything was.

Taking his ancient, beat-up leather satchel from the passenger side, Elliott climbed out of the truck and entered the house, wary over what he might find. God knew Alice was difficult in most situations, but over the course of watching the game film with the assistant coaches, he'd conceded to himself that sending over flawless and confident Peggy might not have been the wisest course of action. Alice was his daughter and he didn't give a damn what she looked like. To him, she was beautiful. He suspected she didn't share his opinion, however, and he didn't have a clue how to convince her.

Voices from the living room brought Elliott to a stop, just inside the door. Peggy was encouraging Alice. *One more time. Better. Once more through.* He of all people knew Peggy could be persistent as hell when her mind was set on something, and he swallowed hard at the reminder of exactly how easily Peggy used to wear him down. Back when his life had taken an unexpected turn and she'd been his only sanctuary. Not anymore, though. His sanctuary was either an actual sanctuary or the field. There would be no deviating. Routine. Routine.

Elliott cleared his throat and listened to the voices cut off. "Dad?"

He started to set down his satchel, pausing when he noticed a purse sitting in his usual spot, outlined by the familiar brick wall. With an unsettled kick in the stomach, he eased his own bag down beside it, staring at them side by side for a breath. "Yeah, it's me."

No sooner had he entered the living room than Peggy breezed past him, back the way he'd come. "I was just heading out." She turned at the mouth of the hallway and sent Alice what looked like a heartfelt smile. "You got that first scene down. The rest will be easier now that you're in character."

Alice's shoulders gave a jerky shrug. "Thanks. For coming over."

"Okay." Peggy seemed relieved. "It was fun, right? Yeah, it was fun." She gave Elliott a fleeting look, then vanished down the hall, calling, "Bye," over her shoulder.

Let her go. Let her go. Let her go.

"I'll just be a minute," Elliott said briskly, turning and striding after Peggy, the image of his daughter's raised eyebrows making him feel like ten times a moron. He wrenched the front door open. "Hey." Peggy spun around halfway down the porch steps and teetered, sending Elliott lunging forward to steady her. "Dammit. Why are you running off so fast?"

"Bet that's the first time you've been annoyed by too *much* speed, huh, Coach?" Elliott's lips tilted, like they hadn't done in so damn long, and Peggy jolted, tearing her eyes away. She stared down at his hands where they circled her arms until he took them back. "Look, tomorrow is a different day. But right now...I just didn't want you to think I'd volunteered to do this, because of us. Or what happened with us. One has nothing to do with the other."

"I never thought that."

"Thank you."

Elliott nodded while performing a mental rundown of what she'd said. "What did you mean, tomorrow is a different day?"

Peggy rested her attention on his belt buckle, which was only a couple inches below her sightline, thanks to his position on the higher stair. "It means I won't always run off so fast. Not if I want to give you the opportunity to catch me."

He was fully erect before the challenge even settled between them, making it necessary to do something he resented. His hand dropped, took hold of his cock, and adjusted the aching flesh. In front of anyone, it would have felt like vulgarity, but he hated the excitement, the gratification that came from touching himself in front of Peggy. The way she clawed into his stomach and reached his basest instinct hadn't changed with the passage of time. Lord, the absence of that rush might have made it even stronger.

"I won't chase you, Peggy," he rasped. "Nothing has changed."

"Everything has changed." She smiled so wide, a dimple popped up on her cheek. "This time, I'm only here through the weekend."

To say he was surprised by the blatant offer was an understatement. Surprised and suspicious. The Peggy he'd known was loyal to a fault. Not the kind of person who would be so casual about fooling around on her husband. Added to that, she knew his faith would prevent him from coveting another man's wife. Acting on it.

Elliott might have laughed if the throb in his groin wasn't so painful. Coveting would be the least of his sins if he accepted her invitation. Kissing, touching, taking was where the real depravity would start. And he wouldn't even admit to himself how badly he needed and wanted to say yes.

Hearing movement in the house behind him, Elliott gestured for Peggy to precede him toward the Suburban. As they walked, he steeled himself against the desire to grab her elbow, to make certain she wouldn't slip on the driveway. His pulse ticked like a clock in his ears until they reached the street.

The next-door neighbor paused in the act of cleaning out his gutter atop a ladder to watch Peggy cross the street. Little wonder. She looked about as out of place in his suburban area code, clicking along the asphalt in thigh-high leather, as a skyscraper might. The man waved hesitantly at Elliott and got the kind of glance in return reserved for players who'd literally dropped the ball.

When he focused back on Peggy, they'd reached the Suburban. As she turned the key in the door, it made a rusted protest and she winced a little, and at once it occurred to Elliott why the Suburban seemed especially out of place.

"This can't be a rental car." He stepped back and eyeballed the dented bumper. "Where did you get this thing?"

Peggy brushed her fingers over the side panel. "It was my mother's."

He absorbed that. "You drove from California to Cincinnati."

"Yes." Her smile was secretive and a little sad. "With a couple of interesting detours along the way."

His stomach lurched at the idea of her solitary figure behind the wheel, air flowing through the open window to blow in her hair. "By yourself, Peggy?"

"Can I ask you something?" Elliott's jaw clenched over not getting the answer he suddenly needed like oxygen, but he nodded, instead of letting on the importance. "When you received my wedding invitation..." Her golden brown eyes cut to the side. "Had the date already passed?"

Lying was a sin. A commandment. The fact that he didn't even hesitate to break it was proof she was bad for his peace of mind. His path. He was already starting to divert his attention from straight forward. "No. The date hadn't passed yet."

"Oh." She breathed the word, her already petite figure seeming to deflate in front of his eyes, but Elliott had no chance to absorb the blow to his gut. She moved like lightning, propping a foot on the steel runner and hefting herself up into the driver's seat. "See you around, Coach. I'm late."

"You said you didn't have plans."

"Huh." Her smile was goofy but distant, as if she'd surprised herself by turning tail so fast. "I did say that."

She started the Suburban, then ran both sets of fingers through her curls, lifting her shirt and exposing the skin of her belly. Elliott had no idea what possessed him to reach into the car and shut off the engine, but that's exactly what he did. For the second time that day, he was about to come away from one of their encounters unsatisfied with the score. Disorder and confusion simply weren't an option for him. "What are you doing?" she asked.

Elliott didn't have an answer to that, so he went with the second most pressing thing on his mind. "Things with Alice seemed to go well."

Peggy watched him closely for a moment, before alighting from the car. "Not at first, but we figured out a happy place."

"Yes, it seemed that way." He shifted. "How did you find it? This happy place."

She molded her back and hips against the vehicle, a position which angled her thighs and pushed up her breasts. His palms started to sweat in response, fingers stretching and retracting on their own with the memory of how those swells felt in his grip. How they shook a little, her nipples spearing his palms, when they'd sinned on their hands and knees. A position that should be reserved only for prayer. "I think I kind of stumbled into the happy place, if I'm being honest," she said, answering his question. "I probably couldn't find it again if I tried. Someone once called me childish, though, so maybe that helped. Just a childish person relating to a child on her own level."

Elliott ground his teeth together. "Said a lot of things I didn't meant back then, Peggy. It was a bad time."

"I was making a joke. You're always so serious," she said on a shrug, reaching out and patting his shoulder, letting her hand linger, thumb brushing the curve of his muscle. "Always. Especially before a game."

"Peggy." He gritted out her name. "I know what you're doing and I won't be persuaded. I won't allow my short-comings to rule me again."

She snatched her hand back as if she'd been burned, but the blanching expression turned playful in no time as she climbed once more into the driver's side of the SUV. "Tomorrow is a different day, isn't it?" Before the door could close, she paused, appearing to wrestle with herself the way Elliott was doing with his guilt for being so harsh. "Alice is terrific. When she says hurtful things to you, she's just being twelve. I said them to my mom. My mom said them to hers, too." A flick of her wrist and the engine roared to life. "She's going to be fine. You're doing fine."

Spikes dug into his chest. "Peggy—"

The slamming door cut him off. Hands on hips, head tipped forward, he watched her drive away, thanking God his life didn't have an instant replay option. When Elliott turned toward the house, he stopped short, finding Alice watching from the front doorway, her face inquisitive. But she ducked out of his sightline, disappearing into the house so quickly, he didn't even have a chance to take a step.

"Shit."

CHAPTER FOUR

It was the sun's fault, really. The shiny fucker reflected off Elliott's sweaty, bare chest as he jogged toward Peggy on the path, shooting a ray into her eye and blinding her, like a sex laser. That was the only reason she stumbled and ate shit, scraping seven layers of skin from her knee. Even in midair, she was already groaning with the humiliation. Bruised vanity made her cheeks bloom with heat. Then, pain.

Still, Peggy tucked and rolled behind a bench, hoping Elliott had missed the whole debacle. Fat chance. They were the only ones out utilizing the jogging path so early in the morning. Why had she chosen a new route, instead of her typical jaunt around the track? This was a disaster. It had been a full week since she'd gone to Elliott in the locker room and he'd made no move to return for seconds. Now she looked like a stalker, creeping on the running trail he probably took every day, at the exact same time. Because that's how Coach Brooks operated.

Her knee throbbed with pain, but she didn't look, know-ing the sight of blood would make it worse. And Elliott was almost even with where she sat sprawled on the grass. Maybe if she just closed her eyes and remained completely still...

"*I can see you, Miss Clarkson.*"

Embarrassment speared Peggy in the middle, along with a wiggling finger of lust. His morning voice was scratchy. Throw in those panting breaths and he might as well be railing her against the locker again. Her eyes flew open at the memory, and that single finger of lust became a bunched fist. Shirtless Coach Brooks. Da-hamn. A big, im-posing mess of dripping sweat and black hair and rounded muscles. Also a scowl. "*I was just watching the sunrise.*"

Of course, his skeptical face made him even hotter. "*Your knee is bleeding.*"

"*So it is.*" *It ached worse for having been acknowledged.* "*It's well known around campus this is the best vantage point for watching the sun come up. I had to fight off at least a dozen students trying to claim my spot—*"

"*I saw you fall.*"

Had his mouth twitched? Maybe just a tad? Peggy blew a loose curl out of her eye. "*Thanks for playing along,*" *she muttered.* "*I'm guessing improv isn't really your jam, huh?*" *Bracing a hand against the bench, she started to rise.* "*While we're tearing down the fourth wall, I think 'Miss Clarkson' is a little formal. Don't you think?*"

Her question ended on a squeak when Elliott scooped her off the ground. "*Do you always ramble when you're bleeding out?*" *He aimed his frown at her knee. Beneath the thunder, she detected...worry.* "*That was a hard fall. Half of my players would be crying for the medic by now.*"

"*Am I being recruited? 'Cause I would look insanely*

hot in football pants. Boom. Ticket sales through the roof."
Her joke emerged breathless, because hello. She was being
carried through the morning mist by a bare-chested legend.
And yeah, she was pretty sure he'd nearly smiled again,
which was almost better than riding the orgasm train to
heaven in her cheerleading skirt last week with him as con-
ductor. "Where are you taking me?"

"There's a first aid kit in my truck." A worry crease ap-
peared between his eyes as he regarded her mangled knee
again. "You're tougher than you look. If..."

Pleasure tickled Peggy head to toe. Men complimented
her on a regular basis about everything under the sun, but
Coach calling her tough was like getting a pink Rolls-Royce
for Christmas. "If what?"

Elliott became impatient. "If I'd been going at my nor-
mal pace, I would have caught you." Showing zero exertion,
he climbed a knoll, bringing them into the parking lot.
"This is why plans and execution are so important."

She tucked her hands beneath her chin and gave him an
exaggerated, starry-eyed look. "Tell me more."

"Yes, I'm sure you're spellbound." There was another
mysterious jump at the corner of his mouth, but he sobered
quickly. "Maybe I'm punished when I deviate from my path.
In fact, I'm certain I am."

"Seeing me hurt is punishment?"

He paused before easing her down onto the bumper of his
truck, surprise coloring his chiseled features. "Yes. It is."

*   *   *

What the hell am I doing?

Elliott forced himself to break contact with Peggy and
retrieve the first aid kit from his glove compartment. Car-

rying her had been a mistake, but it might have killed him to watch her walk on the injured knee. Lord, she was soft. Curved to fit. Made to be lifted and laid down, wherever he chose to place her.

No, not he. Someone else. Elliott wasn't her boyfriend. They were nothing to one another and couldn't be. He shouldn't have given in to temptation—irresistible as it had been—in the locker room, and they shouldn't be spending time together now. Their association was dangerous. Could cost him his job and, hell, his self-respect. The dirt was still fresh on his wife's grave, he had a child to raise, a team to coach. With so many responsibilities on his plate, fraternizing with a student was unacceptable. No matter how gorgeous. No matter how she made him want to laugh. Him. Laugh. He wasn't even sure what it would sound like.

Clutching the kit so hard, the tin bit into his finger, Elliott reached into his pocket with his free hand and rolled his thumb over the smooth bumps of his rosary beads. A reminder that he needed to remain steadfast in his faith. No more mistakes, like the one they'd made together in the locker room.

Groaning low over the memories that winked in front of his vision, Elliott returned to where Peggy sat. She was clearly refusing to show a hint of pain. So brave. Or stubborn. Maybe both. "Turn sideways and prop your leg on the bumper."

"Yes, Coach." *Along with her smirk, that title alone coming from Peggy made blood run south to his cock. And it didn't help his situation when she followed his instructions, stretching out her long leg, tightening the material of her tiny running shorts over her pussy.* "Like this?"

If Peggy didn't seem oblivious to the effect she was having on him, pain finally beginning to make her chin wobble,

Elliott might have addressed the elephant in the parking lot. He'd fucked her. A student. Hard. Rough. Nasty. They'd done something against not only the school's rules, but his own unwritten ones. His focus would not stray, would not change. It needed to be consistent.

If he didn't commit every ounce of energy to football now, he'd been an absent husband, son, father...for nothing. He'd neglected his family for football, choosing the sport over everything and making his purpose clear. It couldn't change now.

Elliott knelt with a curse, smacking open the tin box to remove cotton balls and hydrogen peroxide, applying the latter to the former. But with the necessary items in hand, he couldn't seem to lower the soaked cotton to Peggy's bleeding scrape.

"What's wrong?" she whispered.

"I've never..." Christ, were his hands shaking? "I've probably bandaged a thousand injuries, but never one on a woman."

Peggy didn't laugh as he expected. "It's the same procedure. Leg-wise, at least." He heard her swallow. "If I had a compound boobie fracture, we'd be shit out of luck."

His chuckle was rusty and unexpected. Neither of them moved afterward and the silence grew wider, deeper. Morning fog drifted past, unaware of the time. "I have a daughter. I had a wife. I should have done this before." Peggy's fingers slid into his hair, her nails making light circles on his scalp and he just wanted to sleep, right there with his head in her lap. "I should have done so many things."

She brushed her thumb down his temple, massaging. "I love my mother more than anything in the world. I tell her constantly. And if she died tomorrow, I would still have a million regrets. It's natural, Elliott."

"This is going to sting," he murmured, touching the wet cotton to her scrape. She hissed in a breath and snagged his hair between her fingers—abusing the strands with a yank. Exactly as she might if his mouth were teasing between her thighs. His dick hardened at the image, tenting the front of his running pants. A growl shook out of his throat without permission and they locked eyes.

Guilt trapped him. In one breath, he talked about his failures, his regrets; in the next he wanted to pound this beautiful, perceptive girl against his bumper. Wanted to get lost in her acceptance and feel the squeeze of her pussy. To think of nothing but getting her off. His mind had been a hazard zone since the last time he was inside of her. God, to feel that mental peace again… That level of need-drunk lust he'd never achieved elsewhere.

More guilt. His hands started to work fast, swabbing Peggy's injury, but she slowed him with a touch, capturing his attention. "Tell me something good you've done."

Elliott thinned his lips.

"You're right. That's the last thing you would ever do." She leaned over and snagged a bandage between her fingers, ripping it open with her teeth. "I'll do it for you, then. Last week, after the game, you went out of your way to shake the other teams' kicker's hand, after he blew that field goal. What did you say to him?"

"That he would redeem himself if he practiced hard enough. That there would be chances to make everyone forget the one he missed."

Her smile caused his heart to make a racket. She'd never given him one so bright, not during any of their encounters on campus. This one was pure approval and it hit his bloodstream like a drug. People gave him reverential smiles often, but they came from… the other side of the glass, while Peggy was right there, close, on his side. "I see you. You make positive differences every day, you just don't let yourself have them." She ducked her head to apply the bandage. "Let yourself have them, Elliott."

"I can't be with you again," he rasped. "It makes me forget everything and I don't deserve that."

"I say you do." With barely a wince, Peggy swung her legs off the bumper and stood. Elliott closed his eyes against the urge to wrap both arms around her waist, force her to stay, and make him feel human a little longer. "Come find me when you're ready to be convinced."

* * *

Peggy rolled her forehead against the metal wall of the elevator as it took her to the third floor of the Embassy Suites, where she shared a room with Sage, Belmont right across the hall. She needed to get herself under control before she saw either of them, but the ride over—with windows rolled down to bring cold air streaming onto her face—hadn't helped in the slightest. Even in the metal reflection, she could see puffy eyes and strain around her mouth. Good thing the turmoil taking place on the inside wasn't visible to the other hotel guests or there'd be a mass exodus to the Holiday Inn.

Dammit. Dammit. Round two to Elliott. If it weren't for his clear interest in her physically, she might have already been forced to accept her greatest fear: Time had made him indifferent to her. Had she been an idiot to come back to Cincinnati? Seeing him face-to-face after years and distance—and working toward closure—had seemed doable in theory. But she hadn't counted on the effect he'd had on her as a college senior to be going strong at twenty-five. Tying him up in knots and leaving him reeling in her wake was only possible if *she* walked away intact.

The elevator doors rolled open and Peggy took a deep breath and stepped off, but instead of heading for the room, she plopped down on the bench, just to the left of the elevator bank.

He'd known. He'd known she was getting married and hadn't tried to stop it.

Fucker hadn't even sent a blender.

She muffled her somewhat hysterical laugh with both hands. Four kind, decent men, with dreams for the future, and she'd run roughshod through their lives. She'd tried to convince herself accepting the proposals was a way to force herself into Elliott-recovery, like some kind of penis immersion therapy that would finally blur the past and repair her heart. But until now, she'd never actually *wanted* to get over Elliott, had she? No. No, getting over him would mean shutting off her center of gravity. Pretending she'd never felt the organ race out of control in her chest, just hearing another person's name. Who would want to forget that kind of insanity?

Now, she had no choice but to move on. It was a matter of survival at this advanced stage of her imprisonment.

Something far more troubling than heartache had blipped on the radar of her psyche today, though. She hadn't corrected Elliott's belief that she was married, and there was something hot and dangerous in her belly, simply thinking about his disapproval. His censure when she came on to him, even though she was "attached." A part of her she'd been unaware of grew...excited, over the way he might punish her with his words and hands. All those times he'd referred to her as his downfall were mixed up with images of his body moving above her, sensations of pleasure. Her libido was just confused. That had to be all.

If nothing else, that confusion was another reminder that she'd come to Cincinnati to steal back the love she'd given Elliott. To bury the past and move on with a clear mind and heart.

Resolve firming up her shoulders, Peggy shoved to her feet, already digging the hotel key card from her purse. When she walked inside the room, she expected to find Sage reading or sneaking an episode of their shared *Golden Girls* marathon. But she skidded to a stop on the carpet when she found Belmont and Sage moments from a kiss.

Oh yeah, if she'd lingered near the elevators a minute longer, she would have walked in on a much different scene, because Belmont looked prepared to devour their darling Sage. And while they weren't touching, Sage was clearly prepared to allow said devouring, if her shuddering breaths were any indication. Belmont didn't even glance toward the door when Peggy barged in, merely continuing in his attempts to draw Sage's essence from her body with the force of his will. Or that's how it looked anyway.

Whoa. Just *whoa*.

Sage snapped out of her trance, bounding backward so fast, she disrupted everything sitting on their shared nightstand, mumbling apologies to no one in particular. "She doesn't feel well," Belmont shouted, still not looking at Peggy.

Peggy set down her purse on the closest bed and approached the situation with the caution of a hostage negotiator. "Okay, big guy." She ran a quick look over her friend and deduced that, no, she didn't look as healthful as usual. Her usual glow was subdued, her skin slightly ashen. It occurred to her that Belmont had been planning to heal Sage with a kiss, which was a little too heartbreaking to explore just yet. Maybe ever. "I'm sure she's going to be fine, Bel. Right, Sage?"

"Yes," Sage whispered, giving her that look best friends give each other. The one that said *think about it*. "It's just a stomachache."

Peggy did some quick math and remembered about this time last month, Sage had opted out of going into the gym Jacuzzi because of her period. Knowing modest Sage, however, she would rather die than have this information bandied about in front of Belmont. Or anyone with a pulse. "Uh, hey. Big bro? I'm going to fix her up. She'll be back to herself in an hour tops."

"What is it?" He stepped closer to Sage and she visibly braced herself. Not in fear, but out of necessity, it seemed. "I need to help."

Sage sent Peggy a pleading look. "Some Tylenol, Bel. That would help. Maybe a bottle of ginger ale from the vending machine."

"When I don't feel like myself," he murmured for Sage's ears alone, but Peggy heard anyway, "it helps when I hold you. It could work for you, too, maybe."

A wrench turned in Peggy's gut and she honest-to-God wanted to sob her heart out. Just ached to drop into a fetal position and weep for mankind. It was how she felt ninety percent of the time when in Belmont's company because the storm of emotions building inside of him wasn't hidden anymore. Ever since this trip began and he'd revealed the search for his birth father, she could feel his turmoil every time she came within two feet of his gigantic presence.

Peggy eased closer to the pair, intending to intercept the laser-like intensity Belmont was laying on her best friend, but Sage moved faster, sliding her arms around Belmont's waist, laying her head on his chest and holding. Tight. Belmont rocked back on his heels, eyelids falling like metal garages to conceal his blue eyes, so different from the rest of the Clarkson siblings. He made a sound that could only be described as utter, broken bliss, before wrapping his brawny arms around Sage.

"Please feel better," Belmont said quietly. "Please stop hurting."

"I will. This is already helping," Sage whispered back, her breath hitching when Belmont lifted her off the ground, burying his face in her neck, his back expanding with deep inhales.

Too much. It was all too much. Purse in hand, Peggy backed from the room before she'd even made the conscious decision to leave. As she jogged down the hallway toward the elevator, tripping a little on the plush rug, she'd never felt so alone in her entire life.

No, that wasn't true. Flying home from Cincinnati to California with a shattered heart had been her lowest point. And she hated herself for craving the same coping mechanism as that disillusioned twenty-two-year-old girl. Men. But bad habits couldn't be broken overnight, could they?

The opposite sex was like a drug, even if she rarely partook of them fully. Just a fully clothed taste usually did the trick. Just a flirtation. Enough to make her forget that the one time she'd laid it all on the line, she'd been found lacking. Before the night was over, though, she would feel anything but. Come tomorrow, the game would be back on.

CHAPTER FIVE

It was unusual for Elliott to attend evening mass, since his nights were almost always spent in his office, reviewing the playbook or watching that day's practice film. With the arrival of a certain blond siren that afternoon, however, he'd been compelled to leave his den television paused mid-play to seek refuge from thoughts that continued to harass him. The fact that he'd strayed from his productivity had Elliott's jaw bunching as he parked in the church lot.

Schedules. He lived for the known. Having no confusion over what would happen each calendar day at a specific time. Meals were uncomplicated in his house, but they were nutritious. He cooked, Alice loaded the dishwasher, and they went their separate ways without any fanfare.

Their home wasn't a warm, loving environment, and in truth, Elliott had no clue what that kind of place would look like. His marriage had been a tense, quiet affair that had ended in the same manner. The relationship between him and Judith had been an almost identical reflection of his parents' marriage. Respectful, but not romantic. Being that they were both devout Catholics, it would have remained that way, too, indefinitely.

He could still remember getting the phone call that Judith had been found unconscious in the driveway and taken to the hospital. Receiver pressed to his ear, he'd sat there trying to remember the last time he and Judith had actually spoken. He'd been horrified to realize he couldn't. It might have been a full week of nothing more than brisk nods on his way out the door, football already infiltrating his mind. That's the way it had been since the beginning, but he'd only acknowledged the unfairness of their noncommunicative relationship when speaking was no longer possible.

He'd been a terrible husband. Hell, he hadn't been one at all.

The months that followed had been a blur of trips to the neurology unit at the hospital, where Judith lay in a coma, team meetings, discussions with doctors, interviewing babysitters for Alice, and practice, practice, practice. One afternoon, he'd stood on the field, his neck so tight, he could barely move it in any direction. Then this voice, throaty and musical all at once, forced him to turn around and everything in his world had burst into vivid color as Peggy passed.

From that day forward, he'd lived for the single glances they would trade, even though wanting anything from another woman made him a certified bastard. His only salvation was they'd never exchanged a word. Not until weeks after Judith's inevitable departure.

Now, church served as a reminder not to allow failure again. To keep his focus forward on realistic goals. For him, those goals didn't include relationships with women. One woman, in particular. The structure of mass, the ceremony of it, kept him centered in a way that had gone missing when a certain student had graduated and left, at his urging. With a married Peggy flitting around his town tonight, he needed concentrated routine more than ever, or guilt and regret would worm their way into his consciousness.

So Elliott had taken himself to church. Alice had been closeted in her room since Peggy left, refusing to open the door for dinner, so he'd further hoped she would eat if alone in the house, with no chance of running into him.

The church was located near campus, at the end of a street with several restaurants and small shops geared toward students. Even in the darkness, Elliott could make out a stuffed likeness of himself in the window of a Bearcats gift shop and cringed. Why couldn't the church be in a quieter section of town?

A group of people piling out of a restaurant punctuated the evening with their boisterousness, one of them pointing at him and lifting a cell phone to snap a picture. Elliott put his head down and trudged toward the church steps before they could get brave enough to engage him. Over the last three years, people had begun approaching him less and less. At one time, he hadn't scared everyone quite so much. Had he? No, he recalled shaking hands and suffering through selfies on a daily basis. High-fiving kids. Something about his demeanor now appeared to . . . put them off. He could see it in the way people looked at his face and backed away, as if an emotion he refused to name was etched there. The solitude *suited* him, though. If he engaged with others, their reactions would only confirm what he'd decided to believe. That he was better off alone.

Already pulling the rosary beads from his jeans pocket, a familiar laugh reached Elliott from across the street.

He stopped short, his gaze zeroing in on Peggy where she leaned against the brick wall of an establishment. Surrounded by men. Just…crowded by them on all sides in a way that built a roar in Elliott's throat. His vision seemed to zoom out and in, screwing with his depth perception, so he attempted to focus on the church doors and ignore the compelling instinct to cross the street and extricate the little vixen from her group of adoring fans.

Don't do it.

He didn't have the luxury of walking around Cincinnati without being recognized. They would wonder about his connection to Peggy and that could only lead to uncomfortable questions, including the timeline of their relationship. Furthermore, he'd sent Peggy away with a firm rejection earlier that evening. If he approached the situation now, she would know he'd been full of shit.

Elliott ascended the church stairs—one more, two—and stopped once again, cell phone flashes going off in his periphery.

Closing his eyes, he prayed for patience. Wisdom. But all he could see was Peggy with someone else later tonight. Hands all over her thighs, a stranger's lips kissing her mouth, getting the eye contact she'd once reserved for him.

No. Dammit.

He turned on a heel, hitting the street before common sense could kick in. Satisfaction burned in his gut when Peggy saw him coming and her smile disappeared. And yeah, normally Elliott didn't give a rat's ass about his ridiculous, local legend status, but when the men around her backed away and started hooting at his approach, even more satisfaction found the mark. Having no choice but to shake their hands—even though he sorely wanted to break them all—Elliott kept his focus trained on Peggy.

"You're late for church," he said hoarsely, noting the way her nipples turned to points when he spoke. "The service is about to start."

Her smoky laughter turned every one of her admirers' heads back in her direction. "I've already had enough wine for one night." That dimple appeared. "It was blessed by a bartender, instead of a priest, but I'm not picky. Especially when I can get my version of spirits for free."

The harem of men laughed, one of them having enough nerve to rest his hand above Peggy's head on the brick, bringing them far too close. "Where have you been hiding, beautiful?" the fucker asked, making Elliott's molars gnash together.

"She's been hiding with a husband in California," Elliott ground out, splitting the scene in half. "Let's go, Peggy. You've got a lot to pray about."

Elliott refused to regret the harsh words. He took Peggy's hand and pulled her from the stunned group, crossing the street toward the church as people stopped and stared. She moved at a sedate pace beside him, stumbling along with his strides with an expression of shock frozen on her face. "Wow. You are the king asshole."

"It was for your own good." They moved up the stairs one at a time, organ music beginning to drift from inside. Peggy's hand was icy cold inside his own, but he steeled himself against sympathy. She'd always been good at providing that, while he'd been made of stone. Stone only Peggy had ever succeeded in crumbling, but he'd built it back stronger when she'd left. "Whatever you were planning on doing, you would have regretted it later. When you got home. You're *better* than that."

At the big double doors, Peggy tugged out of his grip. "Better than what? Someone who hurts the people who love them?" She laughed. "I'm not better than that, actually. I've become the master."

Lord, she looked lost and gorgeous and exhausted. His mind sought a way to play defense against the bad parts, but they all involved touching her and he couldn't. *Couldn't.* "You're not the master. That's the most ridiculous thing I've ever heard." She didn't look convinced and he mourned the ability to reach her, even though he no longer had the right. Someone else did, dammit. The reality made him nauseous, but he pushed through because he hated the lack of animation in her eyes. "Come with me. We'll light a candle for your mother."

A sound puffed past her lips. Her hand lifted, rubbing at something beneath the collar of her shirt. Her heart? "Do you ever wish you were a million miles away...and then a second later, you can't stand the thought of being anywhere else, but right where you're standing?"

Countless times. He'd just never allowed himself to articulate the sense that he should be somewhere else. Namely, in California, fighting to get Peggy back. He'd slammed that notion in a box and sealed the lid long ago, pretending it didn't exist. Pretending was how he survived.

The connection between them snapped as it had those years ago before they'd ever formally met. The desire to hold her, touch her, whisper his secrets in her ear was getting too powerful. So he took a pair of mental scissors and tried to cut the connection. "You're talking nonsense, Peggy, and it's making us late for mass."

Relief wrapped around him when Peggy's claws came out, her eyes brightening with temper. She sauntered closer, eliminating the scant distance between them, and tilted her head back to keep their gazes locked. "You know, I wouldn't have regretted anything that happened tonight.

Not even a little. Because at least I'd be living, instead of preparing for my own funeral." Her words tagged him like darts, but nothing compared to the lust that swam in his stomach at having her so close, all that vitality crackling in his blood like it was contagious. "Ten Our Fathers and seven Hail Mary's. That ought to make up for how many times you've thought of fucking me today."

She was gone from his sight in a flash, her curls whipping against his cheeks in the wind, leaving him paralyzed on the church steps. Hurt and rage and need rose up in his throat and expanded, making it difficult to breathe. He couldn't enter the church in that state, would never be able to sit still. Which had to be the reason he went after Peggy, following her where she'd disappeared around the side of the church. As soon as he rounded the corner, he caught sight of her on the stone pathway, arms wrapped around her body as if to stave off the chill.

"Peggy."

Without stopping, she turned, continuing to walk backward, farther into the darkness. "Get lost, Elliott."

God knew he was already. Lost in the pounding of his pulse, the heat gathering in his groin. He'd imagined touching her again for so long, and combined with the fall of night, he allowed himself to believe it was just another fantasy. Not really happening anywhere but in his mind. That hint of an excuse was all he needed to quicken his pace to a determined stride, reaching Peggy in seconds and turning her, shoving her body up against the cold church structure.

Ohhhhh Christ. She was warm, though. So damn warm and pliant, her curves interlocking with his muscle— beating his memory by ten thousand miles—her sweet, forbidden scent tackling his senses. His conscience must have had a little fight left, though, because it prodded Elliott's mind, right when he would have attacked Peggy's parted lips. "I can't. I can't when someone's waiting for you at home."

"Is that all that's stopping you?"

She whimpered the last word, the sound making his balls weigh down with hurt. "Right now it is." He took her wrists, pinning them high on the wall. "When I come to my senses, it'll be fifty other reasons. And fifty more reasons on top of that."

"Come to your senses?" she repeated on a breath. "Because I'm just a mistake to you? A reminder that the Kingmaker has an actual weakness?"

"Yes." Her flinch scalded him with regret, but he fought through the need to take his words back. "I never lied to you."

She closed her eyes for a beat, and when they opened, there had been a change. Plans had been made...and they no doubt included the destruction of his will. Clamping that sweet row of white teeth down on her lower lip, Peggy arched her back, drawing Elliott's attention to her breasts. "We both know how well I can keep a secret, Elliott," she whispered. "No one will know if you touch them."

"I'll know." Despite his denial, he released one of Peggy's wrists, letting his hand slide down to her shoulder, his greedy fingertips dragging lower. "God will know."

"Then I guess it's a good thing we're so close to a church." She pushed up even more, presenting her pointed tits with an innocent expression. "You can go pray about it right afterward."

The head of his rigid cock pressed against his belt buckle, straining painfully inside his pants. "That's not how it works," he rasped. "Prayer isn't an excuse to sin."

Peggy's knee moved up and down the side of his thigh, and

just knowing her legs were apart, her pussy out in the open, blasted another hole in his resolve. "No one will know. Touch them. Be as rough as you want," she breathed. "I remember what you like. How you like to get mad at my body. Frustrated at it for making you want something natural."

"Nothing natural about what we did." His touch moved down, stopping a mere inch from her breast, fingers flexing. "You made me behave like a beast. Some of the ways I took you . . . some of the places . . ."

She groaned and it broke him. Knowing the memories had caused such a harsh sound of longing brought his clutching hand to her breast, where it kneaded the taut mound once before racing under her shirt. Lust railroaded him, and he was out of his mind with need to feel her bare skin. "Yes, Elliott. More."

"They're a little fuller. Bet they'd fill my mouth now."

Before his growl settled, he was already jerking up the hem of Peggy's shirt, exposing her braless tits in the moonlight, and diving forward to suck one peak between his lips. Bad. This was wrong. She belonged to someone else, but denial continued to suppress that fact, shouting instead that Elliott had been there first. How could she ever belong to another after the amount of times he'd taken her to bed?

With a possessive snarl, Elliott pressed her to the wall with the use of his mouth, increasing the power of his suck until she cried out, twisting his hair with frantic fingers. She tugged him away with a cracked sob and then her lips were so close. So damn close. The most tempting of fruit. And he descended on their parted perfection like the Apocalypse was upon them.

"How do you do this to me?" he groaned against her mouth. "I can't even get my dick hard unless I think of you. I bet you love knowing that." The ensuing kiss was brutal, his tongue driving deep and claiming. "Bet you love knowing that sliver of stomach you showed me today in the car made it necessary to jerk off in my office with the door locked."

Without giving her a chance to respond, he crushed their mouths together, Peggy's naked breasts pressing between them as their tongues slipped into a rhythm meant for mating. For fucking. Long, hot slides of lips and tongue that made his cock thicken to such a miserable state, he couldn't help but take it out on her mouth, flattening her against the wall and angling his head to give himself better access. How could God create someone this sweet and not expect him to succumb? Soft. So soft and yet sharp and rounded in the right places. Her ass, her hips, they were moving between Elliott and the wall, goading him, granting him permission to lift up her cock-tease body and release his seed between her legs.

"Feels like I haven't come since you left," he grated against her ear. "Can't wring it out of myself the way you used to. Fuck. The way you'd smile at me when you'd tighten up your pussy, like you enjoyed killing me—"

"I can do it right now. Smile my good little cheerleader smile while you slide me up. Slide me down. I'll tighten it up until you can't breathe." Her voice trembled, that right knee hooking on his hip like an invitation, the heat between her legs finding his stiff groin, taunting him with the promise of relief. Finally. "I can't orgasm without thinking of the time you spanked me," she said in a rushed whisper. "With your rolled-up playbook. You were angry at me for talking to one of the players. Remember—"

"Yes, I damn well remember," he rasped. "The way your pretty cheeks got pinker and pinker. Didn't speak to any of them again after that, did you?"

"No, never," she murmured, pulling his head down for another kiss—

Above them, the church bells began to peel. Shame echoed from the top of Elliott's skull straight down to his feet, as if he were directly inside the bell itself. Even so, taking his mouth away from Peggy's was like being at the ocean's bottom and cutting off his oxygen supply with a hunting knife. But he did it. He managed it, because even if she weren't married to another man—and she *was*, dammit to hell—there was no place in his life for her. For anything other than what was already there.

Elliott's chest heaved as he untangled their bodies and stepped back, doing his best to restore the equilibrium she'd taken. Oh Lord, the way she looked in the moonlight, mouth wet, shirt rucked up above her bare breasts, nipples glowing where he'd sucked them as if he had the right. If her tongue hadn't been in his mouth just seconds before, he wouldn't have believed she was real.

"Did you come back here to make my life hell, Peggy?" he growled. "Answer me honestly. Because you're succeeding."

"You always did equate me with hell, didn't you?" she said, almost to herself, before she seemed to snap back to the here and now. "You're tripping if you think I would drive all the way from California just to bother you, Elliott."

Burning curiosity bled through in his need. "You never answered me earlier, Peggy. Did you drive here alone?"

Peggy covered herself with a jerky movement, robbing him of those incredible breasts. *Want them back.* "No. Not alone."

The ground started to shake under Elliott's feet. "Your husband is here?"

"I'm not married," she near-shouted, coming forward to

shove him in the chest. "The wedding I invited you to never *happened*. I called it off the night before."

There was relief and then there was the almost debilitating rush of calm that dragged Elliott down into a black void of silence. There was no comparison between the two sensations. He'd felt relief after winning a hard-fought game, but nothing in his memory compared to finding out the woman before him hadn't spent the last three years sharing a marital bed with some faceless stranger. His heartbeat boomed in his ears, stress leaking from his shoulders. The stiff fingers of his right hand flexed with twinges of pain.

Pain the invitation to her wedding had wrought three years earlier when it had been forwarded by the post office two weeks after the nuptials date…and he'd broken his hand trying to punch through a brick wall.

And he could see…he could see by the way Peggy watched him that she wanted this information to change something. To change him. But despite the different world he was living in since finding out she was single, the fact remained that his life would never include her. Would never include anyone else.

In the back of his mind, he heard the ring of a phone. Bad news on the other line. Proof of his failure to be what the people who relied on him needed.

He saw Peggy sobbing as she wheeled her luggage toward the waiting taxi. One he'd called after breaking off what they had. Hating himself the whole time for feeling so much agony. More than he'd felt at his own wife's deathbed.

Therein lay the issue, didn't it? Always had. When he looked at Peggy, he felt too damn much, making her a constant reminder of how little he'd felt for someone he'd sworn to serve. In the eyes of God. He would never forgive himself for that.

"Do what's best for both of us and leave, Peggy," he said. "I won't get a moment's peace as long as you're walking my campus again."

Avoiding his gaze, she shrugged. "Deal with it. I'm not here for you. And I'm not going anywhere just yet." She slinked forward and ran a single finger down his belly, increasing the swelling below his belt as if she harnessed enough power to rule every cell in his body. Maybe she did. "You didn't know I was an unattached woman when you had me against the wall. That's called coveting, isn't it?" That torturing finger dragged lower and traced the outline of his erection, bottom to top. "Better get inside and confess your sins."

Peggy was halfway down the pathway before Elliott followed, staying on her trail long enough to watch her hail a cab back on the main street and get into the backseat—alone. He turned to face the church, his intention to join the mass in progress, but found himself walking to his truck instead and driving home. He wasn't fit company for God with Peggy in his head.

CHAPTER SIX

Peggy crept into the hotel room, hoping and dreading—all at once—that she would find Belmont and Sage twined together, pledging their undying love. Instead, she found Sage sitting against the headboard of her bed...scrapbooking furiously. Like it was the final book that would ever be scrapped.

Sage had always been a type A overachiever, but there had been an added nervousness to her on the Iowa to Ohio leg of the trip. Like a cat sensing an earthquake. Her best friend might take pleasure in being compared to a feline and purr in response, but it probably wasn't the best way to broach the subject of Sage's uncharacteristic jumpiness.

"Hey," Peggy murmured, praying she looked halfway human. On the short cab ride home, she'd vowed not to cry even one more time over Elliott—she'd done way too much of that and accomplished nothing—but the lack of tears didn't mean Sage wouldn't know something was wrong.

And wrong didn't begin to cover how right it had felt

having Elliott's harsh words rasped into her ears back at the church. *How annoying.* She'd won tonight's impromptu battle and should be celebrating, not replaying their angry kissing match. But it didn't feel like a win at all, because every time she breathed, her nipples got hard remembering his mouth sucking them. His expression of rapture as he tongued them, pushing that big rod up between her thighs, turning her panties into a wet rag.

Oh sure, now she was *laser* focused on the victory.

She dropped down on the bed beside Sage, taking stock of the mounds of ribbon, magazine cutouts, and lace swaths piled around her petite best friend. With what appeared to be extreme concentration, Sage pressed a finger down onto a pink jewel, holding the decoration in place while chewing on her lip. It seemed like an hour passed before she released it, finally giving Peggy her full attention. Although just like the ribbons strewn across the bed, she could sense a strip of her friend's concentration was elsewhere. Far from this room. "Hello."

Peggy waved. "What have you got going on over there?"

"It's a new wedding idea book." She turned the page, smoothing her hand over the blank space. "I found an art supply store a short walk from here. Picked up some bridal magazines, too, and decided to have a party."

Man, Peggy loved her best friend. She didn't deserve someone as patient and together as Sage. Four weddings they'd planned together and Sage hadn't judged her for calling off a single one of them. Not once. She'd simply made the appropriate phone calls and waited until Peggy was ready to talk. Only, Peggy had never been ready to talk about her inability to commit. Still wasn't. Because vocalizing the kind of feelings she had for Elliott would drown her if she let them loose.

For this exact reason, Peggy had held off on asking Sage what had her so distracted lately. They had an unspoken don't ask policy that had mostly benefitted Peggy up to this point. But what about Sage?

Back in Iowa, Sage had dropped the bombshell that she would be leaving the road trip after Cincinnati, but hadn't confided why. And while Peggy had figured they had time to discuss it, the deadline was looming closer. Losing her best friend, even for a little while, made Peggy anxious. Not only because she loved Sage, but because of what her sudden absence might do to Belmont.

"Where have you been?" Sage asked, ducking her head and letting Peggy know she'd been scrutinizing a little too hard.

"Out." Peggy unzipped her boots, letting them fall on the carpeted floor, one after the other. "Seemed like maybe you and Bel needed some space."

As always, when the subject of Belmont was broached, Sage's cheeks flamed, her fingers fidgeting with the bedspread. "Nothing happened, if that's what you're asking. Nothing ever does, beyond the h-holding. I wouldn't... I mean, he's your brother—"

"Sage." It never failed to amaze her how Sage remained in denial where Belmont was concerned. If Sage asked him for the Pacific Ocean, he would spend his life looking for a big enough bottle to hold the damn thing. "Seriously, whatever is going on with you and Bel has my full blessing. My blessings have blessings."

"Nothing is going on," she whispered. "It can't go on, Peggy. He relies too much on me. I rely too much on him. For comfort and..." A flash of hazel eyes in Peggy's direction. "We're codependent and I've seen where that leads. It's not good."

The silence buzzed in Peggy's ears. Her friend rarely spoke about the past, but she'd just dropped a fat hint that something about it hadn't been ideal. "You've seen where it leads how?"

"In my crystal ball," Sage deadpanned, adding a wink. "It also says we have waffle fries from room service in our future."

"Crafty evasion technique. Maybe you're an ex-spy." Peggy swallowed her disappointment and fell backward on the bed, arms flung out at her sides. "Are you hoping I'll let you get away with that nonsense in exchange for not asking where I went?"

"I didn't mean to evade, Peggy. Call it a bad habit." A hush fell over the room. "Nothing is going on with Belmont that I understand anyway," Sage said haltingly. "He comes at me so fast—so fast—and then he just disappears. It's like he can only take me a little at a time. Or he can only take himself—how he is around me—in doses. But those doses are huge and addictive for us both. I don't know how else to describe it."

Swallowing the lump in her throat, Peggy sat up and reached for Sage's knee, settling a hand there. "He's kind of a mystery to all of us, but I can tell you right now, you're the opposite of his problem."

"I can't be the solution," Sage whispered, flicking her a solemn look. "I'm still leaving after Cincinnati, Peggy." She rolled her lips inward. "It doesn't have anything to do with Belmont...but I need to go alone. Are you going to fight me on it?"

"I'm going to hope you change your mind."

Sage's face broke into a sad smile. "I can't."

Peggy shoved her hands beneath her thighs to keep them from trembling. There had been too many changes in the last couple weeks. Two of her siblings gone, another one seeming to battle demons most days. Elliott back in her life, albeit temporarily. It was like standing in a batting cage, fastballs flying past her before she could swing. "Does Bel know yet?" Her friend's silence gave Peggy her answer. "You never talk about your family. Does it involve them somehow?"

"Yes. But…let me explain another time, okay? You're the first person I would talk to about anything, Peggy, but I'm just not ready. I'm sorry." A beat of thick silence passed. "And you were wrong. I'm not going to let you get away with tonight. I want to know where you were."

The comfort zone Sage usually allowed her popped. "I went to church."

Sage tilted her head. *Come on.*

Elliott's deep voice filtered through her thoughts. *Our father, who art in heaven…*

I'm a reminder of guilt. Something to pray about. Was the very idea of her in church laughable even to her best friend?

"Okay, I get it." The words came out louder than intended, so she took a calming breath. "I get it. I'm the antithesis of holy. I'm going to spark the end of days. Approach with caution."

Sage's brow knit together. "What are you talking about?" She scooted closer to the bed's edge, knocking a few pieces of lace onto the floor. "Peggy, the closer we got to Cincinnati, the quieter you became. Just talk to me." She smiled. "After four almost-weddings together, your skeletons were never in the closet."

"You don't know why I keep canceling the weddings," Peggy said.

"No. You're right. I don't know that." Sage's head tipped

forward, sending forth a curtain of light brown hair. "Everyone has that one thing, you know? That one sore spot. When someone prods it, we get the urge to...banish them and run for cover. My sore spot is my family." She pushed back her hair. "I won't do that to you, no matter how many times you ask, even if I can't talk about it yet."

Peggy frowned over at her friend. "If you prod my sore spot, I'm not going to banish you, either, Sage, that's—"

She started to say ridiculous, then realized...the assumption wasn't ridiculous. At all. Upon returning to San Diego after college, she'd made friends easily. Coworkers from the stores where she'd worked; even some of her customers had become hangout buddies. Where were those friends now? Phased out slowly because they'd been too curious about her serial relationships that ended before they had a chance. Avoided because the flighty answers she'd given to their serious questions left them feeling slighted or unsatisfied. Or not wanting their suddenly single friend around their boyfriends.

Peggy cleared her throat. "Yeah, okay, I can see why you felt like that." She wet her dry lips. "I could never do that with you, Sage. Ask me and I'll prove it."

"Who is he?"

Sage's astuteness didn't surprise Peggy. Not in the least. But having the almighty "he" acknowledged meant she was finally talking about Elliott out loud, and after three years of silence on the subject, she had to brace herself before sharing. She stood up and circled the room, giving a hollow laugh when she saw Sage had paused an episode of *Golden Girls* at a scene where Blanche—Peggy's favorite—was entering the room. Definitely not a coincidence. Sage was so thoughtful she wouldn't let Peggy miss a Blanche scene. Peggy hadn't rewarded that loyalty the way she should have.

"His name is Elliott Brooks. He's the—"

"The Kingmaker?"

Peggy turned with an eyebrow cocked. "Um. Yes?"

Sage squared her shoulders and sighed, obviously regretting that unexpected outburst. "I was down in the lobby earlier and they have this whole section in the gift shop dedicated to memorabilia. They were selling these little crowns that say, 'Elliott Brooks Made Me a King.'"

"Yeah." Pride bombarded Peggy before she could throw up a barrier. "He's kind of a big deal around here."

Sage watched Peggy in silence a moment. "Well, I don't care if he crowned King Arthur, he's dead to me if he's the one who hurt my best friend."

The corner of Peggy's mouth twitched once, before the whole thing moved into a smile. "You're a little bloodthirsty, aren't you, Sage?" She trailed her fingers across the clothes bureau. "It's always the quiet ones."

Sage straightened her back, crossing her legs in a way that made her look prim and proper, belying her outburst. "What are we doing here, Peggy? If he hurt you bad enough that you would cancel four weddings..." Sage visibly reeled herself in. "Maybe he doesn't deserve another minute of your time."

"Yeah, well. Staying away is easier said than done." She massaged her throat. "Every year, I get these e-mails for alumni weekend and I always turn them down. But...here I am." She blew out a breath. "I need to get him out of my head, because time isn't helping. Time has actually made it worse."

"Oh God, Peggy." Sage shook her head. "I'm sorry."

Hating the sadness radiating from her best friend, Peggy forced another bright smile onto her face. "He's the one you should feel sorry for. If all goes according to my evil plans, the next wedding you organize for me and some un-known prince is going to stick. I'll walk down the aisle with my head up, knowing he doesn't have the power to break my heart anymore. I just need to take the power back. To restore balance." When Sage only continued to watch her without speaking, sympathy on her pretty face, Peggy took a chance. "We're your family, too, Sage Alexander. Bel-mont and I. Whatever it is you're leaving us for, we can help you face it. Don't shut us out."

If Peggy had blinked, she would have missed the haunted quality that slipped into Sage's expression then trickled back out. "How about the episode where the *Golden Girls* head to Hollywood for the game show?"

Peggy swallowed the lump of disappointment and re-minded herself to be patient. God knew Sage had been like Mother Teresa with her. "Fine," Peggy murmured. "But it's my turn to be Sophia."

* * *

Shit. It was like she'd jumped into Marty McFly's DeLorean and ended up back in college. There she sat, crossed legged on the cheer squad changing room floor, thoughts of Elliott crowding out everything else. Senior year déjà vu. Around her, faces from her past chatted away happily, as if they'd just been waiting for the chance to re-unite. As if they lived for it. What was she living for?

She wasn't so self-absorbed to think she was the first one in that room to have her heart broken. She could probably swing a cat and hit at least five ladies who'd been hurt by a man.

Until Rita suggested the impromptu road trip on the morning after she'd burned down their mother's restaurant,

Peggy hadn't realized how inevitable this trip to Cincinnati had always been. Deep down, she'd been harboring the need to return. Pretending to be over Elliott, then getting cold feet before pledging her love to another man, was a circular pattern she intended to stop. No more breaking commitments on the off chance Elliott had merely been scared to get serious about someone else so soon after his wife's accident. And that he would come around. To a college senior, their year-long relationship had seemed like a millennium, but in truth, it was a short span of time for a man to get past something so horrific, right?

Now she knew. Time had nothing to do with him sending her packing. He genuinely didn't have room—or want—for her in his life. Yet her body had woken up and responded to his insensitive words last night, her blood blazing like it hadn't—not once—since going back to California. It made her wonder. Was she really back in Ohio to make Elliott's life hell? Or her own?

Discover your inner masochist in beautiful Cincinnati.

That should really be on a postcard.

Jacinda, the woman who'd been her co-captain senior year and now worked as a nurse practitioner, hopped up onto one of the wooden benches and clapped her hands twice. "Okay, ladies. I have some news." She paused for effect, playing with the charms on her bracelet. "Normally we do an alumni cheer with the current squad at halftime of the Saturday game. And we can still pull together that performance. But..." Another smiling pause. "Some of us girls have been talking and thought, why not buck tradition and put together a last-minute fund-raiser?"

A fluttering of murmurs went around the room.

"There's a banquet on Saturday night after the game, which signals the close of alumni week, but those of us

who've attended the last three years know that shit is boring." Everyone, including Peggy, laughed. "Now we all
know the football team is royalty around here, so if we
can convince them to participate, we have a much higher
chance for success. Hell, the cheerleaders are out in all
manner of weather rooting them on, so if they want to stay
on our good side, they'll help us raise a little cash to keep
our digs as cushy as theirs."

"Do you have a specific idea?" someone asked. "Like a
bachelor auction?"

Despite the hoots and whistling that ensued, Jacinda
shook her head. "Believe me, that was our first idea, too, but
it'll never happen. Coach Brooks likes his players to maintain a professional image at all times."

Hearing his name sent a series of little bomb blasts traveling up Peggy's spine, ending at her scalp. The blasts grew
louder when the woman to her left said, "Is it just me or
does Brooks get more delicious with age?"

"It's not just you," approximately eight people shouted
back.

"All that tightly leashed control," another one said, shiv-
ering. "Not to mention those tight buns, am I right? You
could bounce a silver dollar off—"

"What about a compromise?" Peggy interrupted too
loudly, pushing to her feet. Every head in the room swiveled
in her direction as she attempted to rein in the green-eyed
monster whose teeth had sunk into her jugular. "Maybe a
fashion show...where the players model signed jerseys and
the audience bids on them. The jerseys, I mean." When
heads began to bob and Jacinda gave her a thumbs-up to
continue, Peggy climbed onto her own bench, striking an
end of the runway pose that kicked up more laughter. "And
aw, shucks. Once the jersey has been sold, the players will

have no choice but to take the garment off." She gave an innocent shrug. "We might accidentally, innocently forget to mention that to the coach. Whoops?"

Her question was greeted by a round of applause and Peggy gave a sweeping bow, ending with a flourish when Jacinda held up a hand. "Okay, this is all amazing in theory, but the real miracle will be getting Coach Brooks to agree."

A rush of excitement twined through Peggy's veins, anticipation blooming in her tummy. "Not only will he agree, but he'll make a speech at the alumni banquet."

And yeah, that was greeted with skepticism, mainly from her old cocaptain across the room. "Brooks doesn't do speeches."

Peggy winked at her audience. "Leave him to me."

CHAPTER SEVEN

The orange juice in Elliott's stomach turned to acid. Already, he'd been having one hell of a shitty morning, and now this. His star receiver, Kyler Tate, sat across from him, saying the unimaginable. *I can't play in Saturday's game.*

Those words didn't compute for Elliott. Once you'd been recruited and given a full-ride scholarship, the Rapture had better be taking place for your duties as a player to be shirked. In his entire coaching career, he'd never had one of his men say those six hellacious words to him. After a sleepless night spent nursing guilt—and a hard-on for one beautiful, long-legged, *unattached* blonde—a response was not forthcoming. Elliott stared across the desk in his office at Tate, a kid he'd recruited out of an Indiana farm town, and placed the blame squarely on Peggy for his world being thrown into chaos.

There was no other explanation. He'd been perfectly fine, adhering to a schedule. Wake up, eat, drive Alice to school, football, football, football, go home. Now this. Now the unknown. His daughter wasn't talking to him for some mysterious reason. Not that their discussions ever went beyond surface items—schoolwork, mainly—but she hadn't even spared him a good-bye before slamming the car door this morning.

Now this. The receiver he'd groomed from a timid freshman with promise into a contender for the Heisman was prepared to blow off Temple on Saturday. For what? Elliott hadn't asked yet, because the answer flat out didn't matter. It wasn't good enough.

So he sat there still as a statue, not giving a shit about making Kyler sweat, and cursed alumni weekend to the devil. That's why Peggy was in Cincinnati, and his universe had decided to disorganize itself.

"What the hell did you just say to me?"

Kyler started at Elliott's booming question, raking a hand through the mop of sand-colored hair on his head. "I said, Coach, I won't be joining the team for Saturday's game. It truly is an unfortunate thing—"

"Unfortunate." Elliott leaned forward, stabbing a finger down on the desk. "Are you really prepared to lose your scholarship over this, Tate?"

"Yes, sir."

Elliott fell back in his chair, fully aware he regarded the other man the way one scrutinizes a bug beneath a microscope and not caring. Outside in the waiting room, he heard the door open and shut, but ignored the secretary's buzz to inform him of the visitor's identity.

"Ain't you going to ask me why, Coach?"

"This is your job. Showing up is the first requirement. So no, I'm not going to ask. It won't be a sufficient reason for letting down your team."

Tate nodded, a rare display of temper making itself known on his face. "Well, you recruited me because I refuse to back down, isn't that right? You brought me here because I had balls. Those were your words. So I'm going to tell you anyhow."

Elliott experienced a flare of pride, but it didn't dispel the irritation. Not one bit. If he needed to plan an offense around Tate's absence, he'd rather get down to business instead of having a fucking tea party about it. But dammit, he liked this kid. He'd believed in him. "Fine."

Tate seemed surprised by Elliott relenting, but was wise enough not to waste time questioning it. "It's my family, you see. They got a notice just this morning that their farm is being repossessed." His throat worked with emotion. "That land is all they got and—well, the plan was for me to go pro. Not trying to sound boastful, sir, but that was the idea. Then they wouldn't have to worry for nothing." He shrugged. "But time didn't cooperate, so I have to get home and at least try to fix it somehow. Fast. I don't want to let the team down but family is more important."

Such a sentimental attachment to family was something Elliott never understood. His players were constantly going on about their mothers, it seemed, and on the occasions Elliott hadn't managed to tune them out, he'd listened with the mystification of a man trying to decipher a foreign language. Elliott's own mother was still alive and living in Massachusetts, although his father had passed several years back after a stroke. She'd raised Elliott, sent him off to college with no fanfare, and checked in once a year at Christmas, content to lead a separate life, far from the sport she'd never made an effort to understand. Never once had he missed the communication or reminisced about fond memories because the few that were good enough to remember were so paper thin, you could see through them. Not...substantial. Certainly nothing that would choke him up, the way talking about the past did to his players.

"Coach?" Tate prompted.

Elliott picked up the stress ball on his desk and stood, pulverizing the object in his fist as he went to stare out the window overlooking the field. When he realized he was scanning the expanse of green for Peggy, he turned away with an inward curse. "Have you talked to a guidance counselor?"

"I don't much care to have some protocol recited to me." Tate scratched behind his ear. "I was kind of hoping you could do some counseling, Coach."

Elliott stared at the younger man, praying he was joking. There was a comfortable distance maintained by everyone else, and this kid seemed determined to cross it. A lot like someone else he knew. The reminder of Peggy made Elliott feel a definite pressure to help Kyler. Because *she* would expect it. At one time, she would have encouraged him to do good deeds, to try harder. Things had changed since then, though, hadn't they? He'd stopped setting himself up to disappoint others. Stopped trying to be better in her eyes, because she was no longer there to celebrate those small victories with him.

He coughed to clear the discomfort in his throat and refocused on his player. *You're not qualified for this.* What did he know of family and farms and land? He knew football. Church. That was all. "I send players to the draft, Tate. That's what I do. All I do. I don't hold your hand and tell you everything is going to look brighter and shinier tomorrow. I suggest you go listen to the protocol, because in my experience, it's in place for a reason."

Tate's eyes filled with obvious disappointment and Elliott couldn't deny the stabbing sensation in his chest at having let yet another person down. Finally, the young player stood, holding out his hand for a shake, refusing to let it drop until Elliott clasped it with his own. "Football isn't all anyone does," Tate said. "It's mortar, but it ain't the bricks."

"It's the mortar that keeps the whole damn thing standing," Elliott said firmly, stepping back and ignoring the punch of regret. "Best of luck to you, Tate." As he watched the player lope toward his office door, he felt the urge to call him back, but refrained. He knew one way to shape a future. To deviate from that method, to venture out of his depth, could mean failure. And God knew being some kind of father figure or mentor wasn't part of how he operated. He could barely parent his own kid.

Elliott's mental jumping jacks were brought to a screeching halt when Tate paused in the doorway, his exit blocked by Peggy. The younger man wasn't facing Elliott's direction, but his double take was obvious, even though he stepped back to maintain a polite distance.

"Excuse me, ma'am," Tate said quickly. "Or…Peggy, isn't it?"

Surprised pleasure made her lips jump. "Sure is."

Kyler scratched the back of his neck. "You wouldn't remember me. I was a freshman the year you graduated. But you're not so easy to forget." The tips of his ears were red, but he just kept going. "I once tripped over our cornerback on the way out of the tunnel because you'd stopped him dead in his tracks with a smile."

Peggy beamed. "Well. If you're going to get run over by someone, it might as well be a handsome man who comes equipped with flattery." With a groan, she bit her bottom lip and shook her curls. "Oh, wow. Sorry about that. I've been watching so much *Golden Girls* that I've begun to channel Blanche involuntarily."

Tate chuckled, stowing both hands inside his pockets. "I'm a Rose man myself."

"You only said a few words and somehow I already knew that." Peggy cocked an eyebrow. "Favorite episode?"

"Oh, you're going to make me pick, are you now?" Tate looked up at the ceiling. "I'd have to say when those jewel thieves move in next door and—"

"Hate to interrupt." Elliott heard the note of danger in his voice and could do nothing to disguise it. He enjoyed the sight of Peggy flirting with another man about as much as watching live oral surgery. "Some of us have to prepare for a game."

Tate glanced at Elliott, whatever he saw making him take a huge step back from Peggy. "Sorry, Coach. I didn't, uh...I was just being friendly. I didn't know—"

"Didn't know what?"

The younger man tipped his chin at Peggy. "Didn't know you had a girlfriend." He split an amused look between Peggy and Elliott. "I reckon no one in this entire school knows, come to think of it."

"I'm not his girlfriend," Peggy breathed, laying a hand on Tate's arm, causing the back of Elliott's neck to tighten as if someone had turned a deadbolt. "We're just old pals."

Elliott's stomach rebelled at Peggy's smiling pronouncement that she was available. He still hadn't wrapped his mind around that fact, so he sure as hell wasn't ready for everyone else to be aware of it. "Don't you have a train to catch, Tate?"

"I do, indeed." He cleared his throat, giving Elliott what would have been a meaningful look, if he were receptive to such things. "Thank you for everything you tried to do for me, sir. I won't forget it."

CHAPTER EIGHT

Peggy watched the gorgeous athlete move swiftly from the office after just about pouring his bleeding heart out at Elliott's feet. Outwardly, the rigid man standing behind his desk didn't appear to have a damn clue, but Peggy knew better. Down deep inside the coach lurked a benevolent soul. What had happened to it?

"What was that?" Peggy pressed a hand to her chest and slipped through the doorway. "He's one of your players, isn't he? Where's he going?"

Elliott's jaw flexed, a sure sign of annoyance, but Peggy couldn't find it in her to care about his mood this morning. Not when she felt so raw herself after their kiss last night. "Home," Elliott answered briskly. "He's going home." She started to ask why, but the words froze in her throat when Elliott turned away from her, throwing the ball in his hand at top speed, where it ricocheted off the wall behind his desk. "Something I can help you with Peggy?"

"I'll get to that," she murmured, her feet stuck in place thanks to Elliott's rare display of emotion. Off the field anyway. Three years ago, when they were alone in the dark or stealing moments in the light, Elliott had allowed his barriers to fall. Those glimpses had turned her infatuation into more. So much more. But she'd never expected to see the stripped-down side of him again. And she gravitated toward it now. The man beneath the cool exterior he'd once allowed her to know.

Unfortunately, Elliott's shoulders stiffened as Peggy approached. "This is a bad time, Peggy."

"Talk to me about it. Like you used to." She rested a hand on the desk's corner, gripping the wood to prevent herself from getting too close, possibly making him shut down even more. "Why is he leaving?"

"His family farm..." Elliott ripped off the baseball cap sitting on his head, tossing it onto the desk and leaving his hair in uncharacteristic disarray. "It's being repossessed."

Peggy trapped a sob in her throat, wishing she'd given the sweet guy with the molasses accent a bear hug. "That's awful. And...he's going to go save it?"

"I don't know, Peggy." He whirled on her, closing in until she was forced back onto the desk. "I had an All-American on my squad this morning and now I don't. That's all I know." He pointed a finger toward the window. "I solve problems down on the field. Saving people isn't my job."

Saving people. God, there was such a wealth of regret and pain in those two words. But he couldn't hear it and she couldn't address it. Letting him know she saw right through his façade to the hurt beneath might force Elliott to close himself off. "You didn't always limit yourself. Why are you doing it now?"

"Accepting things that can't be changed isn't a limitation. It's realistic."

"But how will you know if something can't be changed unless you try?"

"When it comes to certain things, Peggy, trying leads to losing." He was in her face now, the mint from his toothpaste familiar and inviting where it slid over her lips. "And I don't lose."

No one ever stood up this man but her, and she wouldn't be cowed now. "No? You're out a receiver." She hitched herself up on his desk. "I'd call that a loss."

He gripped the furniture on either side of her hips. "Who do you think you are, little girl? Coming into my office and telling me what I've done wrong?" His eyes were brilliant in their vexation, the attraction he was trying so hard to fight. "Where do you get the goddamn bravery?"

"The bravery is what you liked best about me," she breathed, heat sizzling in a downward V toward her thighs. "Isn't it?"

"No. That bravery is what almost led to my downfall." His hands found her bottom, jerking her to the edge of the desk. "I resented it. Still do."

"Liar," Peggy whispered, easing her thighs wider. "You're dying for an excuse to head for another downfall." When her legs were as open as she could spread them, she leaned up to Elliott's ear and let her breath shake loose. "One thrust."

Elliott's right hand came up out of nowhere, molding over Peggy's mouth as his hips crowded into the notch of her legs. With a quick maneuver to recline her halfway back, Elliott's erection found the apex of her thighs, delivering an aggressive pump against her underwear that sent a scream climbing up Peggy's throat, only to be trapped by his hand. Knees jerking up out of reflex over the rush of sensation, an orgasm almost—almost— broke past the surface, sending her waters rippling out on all sides. Her legs wanted to hug Elliott's waist, her voice wanted to beg for one more, one more, one more, but he shook his head, denying her, even though his gaze was hot, a low groan issuing from his harshly masculine mouth.

He leaned in and nipped the lobe of her ear. "Next time, ask for two."

"God, you can be an asshole," she managed, dropping her trembling legs as Elliott moved away. "I guess that was payback for daring to enter your office without swearing fealty to the Kingmaker."

Elliott's hands were on his hips, sweat beading his brow, offering Peggy some consolation that she wasn't the only one affected. "No? I could have sworn that's what you were doing." His gaze roamed over her rucked-up skirt. "If not, tell me why you're really here."

Peggy wanted nothing more than to sail out of the office, casting aspersions on his manhood and firing off a T-shirt cannon into an imaginary crowd, but that would have been too easy. Elliott achieving his desired result would only justify his asshole behavior and nothing was less acceptable than that.

But his regret over the meeting with Kyler was palpable, fatigue showing at the corners of his eyes. If she hadn't met the receiver, maybe she could have stowed Elliott's struggle in the back of her mind and gotten on with her own plans for closure. Timing was everything, though, and she couldn't forget the way that young man had looked at Elliott, begging for more.

"I was elected as the sacrificial lamb to come ask if you would lend your players to a good cause at the alumni banquet Saturday night."

"No."

"Well, that was easy." Peggy hopped off the desk, smiling over her shoulder as she headed for the door. "I'll go ask that young, new basketball coach. He seems...friendly."

"Wait." She turned to find Elliott glowering at her beneath raised brows. "On Sunday night, my players will either be reflecting on a loss or preparing for the next win. There's no room for anything else." He picked up a folder on his desk and threw it back down. "The basketball coach is a buffoon."

She continued to back out of the office. "I'll have to verify for myself."

"Peggy. Dammit." He jerked on the collar of his shirt. "We're not finished here."

"Tell me about it," she muttered, staring pointedly at the desk where he'd delivered enough sexual frustration to light the stadium. "No finishing last night. None this morning. Nonfinishing is a definite theme with you."

A muscle jumped in Elliott's cheek. "If you ask to auction off my players—"

"Just their jerseys. Signed." Peggy peeked out at the older receptionist, who was humming along to the classical music station, then discreetly shut the door, a move which narrowed Elliott's eyes. Seduction was a valuable weapon, and she never ruled it out, but the need for privacy was for a different reason. Peggy had an idea and didn't want anyone to overhear, because...people didn't take her seriously. *She's lucky she's pretty.* How many times had she heard that?

But she couldn't get Kyler's dejection out of her mind...or Elliott's doubt that he could make a legitimate difference. Maybe this time, this one time, she could be the glue in a situation. "Actually, Elliott..." She took a few steps toward the desk, her fingers smoothing over the covered outline of her necklace. "I have an idea to help Kyler. I don't know if we have time or what his family owes, or if it'll even work, but—"

"Peggy, it's not your fight."

"Maybe it is. Don't you believe in being in the right place at the right time? Could be I was meant to walk in on this meeting." When Elliott only allowed her to see his skepticism, Peggy squared her shoulders and continued on. "The proceeds from this jersey auction would have benefitted the Bearcats cheer squad, but if they knew about Kyler and his family farm, I know they would want to help."

"For all we know, they owe six figures on the land. A few jerseys aren't going to bring in that kind of cash."

"No, but you can." She braced her hands on his desk and leaned forward. "All those players you sent to the NFL would be happy to donate signed memorabilia, especially for one of their own who might not get his chance to go pro." He tapped a finger on his desk, a move she knew from experience meant he was thinking, considering. "It would only take some phone calls and e-mails. What athlete doesn't love hearing from a cheerleader, right?"

There was a flicker of warmth in his eyes. "You would spearhead this whole thing?"

That fleeting glimpse of the Elliott beneath the surface set her chest on fire. *There you are. I see you.* "Once upon a time, you would have helped me or thought of a way to help on your own. You weren't always such a pessimist."

"You're the only one who ever saw the optimist."

Breathe. In, out. Her internal instructions were hard to follow when he'd just hinted that they'd been good together. A bone-deep feeling she'd always kept, no matter the pain. Part of Peggy resented him for the hint, when he'd been the one to let her go. The other part wanted to throw herself across his desk and ask for more acknowledgment that they'd worked. *More.* "Um. Yes, I'll be the quarterback on this one. The other girls will help, too." A lightbulb crackled to life over her head. "My friend, Sage, is traveling with me and she can plan the crap out of anything. I can ask her for help."

Elliott tucked his tongue into his cheek, regarding her for a heavy beat. "Where are you traveling to, Peggy?"

"New York City. To stay," she said without hesitating, trying desperately not to analyze his quick glimmer of panic afterward. "You'll be rid of me soon enough. I promise to get out of town even faster if you say yes to the banquet auction idea. Please. Someone has to help this kid out."

It took him some time to speak, and when he did, he avoided her gaze by rummaging through some paperwork. "You're as much a kid as he is."

Epithets collided in her throat, but she managed to swallow them down. No, her brand of rejoinder was far more effective. It would bruise his pride the same way his words bruised hers. Trailing a finger along the edge of Elliott's desk, she sauntered her way around the expensive, but scarred, piece of furniture. The sound of shuffling paperwork ceased, his big body tensing when Peggy slipped between him and the desk, gliding her palms over his pecs. "Can I ask your receptionist for some contact information?"

"If it gets you out of here, yes," he growled. But his attention roamed over her breasts, his Adam's apple shifting in his throat. "You have the answer you wanted, now leave me in peace."

"You're never at peace," she whispered, letting her fingertips trail down his chest and stomach to his belt buckle, unlooping the leather and lowering his zipper in a few deft moves. "I can help with that for a little while."

"Peggy." Elliott's tone was one of warning, but he didn't stop her from reaching into the opening of his pants, slowly, while he held his breath. Through the cotton material of his briefs, she molded a hand over his erection, riding the hard flesh with her palm. "Fuck," he ground out on an exhale. "There's more, isn't there?"

Peggy hummed. "Will you make a speech, Elliott?"

"No." He widened his stance by an almost unnoticeable margin, pushing his erection into her hand, groaning behind clenched teeth when she stroked him faster. "I've made too many...concessions this morning already."

"For me." Her heart sped up despite the warning in the back of her mind chanting, *Don't ask.* "Why?"

"You think I like seeing you disappointed?" His mouth brushed against hers, his urgent, tortured energy making her inner thigh muscles spasm. "You think I ever liked being the one who let you down? I fucking don't. I hate it."

Peggy's blood reversed direction and she experienced the sensation of floating. He'd never once voiced regret over how he'd dealt with their breakup. How badly he'd hurt her when she'd been prepared to go all in on their relationship. And she could already see his expression clouding over, could see him wanting to take back the telling—they were telling, weren't they?—words. But she wouldn't let him. She couldn't.

Sinking her teeth into Elliott's lower lip, she tugged his head down for a kiss borne of elation and frustration, all at once. Within her hand, she felt his length swell and elongate, proof of her mouth's bad influence. Or good. She didn't know anymore. Had he admitted to making a mistake? A man like Elliott didn't apologize outright; he hinted at an apology and let others draw their own conclusions. Maybe she was getting ahead of herself. Maybe. But when he opened his mouth on top of hers and feasted, hope rose like a hot air balloon above a lush, green valley.

"You had to remind me I haven't finished you," Elliott pulled away to murmur at her lips, dragging the bottom one forward between his teeth. "Had to put your hand on my cock and remind me I left you hungry and wet last night. You and that body God uses to play a cruel joke on me by curving it for my pleasure." He gave a low, frustrated groan. "I'd agree to anything right now up against the crime of leaving you unsatisfied. For wanting to bite all your fingers to prevent you from doing it yourself."

Holy smokes. They blazed back into the kiss, Peggy whimpering and squeezing her legs together until Elliott shoved them apart and stepped into the space he'd created. She attempted to slide her hand inside Elliott's briefs, but he snagged her wrist, holding it out at the side. A power struggle ensued as they bruised each other's lips with a brutal, angry, starving kiss.

"Elliott," Peggy said hoarsely, using her feet, her knees to draw his body closer. "Please, I need the way you do it. So bad. So bad. Please."

Still restraining her right hand, he stooped down to suck on the flesh of her neck, showing no mercy. "How do I do it?" His teeth dug into her shoulder. "How do I fuck you?"

"Like you hate me. I need that. I deserve it." Peggy sobbed, about a split second before her body—along with Elliott's—went rigid. He released her manacled hand and she cupped it over her mouth, every cell in her body screeching with humiliation.

Where had that come from?

Elliott lifted his head, looking equally horrified in his

own stoic way. And for once, she didn't want to hear his response. At all. She wanted to get far away from that confusing confession and fast.

Elliott went to grab her arm, but Peggy performed some kind of genius swim move and danced out of his reach, laughing in a shrill manner that would make her cringe for the rest of her life. "So I guess that's a yes to the fund-raiser and s-speech? The alumni committee is going to be thrilled."

"I don't give a fuck about the committee." Elliott was still breathing heavy as he fixed his pants, buckling his belt while keeping his attention zeroed in on her. "What did you mean? Like I hate you? Like you deserve—"

"Just drop it." Heat seared the insides of Peggy's throat, fanning out into her entire body. She didn't *know* what she'd meant. It had come out of her mouth without warning, but there was no shaking a new sense of almost...clarity. Almost. But right now her embarrassment took center stage, not allowing her room to think. Aware of Elliott's close scrutiny, she managed a smile. "Has it been so long, you forgot how we like it?"

The accusation she'd intended to be playful sounded so incredibly lame to her own ears, but the shittiness was only amplified when Elliott appeared to buy it. She should have been relieved to escape with her dignity intact, but she wasn't. *Get in my face. Demand an explanation*, she silently begged. *I need one myself.* But he only watched her in that inscrutable way she still saw in her dreams. Or nightmares, rather.

"Thank you for agreeing to help," she said. "If you can manage to put a speech together, I'll make the fund-raiser for Kyler as little work for you and the team as possible."

"Peggy."

"Yes?"

A long silence passed where hope lifted and shattered a dozen times. "It's not a bad idea. If you can pull it off."

"Well, you certainly know how to flatter a girl," she responded in her best Blanche impression, waggling her eyebrows as she opened the office door. "Have a great day, Coach."

CHAPTER NINE

This way lies madness.

Elliott pulled the ball cap lower on his forehead, turning his back as two students fell out of the dormitory on a fit of laughter. Look at him. Prowling around campus in the middle of the night, trying to prevent anyone from seeing his face. A relationship with a student would lead to a scandal the likes of which would reverberate for years to come. Maybe decades.

Yet not even the threat of being fired could keep him away any longer.

The need for Peggy had been building without his consent for months. Building so high it towered over everything else now, swallowing his common sense in its shadow.

God forgive him, he hadn't felt anything like this...this yearning in his life. Even before he'd sunk into the sweetest home he'd ever known between Peggy's thighs, the way she'd spoken to him—seen right through him—had been like two charged surgical paddles slapping down on his chest, jerking him a foot off the operating table. Human. You can be human with her.

That was what his faith was supposed to do. Not a woman. Routine, planning, maintaining focus had always been where he found comfort.

The very things that had ruined his marriage.

And yet, here he was now, risking it all for a girl, when he'd held everything back from his actual family. The shame of that, the shame of being absent when he was needed, was a ten-ton weight, pressing him down every minute of the day. It would vanish around Peggy, but his guilt wasn't her responsibility. He shouldn't be there, wanting to give it all over to her for safekeeping. Just for an hour.

Only two days had passed since they'd met on the jogging path. Already the receptors she'd sent firing off in his brain were dimming, giving off no more sparks. He needed. Needed. Her. Despite knowing their relationship was wrong. She called to him like a siren, crumbling his resolve until it was nothing but rubble on the ground. He couldn't get warm, couldn't feel his pulse unless she was making it pound.

With the craving to feel alive blazing in his blood, Elliott entered the dorm, recalling the number Peggy had whispered in his ear on the mostly empty field that afternoon.

His knock was light out of necessity, although she answered almost immediately. Had she been expecting him? Her sleep-wrinkled tank top, panties, and messy curls weren't in keeping with that notion. But they were in keeping with making him so fucking hot, he swayed under the inundation of heat. "Elliott," *she whispered, moving more fully into the doorway and giving him an even better view, as if being provocative came as naturally as breathing to her. "You're here."*

"I'm here," he repeated, not recognizing his own voice. Still, the words were true in so many alarming ways. He was there. More there, more present, than he'd been in ages. Just since she'd opened the door. "Are you alone?"

"Yes. My roommate is spending the night with her boyfriend." She stepped back, an invitation to enter, but Elliott remained in place. "We can just talk, you know." He watched the column of her throat as she swallowed. "If you don't want to touch me."

The words touch me *stopped his breath. Made him think of lithe thighs climbing his waist, her young breasts bouncing beneath her cheerleading uniform. Wrong on so many levels. He should be locked in church, repenting for slipping, for being swayed from the righteous life he'd promised to live. Instead, here he was, being choked by the urgency to do it a second time. A third. A fourth.*

It was more than that, though. The way standing in front of her made his heart lurch proved it. He came for her acceptance. Her honesty.

"I came here to tell you it couldn't happen again." He stepped into the room, his need rising with the way her eyelashes fluttered, her mouth fell open to suck in air. "I was lying to myself, wasn't I?"

Peggy straightened her shoulders and put up her chin in a way that said she was gathering courage. The move endeared her to him, made him picture her in a football helmet and cleats, ready to take on his offensive line. God, she was so full of light, she glowed. Dammit, he couldn't afford to feel anything for this girl on top of wanting to fuck her, but it was no use. She was pulling him into the glow and it felt so damn good. "Yes, you were lying to yourself," Peggy said

finally. "But I'm glad you did, because it brought you here."
Her upper lip curled. "It saves me having to bust my other
knee to get rescued again."

"I rescued you. Is that what you think?" With an effort,
he broke their stare to scan the room, taking in the candles,
the frilly pink rug, scattered textbooks. "I think you've been
the one rescuing me for months. No one can look me in the
eye since it happened. Just you." His attention landed back
on her. "I depend on those eyes of yours most days."

Her breath came faster. "How hard was that for you to
say out loud?"

A curt nod. "Hard."

She smiled, two perfect rows of white teeth showing.

"The other day..." Elliott moved closer, his tongue
heavy in his mouth. "You told me I deserve to forget everything. To find you when I'm ready to be convinced." His
pulse was heading toward haywire. "I shouldn't ask. I'm
not your responsibility—"

"Stop." Peggy tilted her head, coming forward. Reaching up, she slid off his baseball cap and ran her fingers
through his hair, releasing bliss straight down his limbs.
"Talk to me."

"I can't focus." The confession fell from his mouth like a
stone, his forehead dropping down to hers. "I blew a play
call today during a scrimmage. I forgot to send lunch to
school with my kid. Everyone looks at me like I'm going to
blow up. Maybe I am." He clasped the sides of her face and
tugged her closer, as if it were possible. "Stop telling me I
deserve to forget everything. You're making it too easy. It's
supposed to be hard. I earned hard."

Challenging her, making it harder to give him what she'd
so freely offered, wasn't fair. He knew it deep down. But
this was the price people paid for getting involved with him,

wasn't it? Before this was over, she would probably be glad to never lay eyes on him again. "I won't stop. You didn't come here hoping I would stop," Peggy said, pushing back with her forehead. "Tell me something good you did today."

"No."

"Yes." She rubbed their lips together and hunger riddled his gut. Maybe even some resentment toward Peggy for making him feel so much. "Elliott."

"I . . ." He shook his head. "I left practice to bring her a happy meal."

Her lips curved. "Chicken nuggets?" He grunted a yes and her laugh tickled his mouth. "Start making her lunch at night, so it'll be there waiting in the morning. That's what my mother used to do. Mornings are a bitch, even for the Kingmaker." With a groan, Elliott watched her teeth worry that plump bottom lip. "As for everyone looking at you like you might blow up? They're right." Slowly, she untangled from him and stepped back, whipped the tank top over her head, leaving herself in nothing but bikini underwear. "So do it here with me where I can put your pieces back together."

Elliott surged forward like a tidal wave, stopping just short of her, hands poised just above her hips, biting back the urge to crush them in his grip. He could feel the heat of her waist, her belly . . . knew she would be soft to the touch. Warm. Everywhere. His cock stood at attention, dying to slip into the tightness hidden beneath those sheer panties.

In his pants pocket, the weight of the rosary beads heated like a reminder.

"A man shouldn't receive pleasure for his penance, Peggy." His hands finally fell to her hips, tightening until she whimpered. "He shouldn't get to knock on a door, knowing there's a gorgeous girl with a wet pussy waiting on

the other side." Starving beyond the bounds of his control, he turned her around, walked them the final few feet to the twin bed and pressed her upper half down, bracing his lap against the curve of her gorgeous bottom, growing dizzy at the perfect way his erection wedged between her cheeks. "A misbehaving student who whispers in the coach's ear when she damn well shouldn't." His hand lifted and dropped hard, smacking her right ass cheek, the sharp, unfamiliar sound filling him to the brim with lust. More so, when Peggy sagged with a moan. "Christ. This is going to have consequences for us both. Giving in to temptation this satisfying can't come for free."

"I say it does," Peggy whispered, arching her back and sliding her feet apart, ripping a strangled growl from Elliott. She looked back over her shoulder, so courageous and vulnerable and seductive. Sweat began sliding down his temples, his hands fisting at the small of her back. She doesn't realize yet that I have nothing to give in return. She will soon enough. *"We're the only ones here, Elliott," Peggy continued, her voice dreamlike. "You're the ruler of your own world right now." She dipped her bottom, sliding it back up the fullness his pulsing cock. "Wield your power."*

His breath wheezed in and out as he unhooked his belt and yanked down his zipper with shaking hands. "God help me. Who could resist you? Who?" He tore off his sweatshirt and tee, knowing if he didn't press every available inch of their skin together, he would regret the oversight. As if he wasn't already in the eye of the lust storm, Peggy's wide-eyed perusal of his chest and abdomen sucked him into the twisting eddy. "You have something to say, little girl?"

"You're what a man looks like," she breathed. "You're… beautiful."

Elliott reeled under the generosity of her words. Her

body. But Lord, if he allowed an ounce of what she inspired in him to escape, it would all come rushing out and he'd never patch the damage. Never regain his equilibrium. Worse, she might expect more from him and more...more meant loss. More could mean failing her.

Giving Peggy more would mean...all. The all he hadn't been capable of giving before.

The sound of his rosary beads rattling in his hand echoed in his mind. No choice but to ignore them and the guilt they represented for now, Elliott shoved Peggy's panties down to her knees and tested her wetness with a rough finger. Finding her soaked, he slammed his erection home, growling behind his teeth at the utter blanking of his mind to anything but their joined bodies, the slope of her arched back. "Our father, who art in heaven..."

* * *

There was a bee in Elliott's collar, buzzing around, stinging him at will. During a game, when something wasn't quite right on the field, but he couldn't put his finger on the issue, the same damn bee always showed up, the vibrating hum of its wings growing louder and louder until he swatted it away by coming up with the solution. He didn't have an explanation for what bothered him about the conversation in his office with Peggy. Only knew this particular bee was the queen and it stung twice as hard.

Like you hate me. I deserve it.

Those words stampeded like a bull over his concentration, the pencil in his hand having remained stationary going on half an hour. Sex between him and Peggy had always been rough and angry, yes. No denying it. But hate had never entered the equation. He would have remem-

bered. Hell, he remembered everything about those months
with Peggy—that was his life's struggle.

I deserve it. What the hell had she meant by that? Even
though ending his relationship with Peggy had been the
right thing to do, if anyone deserved to be hated, it was
Elliott. He owned up to that fact. The only way to make
her see reason all those years ago had been to be an outright prick.

Words they'd spoken in the heat of the moment tried to
infiltrate his mind, but his throat started to feel strained, so
he shoved those memories to the side. Not today. Not ever.
This was what happened when a man allowed his psyche to
be rearranged. He never got it back the way he liked it.

She'd tried so hard, too. Pulling him into her glow. Urging him to look for the silver lining in everything. She'd
almost succeeded in making him human, but there had been
too many reminders of how he'd neglected his past responsibilities to give the future over to her. As much as he'd
hungered to.

Giving his neck a quick twist to crack it, Elliott jerked
open his desk drawer, the rosary beads inside slithering
to a stop against the wood panel. Surprised he only felt a
passing urge to pick them up, Elliott bypassed them and removed one of the uniform black notebooks and flipped to
the first page—

His phone rang.

"For the love of God," he muttered, picking up the receiver. "Coach Brooks."

"Coach B-Brooks," a woman's voice squeaked on the
other end. "I'm sorry to bother you. I'm so sorry. We've got
that big game with Temple coming up and—"

"Start with your name." Elliott sighed, well used to people shitting their pants when the need to communicate di-

rectly with him arose. Everyone but Peggy anyway. She talked to him like no one else dared.

"Oh! Oh, this is Alice's drama teacher, Mrs. Hughes. I should have said that up front." A groaning laugh. "Um, we have a slight problem down here at the school. I wouldn't call you if it was something I could handle on my own."

Elliott shot forward in his chair, panic dropping like cement on his shoulders. "What's wrong?" He slapped a hand over the receiver, so Mrs. Hughes wouldn't hear his overworked breathing. A flash of memory sliced into view; receiving a phone call while at the stadium, just as he was now. Not being the man his family needed. Not living up to the responsibilities he'd taken on. "Is Alice okay?" When the woman sucked in a breath, Elliott realized he'd shouted the question, so he repeated it in a more reasonable voice. "Is Alice okay, Mrs. Hughes?"

"Yes, yes. Physically, she is fine." The murmuring of excited voices kicked up in the background. "But she has locked herself in the auditorium bathroom. I think it's a case of stage fright, bless her soul." A nervous laugh. "But alas, the rehearsal must go on and Monday night's performance is almost upon us...so we need to get her out, or find a replacement."

Elliott wasn't exactly clued in on the mysterious world of his daughter, but he gathered she would be devastated if the part was given to someone else. And the possibility of Alice crying was undesirable. It made his chest pull tight, right at the center. So...what? He needed to leave his job in the middle of the workday and negotiate a teenager out of a bathroom? Mrs. Hughes had overestimated him if she thought he had those capabilities. He tried to think of one of his players locking themselves in a bathroom and refusing to come out. The ridicule would be endless.

It would be worse among a pack of teenagers, wouldn't it? Shit.

"Coach Brooks? Are you still there?"

"Yes." Lord, he didn't have a choice, did he? "I'm on my way."

The jog to the parking lot did nothing to increase Elliott's confidence in the task ahead. Students and faculty saw him coming and promptly feigned fascination with their cell phone or flat out changed direction. No one said hello. No one asked why he was moving even faster than usual. And maybe the conversation with Peggy earlier was still bothering him in the form of a queen bee in his collar, but for the first time in years, everyone's fear of him seemed amplified. Loud and impossible to ignore. Normally, he was grateful he didn't have to stop and make small talk—and he still was—but now all he could hear was Peggy's voice. *Like you hate me. Like I deserve.*

Peggy was so prominent in Elliott's mind as he reached the parking lot and unlocked his truck, it took him a moment to believe she was there, just across the aisle. Even though he was in a rush, he couldn't seem to move, his hand frozen in the act of opening the driver's side door. None the wiser that he was watching, Peggy lowered the back gate of the rusted Suburban, picked up a gear bag, and attempted to heave it inside, forehead pinching with the effort. Elliott lunged, thinking to help her with the clearly heavy duffel before she hurt her back. A ridiculous notion by the laws of physics, since he was so far away and couldn't reach her in time. But something happened before he could try, cementing Elliott in place once again, at the rear bumper of his truck.

Another man caught the bag in midair and tossed it into the Suburban.

Peggy looked at the newcomer a moment—no expression to speak of—before face-planting in his chest, arms limp at her sides.

The bee in Elliott's collar went crazy, stinging him beneath the hairline, before traveling around to his jugular and sinking its spiky tail in there. Again and again. Before Elliott knew he was moving, he'd stepped out into the aisle. A vehicle to his left laid on its horn, breaks squealing, stopping short of hitting Elliott by mere inches. The force of the wind sailing past finally brought Elliott back to the present.

"*Elliott*," Peggy shouted, stepping away from the dark-haired man, hands flying to her mouth. "What are you doing?"

He couldn't respond. Couldn't take his eyes off Peggy and the man comforting her. Had she lied about being single? Dizziness accompanied his next thought.

Was that man her fucking *husband*?

Peggy's hands fell away from her face. "You could have been hit!"

"Coach Brooks," the male driver was saying. "I'm sorry. I—I didn't see you there. Oh Jesus…right before the Temple game…"

There was a suspicion in the far recesses of Elliott's mind that he was embarrassing himself, but Peggy in someone else's arms was far worse. Far, far worse. When she'd been in an invisible man's arms on the other side of the country, the notion had barely been manageable. In the beginning, he'd been forced to numb his brain. By working until exhaustion caught up with him and he passed out, not waking up for full days on occasion. Blocking out the world until it became absolutely necessary to formulate responses outside of coaching. Yeah, it had been murder on his sanity thinking of her with someone else, but he'd never expected to see it happening live. "Step back." Elliott cleared the cobwebs from his voice. "Step back from him."

Confusion replaced Peggy's worry. "Excuse me?"

Elliott strode toward the pair, no idea what he'd do once he reached them. He never found out, though, because the dark-haired man stepped into his path, his features arranged in the quietest fury Elliott had ever seen. The singular layers of curiosity, rage, and calm might have fascinated Elliott on a different day, but all he could think of was making blood run through the center of them.

"Are you the one?" the dark-haired man asked.

"I was just going to ask you the same thing," Elliott returned, surging into the intruder's personal space, hands fisting in preparation to swing.

"Bel," Peggy said, attempting to wedge herself between them. "Elliott. Stop."

Bel. He'd heard that name before. Somewhere in the dark with Peggy's fingers combing through the hair on his chest, her voice dreamy as she talked about her family, San Diego. Relief and yearning kicked in at the same time, making his voice emerge like gravel. "Your brother. This is your brother."

"Yes. Who did you—" Peggy broke off, dismissing him with a waved hand. "Never mind. I'm afraid to find out."

"I asked you a question," Belmont said, his cold anger still visibly intact. "Are you the one?"

A pit opened in Elliott's stomach. "The one what?"

"Bel, please." Peggy slid her arms around her brother's waist and it took every ounce of Elliott's willpower not to separate them, siblings or not. "Please, don't. Please don't."

"You didn't really see her," Belmont said, his eyes narrowing. Blue eyes. Not that rich golden brown like Peggy's. Different fathers, he recalled fleetingly; the other man's words were so packed with gravity, they demanded attention. "You're still not really seeing her, so you'll get no sympathy from me. It's going to happen too late and you'll be nowhere. A goner."

A beat of time passed wherein Elliott wondered if he'd actually been hit by the car and Belmont was the keeper of the gates of heaven, listing his sins. Ridiculous. But there was no denying the note of truth in the man's tone of voice. Elliott couldn't recall a single time he'd been so certain of another person's... authenticity.

Elliott opened his mouth to question Belmont, but the cell phone in his pocket went off and reality sped in like a silver bullet. He snatched the device from his pocket to find his secretary had called several times, probably since he'd been in the parking lot behaving like a lunatic. "Alice," he said, already turning toward the truck. "I have to get down to the school."

"Wait," Peggy called, making him pause mid-aisle. Thankfully, no cars almost killed him this time. "Is everything okay with Alice?"

After walking through campus, everyone avoiding him like the plague, her genuine concern was almost too much. "She got stage fright. Locked herself in the bathroom."

Belmont reacted right along with Peggy, mirroring her concern, as if the last five minutes of all-out animosity hadn't taken place. Peggy noticed it, too, and tension crept into her frame the more rigid Belmont grew. That obvious connection between siblings made Elliott anxious. He didn't like her having that kind of bond—not with anyone. To hell with caring that it made him a selfish prick.

Finally, Peggy's gaze cut through his jealousy. "Well, let's go get her out."

CHAPTER TEN

As if the return to her alma matter hadn't been enough of a blast to the past, now Peggy was venturing into a middle school auditorium. Everything from the plastic bucket seats and stale granola smell to the stage ahead looked like doll furniture, but she imagined all those components appeared massive and important to the students. Students who were currently huddled in groups, speaking in whispers and failing to disguise their laughter. Over Alice?

Peggy's stomach flopped over. Elliott thought he was out of his depth? She'd been a fucking cheerleader—about as far as one could get from a drama geek. And yet the heft of this mission rested squarely on her shoulders. She could feel it, weighing her down into the cheap carpet as she and Elliott approached the harried teacher. For once, Belmont was no help at all, his claustrophobia keeping him stationed at the auditorium door, arms crossed like a sentry. Not that he'd said a word about his agitated condition to

Peggy, but she knew seeing Alice trapped in a small space would bother him, so she'd squeezed his elbow to let him know she understood.

See? Easy. Teenager having a meltdown in front of her peers? Not so much.

What to say to Alice? What to say? Just like her first encounter with Elliott's daughter last night, she could very well blurt out the dumbest thing to enter her head and blow this undertaking to smithereens. The girl would be found seven hundred years from now, her bones uncovered by paleontologists, still locked inside the bathroom. *Theorists have concluded that this specimen's father's ex-lover was responsible for her rather awkward demise. Now, on to our next exhibit…*

When the students began taking notice of the legend in their midst—Elliott—a hush fell over the groups, elbows nudging, mouths dropping open. Sensing how much Elliott was discomfited by the hero worship, she let her hand graze his, just a touch, in a way that would appear accidental. Or might have, if he didn't raise a stately eyebrow in her direction.

"Do you have a game plan?"

Peggy pulled him to a stop mid-aisle. "This isn't football, Elliott." She cast a glance toward the awed students. "This is middle school. It's far bloodier."

"You're exaggerating."

"Were you born an adult or did you manage to wedge a childhood in there?"

"I assume you don't expect an answer."

"Oooh." She gave him a narrow-eyed head shake. "You're so condescending sometimes. It's even in the way you look at people."

He rolled his tongue along the inside of his lower lip. "I

don't have a mirror, Peggy, but I'm pretty damn sure that's not how I look at you."

"No." She drew the word out while mentally reminding herself of her ulterior motive. Just because she was there to save Alice didn't mean she couldn't tick a box on her seduction checklist. "You look at me like a dieter ogling chocolate cake. But you should know something."

"What's that?"

She moseyed a step closer. "Even the most dedicated dieter eventually takes a bite."

If they were alone in that moment, she had a feeling he'd have taken a few bites, but as it were, they had a rapt audience. Peggy was just getting ready to remind Elliott of that when he slanted his head to the side. "What did you mean earlier when you said, 'I deserve it'?" He gave a tight head shake. "It's not sitting right."

Fast as Peggy could manage, she pushed through her surprise. She hid the achy, breathless shock that he'd even been thinking about their encounter by brushing off the question with her best *Whatchu talking 'bout, Willis* look. She still didn't know what she'd meant by her unexpected outburst earlier. There had always been something poking beneath the surface, preventing her from moving on from Elliott. Was this buried belief that she deserved punishment the cause? "You Catholics really know how to dwell." Needing to distract him, she cast a glance toward the buzzing students. "While I'm salvaging this seventh grade Armageddon, why don't you go sign autographs for these kids? It'll make their year."

"Autographs," Elliott repeated slowly. "I haven't exactly been friendly since..." He stopped himself, cutting her a quick, sidelong glance. "You sure that's something they'd want?"

"Of course it is," Peggy murmured. "Everyone wants one. They're just too scared of you to ask."

"You're not," he blustered. "Today alone, you've had me agree to a speech, a fund-raiser, and a signing."

Her smile bloomed. "That sounds like a yes."

Elliott grunted.

Even though he'd broken her heart and stood between her and potential happiness with someone else, Peggy was so happy with him for agreeing, she went up on tip-toes and laid a smacker on his cheek, lingering there to speak near his ear. "Right about now, I'd let you auto-graph my naked body in Sharpie. Anywhere you wanted. As many times as you wanted. And I wouldn't even try to wash it off." She pulled back and started toward the stage, throwing him a little wink over her shoulder. "Makes you wonder why you aren't always so agreeable, huh?"

His wolfish growl imbued Peggy with the confidence she needed. She'd never been much of a planner, but she'd been born with enough bravado to sink an ocean liner. At times like these, mama worked with what the good Lord gave her. "Hello! Hi!" Peggy chirped as she reached the drama teacher—Mrs. Hughes, Elliott had informed her on the way in—who could have passed for one of the students in stature, but the character lines around her eyes set her apart as the adult. Peggy took her hand and shook it vigor-ously. "So lovely to meet you. Can you please direct me to my acting pupil, Alice Brooks?"

"Your pupil?" Despite her clear confusion, the woman's warm smile never faltered. "Are you her—"

"Acting coach. Yes." Peggy threw her arms out with abandon and turned in a slow circle. "Ah, to be back on the middle school scene. It hasn't lost its magic and it never will. Not as long as there's a stage to serve as our magic wand, right, Mrs. Hughes?"

"Sure. Yes. Yes!" The woman actually began to shake when Elliott joined Peggy, the dozen or so necklaces looped around her neck clanking together. "Coach B-Brooks. It's an honor. Can I get you a glass of water?"

"I'm fine."

Two words from Elliott nearly sent the teacher into a swoon and Peggy started praying they kept smelling salts backstage. "Since I don't see Alice," Peggy continued, loud enough for everyone to hear, "I assume she's still mid-exercise."

Mrs. Hughes glanced toward the right auditorium wing, probably where the bathroom was located. "Mid-exercise?"

"Yes." Peggy walked past the drama teacher toward the stage, running her finger along the edge and picking a few boys to smile at. "She's getting into character, just as she's been instructed. Time doesn't exist until the curtain call, isn't that right, Mrs. Hughes?"

"Well, I suppose—"

"If a butterfly emerges from its cocoon before it's ready, it might never fly as magnificently as it could otherwise." Peggy threw herself into a chair between two female students in the front row and took their hands. "I encourage you all to follow Alice's lead pre-performance and close yourself off from this world until you're ready to fly into the next. Just like the butterfly. You are all butterflies."

"Uh. Thank you," one of the girls muttered.

Swearing she heard Belmont's low chuckle from the entrance, Peggy surged to her feet. "Alas, every pupil needs a mentor. Does the butterfly not receive assistance from the wind?" She blew a kiss at a male student who sat three rows back with his mouth hanging open. "I must go to her."

Mrs. Hughes lifted her arm in slow motion. "She's that way."

Peggy caught only a quick glimpse of Elliott's astonishment before sailing off toward the ladies room. "Oh!" She stopped short and turned. "While I consult with my actor, Coach Brooks would be pleased as punch to sign autographs for—"

Everyone moved at once, diving over chairs and riffling through backpacks for writing implements. Peggy couldn't help but watch for a few seconds, arrested by the utter disbelief on Elliott's face when the kids formed a line, excitement rolling off them in waves. The quiet grit of his voice had Peggy closing her eyes and sighing as she approached the bathroom and knocked.

"Malice Alice. Your rescue has arrived."

"I heard you from in here. Are you from another planet or something? Oh God, there's no way they bought that."

"Yeah, there's a pretty good chance some of them didn't." Peggy leaned to the side so she could get her eyes on the autograph proceedings. "But I think your pops is tidying up any loose ends."

Silence. "I can't believe he's here."

Peggy frowned at the door. "Did you think he wouldn't come?"

"I don't know." A gusty sigh. "But I've been in here for, like, ten hours. No way I can come out now."

"Yes, you can." Peggy leaned her side against the door and crossed her ankles. "Tomorrow there will be something else for them to gossip about. Maybe we can even frame someone as a diversion tactic."

"Chess Club Moonlights as Strippers." Alice sniffed. "The middle school paparazzi will eat it up."

Peggy snort-giggled. "You're a funny kid, Alice." There

was no response from the other side of the door, which could have been a good or bad thing, but Peggy had no way of knowing without seeing the twelve-year-old's face. She needed to do better here. Unfortunately, she'd never been so aware she was winging something. Peggy blew out at a breath and turned, bracing both hands on the door. "Look, you might not see it now, but you have the advantage here."

"Wow."

"Stay with me." Peggy patted the door. "Like I said, you've got a great sense of humor and...reality, which puts you ahead of those kids out there. You can see this situation for what it will be in the future. A great frickin' story. You're going to slay with this one someday at a party." There was no answer. God, she was sucking balls. Before Peggy could turn away from the door, however, a giant hand came to rest on her shoulder. She didn't have to turn around to know it was Belmont because the peace that cooled her head to toe was his signature effect. "Listen, Alice," Peggy tried again, voice firmer than before. "When I was in middle school, I worried about things like my hair and brand names and...okay, I still worry about things like that. But you're different."

"That's the problem."

"No, it's not." Peggy drew a heart on the door, then filled it with little finger scribbles. "You're already looking back on this day with an adult perspective, aren't you? The way you talked about what's-her-name...Kim Steinberg—"

"Oh my God." An agonized groan hurtled through the door. "Lower your voice or she's going to hear you."

"Ooh, sorry." Peggy winced. "But seriously, that's the kind of outlook I never had going for me. Not many people do. You know middle school isn't where life ends, but you're living in the moment kind of grudgingly anyway.

You're going to make the ultimate adult." Peggy turned to Belmont with a how-am-I-doing expression, but he only shrugged. "Go out there and take it all in, Alice. Laugh about it and move on. There are bigger and better things ahead for you. Like the best ice-breaker story ever. Some dopey ex-cheerleader pretended to be your acting coach while you lived in the bathroom for an afternoon. Plus? Chess club strippers."

"Sounds like this is going well," Elliott remarked from the hallway entrance. "Alice—"

The door opened.

Peggy almost fell headfirst into the bathroom, but Alice and Belmont caught her just before she busted her ass. She straightened, brushing both hands down her skirt. "Well. When you gotta go…"

Alice laughed, then seemed almost embarrassed for cracking. "I better not keep them waiting out there." She peeked up at Peggy. "Thanks."

Lightness inflated in Peggy's chest. "No problem."

Alice's head tipped back, her face turning red as she saw Belmont for the first time. "Who i-is that?"

"That's your bodyguard." Peggy nudged her brother with an elbow. "Bel?"

He nodded at Alice and stepped aside, indicating she should lead the way. "After you."

"Whoa," Alice breathed. "I wouldn't mind him being one of the bigger and better things ahead." A beat passed. "I just said that out loud, didn't I?"

Laughing, Peggy gave Alice a side hug and sent them on their way.

Before the pair could enter the auditorium, Alice paused in front of Elliott. "Hey, sorry about making you come down here. I just—"

"Don't mention it," Elliott said brusquely. "I'm glad it all worked out."

"Yeah." Even though there was a definite note of disappointment in her voice, Alice's shoulders stayed squared as she threw a glance at Peggy. "Can you come over for dinner tonight?" Clearly startled by her own invitation, she didn't take it back. "It's just spaghetti or whatever, but…"

"I, um…" Peggy didn't have to look at Elliott to know he didn't want her to accept. "I don't know if I can—"

"Please?" Alice asked, the flush on her face deepening.

There was no way in hell Peggy was going to turn down Alice and let her be embarrassed twice in one day. Elliott could just suck it up for an hour and deal with the fact that she existed. "Sure. I'll bring the Kool-Aid."

Alice rolled her eyes, but her pleasure was obvious. "See you later." She looked up at Elliott. "Bye."

"Bye, Alice."

When Elliott and Peggy were alone in the hallway, the silence was thick. Too thick. Before she had to endure a lecture or listen to him explain why dinner was a bad idea, she breezed past him. "Relax. It's not about us."

"Hey." He snagged her elbow before she could pass. "I appreciate what you did." His voice sounded rusted. "She'd still be in there if I'd come here by myself."

"You have no idea how wrong you are. She would have flung that door open before you got through a hello." Between his statement and questioning earlier if the students really wanted his autograph, those insecurities the great Coach Brooks used to reveal only to her were shining through. Letting her in just enough to make her ache, dammit. But she'd never been able to turn away from him, especially when he needed reassurance. "Tell me one good thing you did today."

His features tightened, the air growing heavier around them as past collided with present. "After all this time, after everything, you're still trying to redeem me?"

Further proof she was a glutton for punishment. "No. You have to take care of that yourself now." Feeling his scent, his magnetic presence, and his hypnotic voice begin to take hold, she tugged out of his grip before she could make a fool out of herself and beg him to let her in again. That's not why she was in Cincinnati. "Just like I have to take care of myself. Later, Elliott."

CHAPTER ELEVEN

And just like that, Elliott was more focused on dinner than the game with Temple on Saturday. Which was unsettling to say the least. When he'd dismissed practice half an hour early, his players had looked at him like he'd donned a dress and started tap dancing on the field. For good reason, too. The offense he'd designed specifically for the upcoming game still needed tweaking due to losing Kyler, an announcement that had cast a dark pall over practice all its own. Not to mention, he now had a speech to work on.

Yeah, he'd known Peggy's return would throw a wrench in his engine, but he'd forgotten exactly how much he enjoyed being thwarted by her antics. Hadn't allowed himself to remember how much she calmed him and crucified his control at the same time. How addictive that combination could become.

He'd heard far more of Peggy's speech to Alice than he'd let on that afternoon. Standing there, he'd been so aware of his pulse, he could have closed his eyes and counted each little bump. That is, if he'd been capable of removing his focus from Peggy. She'd always been earnest and bright, but the additional maturity to her now? It got his blood flowing even hotter. He wanted to pin her down and ask what she'd experienced during her three years away. Maybe ask what gave her the nerve to be even more fascinating now than she'd been at twenty-two.

She was doing damage to his peace of mind. Always had. But there was a new sense of urgency in his belly making him crazy.

Elliott pulled up to the house and exhaled slowly when he didn't see the Suburban. It was entirely possible Belmont had dropped Peggy off, though, meaning she could already be inside his home. Inching toward the tennis ball that hung from the ceiling, his foot slammed on the break when an image of Peggy in his bed blindsided him. He threw the truck into Park with a curse but didn't try to dismiss the image, knowing from experience it would haunt him until he allowed it to play out.

Dinner would be over, Alice gone to bed. Peggy would ask for a tour upstairs and they would move quietly, careful not to be heard. She would tease him a little, slinking around his bedroom and picking up his watch, his aftershave—sniffing it—all while he followed on her heels, waiting for the right moment to strip her naked. She'd be wearing a thong—that little nude-colored nylon one from his memory—and he'd slide it down her legs with his teeth, watching her back arch on the bed.

Elliott groaned in the truck's silent interior, pushing his erection down with the heel of his hand, but succeeding only in chafing it into something bigger, more urgent. And when he opened his eyes, Peggy was looking right back at him from the garage entrance, holding a glass of soda in her hand. Smiling knowingly.

She saluted him with the glass and retreated back into the house, her skirt molding to her backside in such a taunt, he would have put her over his knee and given those cheeks hell if they were alone. It wouldn't have been the first time.

Rein it in, Elliott.

The scene he was about to walk into would be dangerously homey. Alice cooking dinner, Peggy setting the table or helping cut up salad ingredients. If he wasn't careful, his mind might play tricks on him. Confuse him into thinking he were the kind of man who welcomed the idea of home. Family. Togetherness. He'd tried it once and hadn't succeeded. He'd failed to be a good husband and proved every day how deeply his abysmal parenting skills ran.

This was a one-off deal. Peggy acknowledging earlier that day that this dinner wasn't about them might have made him feel hollow, but the sensation would pass. What wouldn't pass was his inability to be the kind of man who comes home to spaghetti and small talk every night. He wasn't built for those comforts.

So why was he so damn anxious to get inside?

Elliott brought his libido back under control and climbed out of the truck, the smell of red sauce and sautéed mushrooms wrapping around him. Not the usual scent of Alice's spaghetti, and when the kitchen came into view, he saw why. Peggy stood side by side with Alice at the chopping block, a sprig of rosemary tucked behind her ear, instructing her on how to judge when you're adding too much garlic.

"Dad." Alice looked more animated than he'd seen her in a long time, and warning bells went off at the same time his pulse went haywire, the scene way more real than he'd been expecting. Especially the way Alice regarded Peggy with such blatant hero worship. If he'd allowed the moving picture in his kitchen to be the norm for the last three years, would he have already fucked it up? "Did you know Peggy's mother used to have her own cooking show on TV?"

How were they playing this? As far as he knew, Alice had been told Peggy was a professor at the college, but who knew if she'd even bought that explanation? Still, it was a big jump from Peggy being his colleague to an ex-student with whom he was formerly involved. When Alice blinked at him, still waiting for an answer, he decided honesty was the best policy when dealing with someone as sharp as his daughter. "I did know that." Alice looked a touch surprised by his answer, but didn't comment. "Is there something I can do?"

"Got it under control, Coach," Peggy said, without looking at him.

Elliott nodded once. "I'll be in my office."

A few moments later, he closed the door behind him and propped both hands on his hips, running through the team's offense in his mind to erase the vision of Alice and Peggy huddled in the kitchen. To block the way it made him feel; a sensation far too close to content. The contentment he'd experienced with Peggy years back had been so brief, he shouldn't recognize the return of it now. But there it was, like green sprouts trying to push through dead weeds.

There was a gentle knock on the door behind him. Thinking it was Alice, he turned and opened it, surprised to find Peggy on the other side. The stress of what he'd come home to must have shown on his face because Peggy gave a low whistle. "Brought you a beer." She held it out to him. "Looks like maybe you need whiskey, though."

Maybe it was the way she made light of something he found so heavy. Maybe it was simply a buildup of tension inside of him, starting on the day she'd left town. Or the day she'd returned. He didn't know. Only knew he was so damn aware of the strain in his hands, his neck, his chest… and it needed to go somewhere. Preferably to the person who'd caused it.

When he clasped Peggy's wrist and jerked her into the office, beer sloshed over the bottle's rim, but neither of them stopped to clean it up. Elliott kicked the door shut and moved up behind Peggy, burying his face in her hair, pushing against her ass with his growing erection. "Lay your hands flat on the desk."

"W-why?"

Despite questioning him, she set the bottle down so fast on the wooden piece of furniture, it suggested her arms had lost strength. "Did you really come in here to bring me a beer?" He hooked a finger beneath the hem of her skirt, drawing it up to find a neon orange thong running between her cheeks. "Or were you wondering if that little salute you gave me in the garage might have earned you a spanking? Is that what you came in here to find out?"

She seemed to deflate a moment, before her shoulders heaved back up. "Yes."

"Well?"

Even as he reached over to lock the door, Elliott couldn't drag his attention away as she bent forward, angling her hips up so he could see the entire underside of her body. Her stockings ended mere inches below her upturned ass, the skin above them a smooth sliver of a taunt. And God, the orange silk hugging her pussy was already beginning to darken. "Hard, please," she whispered. "Please."

There was a voice in the back of his mind telling him to step back, but he'd been denying the impulses too long. Hell, there'd been no one before or since Peggy he'd wanted to loose them on. Now? He wanted to hear that snap of flesh on flesh so bad, he couldn't have held back, even if the quiet warning voice had been a shout.

Elliott removed the ever-present rosary beads from his pocket and placed them on the desk, out of respect for what they symbolized... and the action untethered him even more. He felt unexpectedly light-headed. Hungrier then he'd ever been before, as if setting the beads aside had given him permission. Stepping forward, he conformed both palms to her curved backside, groaning at the memory of propping it up, meeting the tight buns with his abdomen while thrusting inside of her. "Been begging for this since you got here, haven't you?"

She pushed her legs apart a few more inches with a breathless whimper. "Don't take your ring off."

Twisting the gold championship ring in question—and painfully aware that they didn't have much time—Elliott stepped to one side, giving her a warm-up slap. That single sharp sound had him nearly doubling over, the possibility of needing to change his pants before dinner a definite reality. From his position, Elliott could see Peggy's teeth digging into her lower lip, eyes closed tight. So beautiful. So... dutiful. Again that electrified zap of forewarning bashed into his subconscious. *Like you hate me. I deserve it. Like you hate—*

"Elliott, please," Peggy breathed, swaying her bottom side to side, the seductive movement forcing him to swallow a groan. "Don't stop." And he couldn't. His hand seemed to move all its own. It lifted and rained down a series of smacking blows, one right after the other, until Peggy fell forward onto the desk, breath wheezing in and out. Her tight ass shook with each crack of his palm, the muscles in her thighs straining, hips angling to encounter his hand as soon as possible. *So soft.* Was a man supposed to strike something so soft? Crave it? As if answering him, she chanted, "Yes, yes, yes."

He should never have made contact with her in the first place, because moving forward with the evening without fucking Peggy first was unimaginable. Yet it was their only option. His stomach constricting with the need to claim her, he snatched a Sharpie out of the pen holder on his desk and signed his name across her right ass cheek, before letting the marker drop to the ground.

Shame and pride mixed inside Elliott as Peggy straightened and smoothed her skirt back into place. It was huge and constantly shifting, shame winning out by a mile when she refused to look at him.

"Peggy," he said hoarsely. "Wait."

She surged forward, fusing their lips together. Not kissing him, just stopping the flow of his words. Then she pulled away, licking the seam of her lips with a smile that didn't reach her eyes. "I don't know about you, but I just worked up an appetite."

CHAPTER TWELVE

Today was Peggy's birthday.

Growing up as the youngest Clarkson, a big deal had always been made over the day. Pink streamers? A new dress? A tiara? Bet your ass. Even the first three years of school, her squad had thrown her a bash, complete with a grand entrance on the back of whichever frat guy drew the longest straw. She'd primped, imbibed, danced…

Over the last few months, though, the time she'd spent with Elliott meant less time with her friends. And while there were definitely no rifts or open animosity, she'd heard no rumblings of party plans, either.

Peggy toed a rock out of her path as she walked back to her dorm from class. Someone she only vaguely recognized whizzed past on a bike calling hello, so she smiled in response, but there was no answering pleasure in her chest. She hadn't told Elliott it was her birthday, or even that the date was approaching, so feeling let down was ridiculous.

They'd gotten closer with each passing day—sometimes it felt like each passing moment—but she still sensed him holding back. When he didn't think she was watching, there were shadows in his incredible eyes, thoughts deeper than the ones he shared. And still—still—being with Elliott was better than a birthday party with male belly dancers and a keg.

She'd fallen in love with him. Bad. No way out bad.

So sometimes it was hard. Sometimes they couldn't see each other for a handful of days because of traveling for his coaching responsibilities. Or he couldn't get a babysitter for Alice, the daughter he'd never offered to introduce Peggy to, although she still held out hope. Most difficult of all, they were a secret, which meant no going out in public together. No confiding in her friends that the legendary football coach they all went horny-faced over was her...

What?

Her boyfriend? Ha! Men like Elliott Brooks didn't do boyfriendom. If Peggy asked him to define their relationship, he would give her that quizzical, narrow-eyed, Dirty Harry stare. And then he'd probably kiss her until she forgot the question.

Peggy stumbled on the walkway when licks of heat traveled up the insides of her thighs. About normal, since they hadn't been together in three nights. Which probably accounted for her pointless, melancholy mood.

It started to rain.

Shit.

Holding her messenger bag over her head, she ran down the path to her dorm. There wasn't another soul in sight, everyone else having noticed the gathering thunderheads while she'd been lost in an Elliott-induced daze. Only a hundred or so yards from her dorm, she cut through a park-

ing lot, skidding to a halt when a car door opened to her right.

"Peggy."

"Elliott," she breathed, dropping the bag and letting herself get rained on. "What are you doing here?" Subtext: during the day. Although it could have been midnight, the sky was so ominously dark. Black.

"I wanted to be where you are." His chest fell heavily and lifted as he looked her over, head to toe, settling on her eyes. Wow. The intensity kindling in his gaze knocked the breath straight out of her lungs. "Can't stay away."

Had he been trying? The idea made her stomach ache.

She nodded in the direction she'd been traveling. "Come on."

It was risky. They both knew it. But after a curt nod, he followed Peggy, staying a good distance behind her until they reached the exit stairwell the students kept propped open to bypass the dorm's notoriously slow elevator. His tread echoed in her belly as they climbed the steps, Elliott remaining in the stairwell until she'd unlocked her door.

She held her breath and waited once inside. Only a couple seconds passed until he blew through her doorway—sexual and intimidating—kicking the door shut, lifting her off the ground to attack her mouth. Peggy moaned into the kiss, her thoughts going fuzzy when Elliott's tongue slipped past her lips, his free hand stroking down the side of her face, smoothing her hair in an affectionate gesture that made the last three lonely days worth every second. God. God. His huge presence combined with the passion of the kiss to rock the atmosphere. Thunder boomed outside, but she swore it was happening in her chest, between her legs. The smell of him and rain and . . . chocolate . . . was amazing.

"Shit," Elliott rasped, pulling back. Rubbing a thumb

against her lower lip, he dropped a kiss on her forehead, then reached into his jacket to remove a small, crushed bakery box. "This didn't go according to plan," he grumbled. "Nothing with you does."

"What's in there?"

"A cupcake. For your birthday." He cleared his throat. "Happy birthday."

Man oh man, he looked crazy uncomfortable. And she took exactly zero mercy on him, because jubilation was spinning inside her like syrup-soaked yarn. "How did you know it was my . . . you brought me a . . . Elliott."

He opened the box and they both peered inside to inspect the damage. Pink sprinkles. "You left your wallet out on my coffee table a few weeks back and I looked at your license. Thought maybe having your age staring me in the face would knock some sense into me."

She hated when he admitted to having doubts about the wisdom of their relationship. Every time they were together, he seemed to remind her at least once. "Since you're here now, I guess it was an unsuccessful mission."

Elliott tilted his head, an eyebrow lifting over her tight tone. "I just walked into a student dormitory in the middle of the day to be with you, baby. Safe to say the mission bombed."

Thrills raced up and down her arms. Was he being extra dreamy because it was her birthday or what? God, if he could just be like this all the time, instead of brooding at her so much. "Guess so, Coach."

"You didn't look happy out there. Before you saw me." He dragged a finger through the icing and slipped the digit between her lips, his breath going shallow as she sucked off the decadent chocolate. "Something wrong?"

"Everything is fine," she whispered. "Sometimes I get

homesick on my birthday. Which I shouldn't even tell you, because you're already hung up on my age and it makes me sound like a whiny toddler."

His eyes were full of concern, even though she'd pushed him out of his depth. "How do I make it better?"

"You brought me a cupcake." She licked another offering of chocolate off his finger, watching his jaw tick. "That's a great start."

"I brought you nail polish, too."

Peggy reared back. "What?"

She could hear his swallow. "You're always painting over that black mark on your finger." He looked away, his frown lines fierce. "I bought the clear kind, because I think you should just let me see it. The mark."

Dumbstruck. That's what she was. Maybe it was the rain or the dark sky afternoon, but there was none of the usual tension between them. Like they'd been given a reprieve, just for her birthday. Or maybe Elliott not shutting down was her real present. "Why?"

"I don't like you holding back any part of yourself from me. I hate it." He dropped his hand to the pocket of his jeans, brushing the rosary beads Peggy knew were inside. "It's wrong to expect so much from you, when I can't give the same."

Wrong. That word was famous around these parts. She covered his mouth to stop the outpouring of regrets. "Please. Not today, okay?"

After a beat, he nodded and Peggy dropped her hand. Rain ticked on the windowsill, thunder rolling in the distance. Desperate to maintain the spell, she smiled. "Can I see the polish?"

Setting aside the cupcake, he reached into his pocket and removed the tiny bottle, clear with silver writing. It looked so out of place in his big, rough hands, a giggle broke free. But it cut right off when Elliott pulled out the chair from her desk, sat down, and patted his knee. In a trance, she went toward him and perched on his lap, holding her breath as he smoothed her right hand out on the desk's surface. Lips pressed to her neck, he unscrewed the bottle. And with an expression of sheer concentration, the Kingmaker painted her nails. Clear.

It was the best birthday of her life.

* * *

Peggy didn't do awkward. She could chat her way out of weird silences during phone conversations, running into an ex-fiancé in public, while on a movie date with the new one—ouch—or smile when a customer broke a zipper by force, instead of asking for the next size up. You name it, she had a way to put herself and the equally uncomfortable party at ease. When called upon to use her linguistic skills to combat social ickiness, however, she usually wasn't fresh off a spanking for the ages.

It wasn't necessarily her tender rump that forced her to keep shifting around while twirling spaghetti onto a fork, though. Her reaction to being punished was what continued to trap words in her mouth, like fireflies in a jar.

Okay, so she had a kink. One that had been unintentionally discovered and fostered by Elliott. She liked to be bossed around in the sack, except…she'd only ever enjoyed it with the coach. Technically, the only way she could have a satisfying orgasm was to have that discipline doled out by him. Just one man.

What happened in the office didn't feel like it did before. At twenty-two, the spankings, Elliott's domination, had been about sex. Right? About lust for one particular man? Just now, though, as she'd bent over the desk and taken those slaps to her bottom, she'd felt a click unlike anything she remembered. A registering in her mind that she was getting her due. Being punished for something, rather than being punished for pleasure. Yes, there had been the sticky hot bliss of orgasm shooting from her internal firearm, but something in her mind hadn't allowed the bullet to strike.

Had she experienced the same foreboding at twenty-two, but her younger self hadn't recognized it? Or perhaps, in the blinding bright white glow of infatuation, the invisible grip on her spine had been equated with something new and exciting. But in the office it had felt... wrong. All wrong.

Between her thighs, she was still damp. In fact, every time she caught a whiff of Elliott's apples and mint scent, her vagina muscles seized. The way they do when your stomach lifts during a roller coaster and you can't breathe, squeezing your legs together until it drops back into place. But there was a new layer, too. Like a thin red lining to her attraction, throbbing with light.

She'd bent over for that spanking because something in her psyche craved Elliott's anger. His disapproval. Not just the façade of it, though. The real thing. That click she'd heard, clear as day, had been like shaking hands with a villain and recognizing her foe. Some part of her she'd grown to despise since sitting down at the table... enjoyed Elliott making her feel bad. Believed he was right.

And that. That was not okay.

Peggy glanced up from her meal to find Elliott observing her over the rim of his glass. Milk. He'd exchanged the beer she'd brought him for the wholesome white stuff, and she suddenly wanted to slap it out of his hands. She'd come back to Cincinnati to jar him into realizing what he'd lost. To make him pine and lust, so she could ride into the sunset knowing she'd had the last laugh, after years of misery. She would have broken Elliott's hold on her. The control would be in her hands, instead of the other way around.

But in that moment, even with her soaked panties clinging to her flesh, she wondered if this Ohio detour was a huge waste of her time. Perhaps three years had earned her some perspective or taught her about human nature. Because the curtains were lifting to reveal what her heart should have been telling her all along, instead of mourning the loss of her first love. Elliott didn't deserve her.

All those times during their relationship when she'd stumbled her way through pulling him from black moments...and he'd never done the same for her. She'd been stuck in a perpetual one for three years and he hadn't come. Hadn't appreciated her enough. He'd made her feel like a weakness, a transgression unfit for anyone else, but all this time *he'd* been unfit. Not her. A man who took her love and made it something ugly. Maybe her crusade to make him miserable was overkill. Elliott already was miserable...and perhaps she should simply leave him to it.

Until that moment, moving on had seemed like a distant goal, but now...now it was close enough to grasp.

She would explore this more later, but right now, she had a dinner to get through. Alice sat to her left, staring down glumly at her own food, probably lamenting her impulsiveness at inviting someone over for dinner who'd turned out to be lamer than dry wheat toast.

"Alice," Peggy started, coughing into her fist when it sounded like she'd just guzzled ice chips. "How did rehearsal go after I left?"

"Fine." She sat up a little straighter in her chair. "Mostly the girls were asking about Belmont, so that was good. He distracted them from my social suicide."

Peggy chuckled. "I won't tell him he caused a stir. He wouldn't know how to react and we'd get trapped under a frown avalanche."

"Huh. I think that's why I liked him," Alice said, stabbing at her spaghetti. "He's different. Like me."

"Yeah," Peggy responded softly, kind of shaken up over having Alice echo her words from earlier. The ones she'd lobbed through the bathroom door in the auditorium, praying they found their mark. Had she actually made some kind of difference? She hoped so, because there was something about Elliott's daughter that was so authentically beautiful, Peggy hated the idea of her spirit being nicked by the cruelty of others. And even though she knew it shouldn't, even though the thought bubble trying to float into her consciousness was the kind that could burst too easily, it entered anyway.

Alice needs a mother.

Not Peggy, obviously. Hell to the no. Someone else. Someone without obsessive hang-ups on unavailable men or the newfound realization that she thinks herself in need of chastisement. No, Alice needed a woman with the warmth and steadfastness Peggy didn't have. All she had was a great fashion sense, the ability to recite entire episodes of *Golden Girls*, and apparently a knack for impersonating a theater coach.

Knowing she could never be the kind of woman who would bring stubborn Elliott and Alice together, right on the heels of the realization she'd developed something unhealthy inside of her, had Peggy wanting to make a breezy excuse to leave. Talk about being clobbered. She couldn't even get a bite of food down her gullet and it didn't help

that the perfect amount of spice and garlic reminded her of
Miriam. Oh God, what would her mother think if she could
see her? Breaking bread with the man who'd shattered her
heart just as soundly. Punishing herself on purpose.

"Peggy," Elliott's rasping voice broke into her thoughts.
"You've barely eaten."

"I—yeah. Look at that." She tapped the fork against her
plate, sending a tinny sound winging through the room. "I
think I tested the sauce a few too many times and filled up."

Elliott's own eating utensil was paused on the table, held
tightly between two thick fingers. "You should try."

"Stop," she whispered.

When silence seemed to boom loudly from her left,
Peggy looked over at Alice, who was transferring a narrow-
eyed glance between her and Elliott. "Um." The preteen
took a long sip of her soda. "Dad said you were a professor
at the university, Peggy?"

The air in the dining room went very brittle, stagnant,
but Peggy didn't pause before answering because she didn't
need to think about telling the truth. Not this time. You
didn't attempt to build someone's confidence and get to
know a private part of them—the way she'd done that afternoon with Alice—and then lie to them. Or lie more, rather.
"No, I'm not." She took the napkin from her lap and laid it
down carefully on the table, noticing Elliott did the same.
"I'm here for alumni weekend. I was a student, back in
the diz-ay." Her attempt at levity smashed to pieces on the
ground. "Just here to see old friends."

"But how do you know my dad?" Daughter scrutinized
father. "As long as we've lived in this house, no one has
been inside of it besides us and a couple repairmen and
my aunt. You've been in it twice. So you have to know
him…somehow. I just…" She shook her head and Peggy

saw a resemblance to Elliott in her frustration. "When did you graduate?"

Oh now. Now they were on shaky ground. Elliott seemed to realize it, too, but like Peggy, he seemed disinclined to fabricate a story. There was no pretense in his gaze, only resignation. "Peggy graduated three years ago."

A puff of air left Alice's mouth. "That's the year after Mom died. Or the year we took her off life support anyway." She laid her right hand flat on the table. "Did you two...have a relationship?"

A buzz of silence met Alice's question and then the twelve-year-old was pushing away from the table, knocking her chair onto the ground. "Oh my God." She leveled her next question at Elliott with the kind of brutality only a pre-teen can muster. "You probably wanted Mom to die, didn't you?"

"Alice." Elliott's voice was steady, even though his eyes were turbulent. "Sit down and we'll talk about this calmly."

"No. No. Everything we do is calm and I don't always feel calm. Actually, I never, ever feel that way."

It felt as though a manacle were cinching tighter and tighter around Peggy's throat, but she managed to speak past the pressure. "Alice...what happened. It was after. Not during. And—"

"I thought you were here for me." Alice broke off with an awful keening noise that had Peggy shoving to her feet, but she froze on a dime with the girl's next words. "Stop. You're just some mistress, or a...whore."

"*Alice.*"

Elliott's voice boomed the way it only did on the side-lines, sending his daughter falling back three steps, hand flying up to cover her mouth. For Peggy's part, she didn't move. Couldn't move. A tremor started in her midsection and grew more intense until she swore she had to breathe in and out through her nose or risk vomiting.

Elliott slammed his fist into the table, clattering the plates. "Apologize, Alice."

"She doesn't have to," Peggy forced out between numb lips, refusing to break the furious gaze Elliott turned on her. "I'm going to just…"

Peggy eased out of the scene, as if she were the only component that hadn't been paused in some gruesome family portrait. Regret pushed down on her lungs. Being called a vile word by someone she liked caused a thick ripple of pain. An invisible sword made entirely of shame tried to prod her, too, but she forced armor to close around herself, welding it shut so nothing else could hitch a ride. As soon as she reached the hallway leading to the front door, she heard running feet and a slammed door behind her, presumably Alice locking herself in her room for all eternity.

Feeling like a stone statue walking for the very first time, Peggy moved through the door, into the night, unfamiliarity bombarding her from all sides. Houses she'd never seen, cars full of people she didn't know, a sky that looked so different from San Diego's sky, it seemed to be projected from a television screen.

She had no idea how long she'd been walking when Elliott pulled his truck up alongside her, parking at the curb and getting out. Following her.

"Peggy."

"You should be home with Alice. She needs you."

"You need me."

Peggy halted and turned slowly, eyebrows somewhere near the clouds. "Huh?"

"You need me to drive you back to the hotel," Elliott clarified. When Peggy made no move to climb into the truck or even respond—and honestly, she wasn't sure if she could respond to anything every again—Elliott tapped a closed fist on the hood. "I need to take you back, too. It would drive me crazy knowing you were walking around in the dark under normal circumstances. But after that...after that, I won't have you alone in the dark. Thinking about it."

"And you're going to distract me, are you?" She heard the invitation dripping from her voice and hated herself for going there, like it was some kind of unavoidable default. "Forget I said that, okay? Just forget everything I've said since I got here."

"I'll try and fake it, if you get in the truck."

That spun a laugh around in her throat. "Wait. Let me say one more thing before we start faking." She started toward the truck, moving past him and resting one hand on the door. "I came here to make you miserable, just for old times' sake. Okay? You were right about all of it. I thought I could get you out of my system if I was the one to end things this time around. But it turns out, I might have already accomplished that." She yanked on the door handle, heaving a sigh when she found it locked. The impediment, however, spurred the rest of her confession. "We're bad for each other. I finally believe what you've always told me. So I'm done now. Maybe we can just be...*nice* to one another until I leave."

Appearing to be in a daze, Elliott lifted his keys and pressed a button to unlock the door, allowing Peggy to climb inside and click her seatbelt closed.

CHAPTER THIRTEEN

Elliott couldn't feel his hands around the steering wheel. He should probably pull over, but then he would have to confront what Peggy said before he was ready.

Yeah, like he would ever be ready.

The times he'd accused Peggy of coming back to Cincinnati—or hell, being put on this earth—to make him miserable, he'd meant it in terms of temptation. Trying his faith, his convictions, his routine. Had he meant those callous words, though? Or were they just a practiced speech from three years ago, when she'd blazed her light through the darkest period of his life? Back then, her sympathy and understanding had made him feel one of two ways. Healed. Whole. Or like she'd thrown salt in his open wounds.

Right now, his wounds were bleeding, but Peggy hadn't been the one to put them there. Had he made her believe otherwise? She'd stumbled on a broken beast in the woods and tried to bandage him up, but he'd bitten her instead.

Continued to bite her. The way he'd felt about Peggy had been a thorn in his paw. His own wife had never been on the receiving end of those feelings, and as a result, she'd died alone.

Peggy had merely come to him at the wrong time. He'd looked at her and seen his own shame. Had it reflected back off him and trapped her, too?

Whore.

His insides were on fire at the memory of her face, how her positive energy faded into the expression of someone who'd walked into a brick wall.

It was the same way she'd looked after he'd spanked her in his office.

He pulled into the hotel parking lot, watching the headlights crawl along the black asphalt, and experienced the sinking horror that he'd been living in darkness himself, failing to switch on even the smallest lamp to see what was around him. Three years. She'd been gone three years. And it felt like she'd left yesterday. But she hadn't—and while he'd numbed himself to the reality of her stark absence, Peggy had been living without painkillers. She'd been living in *awareness* this whole time.

His blood ran cold when he tried to imagine what that felt like. How he would have been living if he'd allowed himself to fully register the fact that he'd sent her away. Sent her away to California.

"Thanks for the ride."

Peggy pushed open the door and started to climb out of the truck, but Elliott—needing to have himself in motion—rounded the truck's rear end before she could vanish into one of five hundred rooms, the number to which he probably wouldn't be able to find out. "Hold up."

She riffled through her purse and removed a pack of

gum, popping a little white tab into her mouth with a sigh. "I'm not one of your players."

"Peggy, if I'm aware of one thing, it's that." She'd obviously had a pep talk with herself in the truck while he'd been brewing in his own shit. He could see it in the determined set of her shoulders, the forced flippancy in her eyes. But for the first time in seemingly forever, Elliott was desperate to reach someone on a level that had nothing to do with football. To reach into Peggy's mind and rearrange something that had been put in the wrong place, thanks to him. "If you were one of my players, I would know what to do here. I'd be capable." He took her shoulders and watched her chin lift, felt her inhale deep in his bones. "That name you were called tonight is so far beneath you, Peggy, you shouldn't even be aware it exists. I need you to nod and tell me you understand that."

Humming in her throat, she looked away. "That word is beneath anyone." She exhaled. "I know she didn't mean it, okay? Maybe she'll mean it for the next decade, but someday when she's an adult, she'll understand. I...hope she does."

"I'm going to make sure she does."

For a few beats, Peggy just watched him. He would have felt awkward standing between two parked cars in silence with anyone else. No doubt he would have made an excuse to get back in his truck and leave. But the quiet felt like due course with Peggy. A lead up to something else he didn't want to miss. "There's a park around back of the hotel." A puff of cold breath hung in the air near her mouth. "You want to go for a walk?"

Normally, he would say no, even if he wanted to remain with her long as possible. But he wanted to say yes to the walk. Had a sick feeling that he should have said yes a lot more often to this woman. Too late, though, wasn't he? He'd turned on a small lamp in his dark room way too late—and he was afraid to turn on any more. To see what he might reveal. His hesitation brought the glazed quality back to her eyes, though, and an answering stab in his chest pushed a single word out. "Yeah."

Elliott moved to put himself between Peggy and any cars that might drive through the parking lot as they walked, wondering if she was laughing on the inside over him being old school. If so, she didn't betray it on her face. There was only surprise arranging her features, probably over his agreement to go for a walk. Elliott could barely believe it himself, truthfully. Any time spent with Peggy was an opportunity to slip into a bad habit.

Bad habit. That's how he'd always seen her. Spoken to her. Touched her.

Thank God she'd finally realized he was bad for her. Thank God.

As they entered the deserted park, Elliott realized his lungs were burning from lack of oxygen and he tried to be discreet about filling them. "So." He rolled his neck, trying to match Peggy's casual pace on the path, even though his usual fast stride tried to send him ahead. "You're traveling with only your brother?"

"My best friend, Sage, is here, too. She's a wedding planner." Peggy glanced up at the hotel. "She texted me earlier to let me know she spent the day visiting venues in town, just to get ideas. This whole trip is about my family and she has been so patient with us. I don't deserve her."

There was that word again. *Deserve.* The need to address it was like a spoked wheel turning in his throat, but something else snagged his attention and wouldn't let go. "Wedding planner. Is that how you met her?"

"Yes," Peggy said after a moment. "She planned my wedding. She planned all four of them. And I didn't show up to a single one."

Elliott stumbled to a halt, his pulse speeding up so fast, he got dizzy, vision doubling. "Four?" he wheezed. "Four, Peggy?"

"That's right."

When she stopped on the path and turned, her eyes tightly shut, he could see she hadn't planned to make the confession. Maybe wished she hadn't. But now that it was out there, she was hardening herself, ready to embrace it. A player who'd been injured, but was ready to get back in the game and ignore the potential damage that could be done. "Four great guys and I couldn't commit to a single one." Pain sliced across her features. "I gave them all different reasons when I broke it off. I'm scared of getting old and boring. I want to focus on my career. I don't want kids. But you know what it was, Elliott? You know what it really was?" She braced herself, and he got the distinct impression she'd never told the next part to anyone. "They were all too nice to me. I couldn't stand it. Every time they complimented me or bought me a gift, my fucking skin would crawl. I hated it. And I hated me for hating it."

"Peggy," Elliott managed. This was his doing. All of it. Lamps were flipping on all over his pitch-black room, revealing monsters and shortcomings and screwups. They were everywhere. They'd been there this whole time, waiting to be illuminated. "Ah, baby. What have I done to you?"

"That's not the worst part," she half whispered, half laughed. "The worst part is I let you."

"I told you..." His words emerged choked. This was why he avoided relationships of any kind, even when he was an active part of them. There was no way to circumvent the inevitable destruction he caused. The memory of a phone ringing caught him in the neck, that devastating stretch of time where he tried to remember if he'd done his job as a husband, a father.

Being hit with the certainty that his lack of caring had killed someone for whom he'd been responsible, knowing he was more than capable of doing it again, had torn him down the middle. Rendering him incapable of being healthy for Peggy.

"I told you to stay away."

Peggy moved into Elliott's space, peering up at him from beneath her eyelashes. Seduction mixed with curiosity. Could she see the cracks in him? Yes, she always could. Always knew exactly where to insert the crowbar to pry him farther apart, but nothing compared to now, because she'd finally shown her own cracks. Fissures that he'd hammered into her, sure as they were standing there.

I'm cancerous. I didn't send her away in time.

"So are you going to let me?" Peggy breathed, walking closer until Elliott was forced to back up, his knees hitting the edge of a wooden bench.

"Let you what?"

"Get you out of my system." Her answering smirk said, *Keep up.* "Remind you what you'll be missing when I leave again?"

She shoved him hard and he allowed himself to fall back onto the bench. A battle went live in his chest, complete with cannon blasts. One side fought against the critical need she stirred in his belly. But the opposition was far stronger, because it had the desire to soothe her on its side. To take the deeply etched hurt he'd seen in her eyes tonight and obliterate it, make her forget every single negative thing in her mind. And above all, he was so fucking jealous over four unknown faces, his cock was swollen with the urge to erase them from her memory bank. Forever.

The years that separated the last time he'd been inside of her were nothing, nothing, compared to how damn good they were together. You didn't just find someone else to take the place of perfection. Hot, rough, perfection.

But as Peggy's knees planted on either side of his thighs, the things she'd said—not just tonight, but that afternoon—replayed in his mind like a determined broken record. *Like you hate me. I deserve it. They were nice to me. I hated it.*

"Peggy, slow down a minute."

She unzipped his coat and rubbed her hands down his chest, all the way down to his lap, where she ran a knuckle along the seam of his fly. "It doesn't feel like you want me to slow down."

God in heaven. "Want is a different animal than responsibility."

Her eyes flashed. "I'm not your responsibility." She cut herself off at the end of the last word. "You know what? My mind is my own, but this unsatisfied part of me *is* your doing. You made me need something and left me with no way to get it. Or feel it." The touch of her hand left his erection and he almost—almost—growled at her to put it back, had to battle his instinct to keep from making the order. Instead, he watched as she slipped her skirt high on her thighs, revealing the top of her stockings, so close to her pussy—and his dick pulsed hotter. "I want the wrong kind of sex, Elliott. The kind only you gave me."

"I was, am, the wrong part." He was vehement. "Not you."

She carried on as if he hadn't spoken. "The difference between then and now is this Peggy finally figured out the score. Just show me one last time, so I can walk away knowing without a doubt I'm better off." She unzipped his jeans and slid her hand into the opening, massaging his aching shaft through his briefs. "Do that for me, Elliott?"

I'm not prepared for this. Proving beyond a shadow that he was a negative influence on her mind, her body...God, her heart. Letting her go. None of it. He hadn't woken up this morning with the willpower for something like that—and it was possible the willpower he'd employed to send her away in the first place had only been an illusion to begin with, because having her on his lap, her voice in his ear, was like seeing again after a three-year bout with blindness.

"Peggy..."

She must have heard the hesitation in his voice because her eyelids flickered, a *huhhn* sound leaving her lips, then she grabbed his hand, pressing the palm up against her panties. Damp material greeted him. Elliott and his balls constricted hard enough to grit his teeth. "Finger me, Coach Brooks," she murmured. "Wet me up. Make me shiny. Isn't that how you like me?"

"Yes."

Elliott was fast losing any notion of self-control, but he dragged it back with determination. There was no stopping the bullet train that was their sexual chemistry, or the pounding, driving need inside him to take her, especially after seeing her so disillusioned, but he could make the encounter good for her. Make it healthy. If he did any more damage, especially after witnessing the aftereffects, he would never forgive himself.

He pressed the heel of his hand to her clit, chafing the silk up and down. "Maybe I did one or two things right in my life, huh?" Knuckling aside the edge of her underwear, he pushed his index finger into her heat, issuing a low curse between her breasts. "Seems impossible, but I must have, if

I'm about to have your slippery pussy ride me again. God knows that's the sweetest reward life has to offer."

"No." Her breath hitched. "No, you stop that. I don't need to be told I'm pretty or I have a nice body." She nipped at his mouth and he nipped back, both of them bearing their teeth. "You rip off my panties, fill me full. Hold me down while you take and take a-and repeat the Our Father."

How many times had he done that?

The question reverberating in his mind, Elliott slid his fingers free of the tight spot between her thighs, a lodgment the size of a fist jammed in his throat. He'd made her the embodiment of sin. He'd foisted that on her when she'd only wanted to comfort him in a dark time, offering her body and heart as a way to forget. Because she'd felt something for him. A feeling he'd returned, but hadn't known how to handle. So he'd twisted it, turned it into something shameful. Goddamn him.

"Peggy, no. That wasn't right of me—" Elliott cut himself off as a necklace winked back at him from the V of Peggy's coat. Was that a diamond hanging from the chain? Urgency bit him in the sternum, making it impossible to go another minute without getting a look, and before he knew his own intentions, Elliott had pried apart her coat, snatching up the necklace. "What the hell is this?"

Color stained her cheeks, but she lifted her chin defiantly. "The heads I've hunted."

"These are engagement rings," he gritted out. "You wear them around your neck?"

"Yes." She tried to jerk away, but Elliott held fast to the piece of jewelry. "I'll be buried in them, if I want."

The blinders he'd been wearing since Peggy left were long gone, and he might as well have been standing right there in the moment she drove away, watching her leave from his garage, the smell of her still on his skin. If he hadn't shut himself off as her cab kicked up dust, he would have gone after her. Dragged her back and admitted everything. How badly he needed her. All of it. And those long-buried admissions clashed with his jealousy now, so righteous he could barely think straight around the desire to take. To claim.

"You want my fuck, baby?" he gritted out. "You take them off now."

She glided into his space, bringing their mouths a hair apart. "Go to hell."

"I've been there. I own property in it." Holding her gaze, Elliott twisted the necklace—and snapped the chain, feeling the night wind howl in response. But the sound was nothing compared to Peggy's reaction. Oh no. He would remember it until the day he took his last breath.

The way a sob seemed to surge up inside of her, fleeing her mouth in a terrible rush. She was a suspect in a courtroom hearing a not-guilty verdict. She quite simply broke, falling against his chest in a way he never expected from positive, bubbly Peggy. "Please, Elliott. Don't do this to me. I haven't..." Her voice bathed his ear in heat. "I haven't been able to. Not since you. And it hurts, it hurts, I hurt everywhere."

"You haven't what?" He tried to duck down and meet her gaze, but she evaded him by pressing her face into his neck. "You haven't had an orgasm, Peggy? Since..."

She shook her head.

A ringing began in his ears, too many reactions to count clashing in his chest. Responsibility, shame, pride. Pride that he hated, because she'd been in pain, but couldn't deny nonetheless. He fixated on responsibility, grabbing on like a rescue raft being tossed into the ocean.

Give her what she needs.

CHAPTER FOURTEEN

Peggy kept expecting to be embarrassed. Maybe she'd simply filled her quota for humiliation that day already, but somehow admitting her inability to climax to Elliott only seemed inevitable. Like she'd just been waiting for the right moment in the dark when their facades came down, so she could be honest.

Honesty. Was she ever honest with anyone? Even her best friend only received half-truths and evasions, her family only seeing the happy-go-lucky baby sister. Maybe sexual release wasn't the only thing she could share with Elliott alone. Maybe it went hand in hand with the truth. Sex, honesty, Elliott. All the times in between when she couldn't succeed in finding pleasure...it was possible she'd just been weighted down by her constant pretense.

Vanity reared its head to save her. Probably from placing too much importance on this last time with Elliott. Ruining herself forever. Because after this, it would be over. No more lying or fronting or pretending she was fine when her chest felt split down the middle. Admitting your problem was the first step toward correcting it, right?

"This isn't why I came back here," she whispered against his neck. "I didn't drive all this way just so you could orgasm me. So don't get a big head about it, okay?" His hands were everywhere, big and commanding, teasing over her bottom, roughing up her thighs with scrapes of his calloused palms. God, nothing had felt that good in so long. "This is about m-me moving on. I don't want your pity."

"No?" His mouth opened on her neck, delivering the exact amount of suction to make her legs jerk, to start a miserable/wonderful quickening at the juncture of her thighs. "Let it be about pity for me, then. I might come on occasion, but it's never near as satisfying as when I did it in your pussy. Not even close. And the idea of looking for someone else? Fucking laughable. I haven't glanced at another woman since you drove away. They might as well be invisible."

"Stop." Behind Elliott's head, Peggy's hands curled into fists that shook with the urge to strike out. The impulse stemmed from the center of her chest, colliding with the flare of unwanted pleasure that he'd been celibate without her. "I don't want to know it was hard for you. You're the one who kicked me out."

Beneath her body, his muscles went tight, his breath going shallow. "Baby—"

In a panic, Peggy cut him off with her mouth. For a few beats, he resisted, that stubbornness radiating from the hard lines of his body, but she couldn't allow him to say whatever it was. Premonition told her it would be counterproductive. Ha. Such a technical term for taking a scalpel and carving words into someone's heart.

His resistance abated in seductive degrees, his right palm sliding beneath her skirt on a dark groan that increased in volume as he found her wetness again. Yes. Elliott had this way of fingering her that she'd never been able to mimic, no matter how many times she attempted it alone in the dark, her head tossed back on the pillow. A man testing out the goods. That was the only way she could describe the manner in which he shoved his index finger deep, his brow furrowing as he drew that single, blunt digit in and out. Sampling her resistance, checking for the right amount of wetness…and always, always, being over-the-top satisfied with the results.

Elliott's jaw fell as he added his middle finger, curving them inside her to find the gathering of devastating nerve endings on her front, inner wall, and exploit them. "Why aren't you stroking me off right now?" His chastising tone flowed from the top of her head down, down, like warm water. "I'm about ready to rip through these briefs. Were you waiting for an invitation?"

"No." A buzzing current replaced her blood, lightning flickering in her veins. She couldn't get her hands on his erection fast enough, was dying to hear his approval, his pleasure, punctuate the air between them. And it did. It did. As soon as her palm dipped beneath the waistband of his underwear and began to rub that ruddy trunk, he gave a gritted curse, hips jerking.

"Shit." His fingers crammed deep inside of her with that single word, forcing a tight-lipped cry from her mouth. "Your skin on mine. That's what was missing. Skin on skin." Barely able to stay upright under the weight of lust, Peggy closed him in her fist and pumped his flesh, tight and slow, loving the way his jaw loosened. "That's right. You remember how I need it done. How to make me so hard, I have to concentrate on not coming the whole fucking time I'm inside you. Because that's what you need. Isn't it? You need me to sweat and get angry and shake over how good your pussy feels. You get off on my torture."

"Yes. Yes. The things I do to you are bad." She released his rigid length in favor of quickly unbuttoning her top, shoving the sides open to give him a view of her braless breasts. He loved it. Loved them on display, because his fingers began working her center with fervor, his eyes glittering with the kind of lust that swelled her nipples, the nub between her legs. "Can I ride you, please?"

"You'd love that, wouldn't you?" Elliott rasped, and she swore—she swore—a flicker of regret crossed his face, but she ignored it, using her sliding grip on his huge arousal to make that unwanted emotion vanish into nothing but blatant hunger. "Having a front row seat to me giving in to temptation?"

Heat seared her from all sides, firing even hotter when his thumb started fondling her clit, dragging a ragged moan past her lips. The way he looked at her, perusing every inch of her with a hooded expression, turned back time to when she was his downfall. The downfall of mankind. "I bet if I check your pocket, I'll find a condom. Won't I, Coach?" She tucked her fingers into his jeans and closed them around a foil square, euphoria making her lightheaded. "Did you hate it? Did you hate going into the store and buying this, knowing you shouldn't use it on me, but secretly hoping you would?"

"Yes. All right? Yes." He levered his body forward to catch one of her nipples in his hot mouth, abusing it with his tongue as he sucked. Her center clenched so tight, she knew if she didn't get Elliott inside her soon, she would climax right there on his lap. And she needed so badly to have that completion while filled, every inch of her crowded and stretched the way only he could do it. "Can't stop thinking about how hard I used to fuck you. How hard you used to let me. Just driving you up the bed until you were bent in half, that blond hair tangling around your ankles."

Holy shit. Peggy shoved at Elliott's shoulders, putting his back up against the bench, his expression rife with lust and anticipation as she applied the latex, sucking in a breath when she felt him pulsing against her fingertips. Using the bench's wooden back for balance in her left hand, she moved higher on his lap, guiding his erection home with her right. "Oh God, oh God," both of them groaned in a seemingly endless loop, as she sank down—

With only half his erection inside her, Peggy started to shake, the orgasm she'd spent so long chasing, busting through the dam of her middle and drowning her, dragging her under the churning relief. She felt Elliott's hands in her hair, his powerful grip steadying her, mouth blocking her scream with a kiss. The kind of kiss you gave someone you might die without. Fast, slow, heads turning, bodies twisting. A full body kiss. "More. Elliott. More."

He searched her eyes a moment before laying another one of those bruising, soul-crushing kisses on her mouth. Reeling over the sensation of ultimate fullness—possession—she wasn't prepared when Elliott shoved her hips down, impaling her completely. Another crest of pleasure sailed through her, making her quake on the thick perch of his manhood. Her muscles were already brutally sore from the first time, she realized in a far-off way, before Elliott's harsh voice pierced the fog around her.

"Hey. Baby." He shook her by the shoulders. "Where do you think you're going?"

"N-nowhere. I'm..."

"You're here with Elliott." His hands cupped her backside and ground her on his erection, a strained growl drifting from his mouth. "That's where you are. Right where I need you."

Peggy's head shake was disjointed. "But w-we shouldn't be, right?"

Even in the midst of his visible, gripping need, he seemed to be grinding his jaw, but that made no sense. "No, we shouldn't be. But that's not going to stop you, is it?" He tugged her ass close and rolled his hips, at the same time, leveling a strangled fuck in her direction. "Do it. Drive me insane. I'm dying."

"Send you to hell?" she whispered.

His Adam's apple lifted and plummeted. "Send me to hell."

Bliss obscured her vision with a blurry screen as she started to ride. She gathered his head to her bouncing breasts, increasing her pace out of necessity when he sucked her nipples like a savage, his grip on her ass urging, urging. If it were anyone else on the entire planet, she wouldn't have sensed the small part of him holding back. Elliott never did anything in half measure once his mind was set to the task, whether it be winning a football game or giving her pleasure. But something was off in the tight set of his jaw, the way he lifted his head to watch her under his half-mast eyelids, as if he were seeing her, finally seeing her and—

No. It was too late. She didn't want to know what he would find. Was terrified to know if it would change anything. *Push him.* Pushing him that final few meters toward the abandoned, animal mating they'd always known, without a thought to the consequences, was her only option.

Peggy contracted her most intimate muscles around Elliott's girth, listened as rusted epithets married in his throat, felt his fingers dig into the flesh of her backside. "These inches of yours," she breathed up against his ear, licking the lobe, catching it between her teeth. "They're the only ones that know the right spot to hit . . . the only ones that can make me scream. Or feel a damn thing. *Please.*"

Her back landed on the bench, the wood's coldness reaching through the back of her jacket to wrap around her spine. But the rest of her . . . oh God, the rest was so fucking hot, she knew the word *fever* would forever hold new meaning. Elliott descended on her with the power of a pack of wolves, caged inside one man.

"Get your knees up. *Get them up,*" he snarled. Without waiting for her to comply with his command, he reached back and pulled her knees even with her hips, just out to the side. And that first drive with Elliott's full weight on top of her was so glorious, it might have topped the orgasms he'd already given her. The positivity that she was being dominated, that she was prey and couldn't escape his pinning heaviness, the thick evidence that he was man . . . it caused starburst to erupt behind her eyes, in her belly, all along her nerve endings.

"Yes, yes, yes," she whispered, throwing her arms up over her head to grip the bench's edge, just a foot or so from the top of her head. Already, her stomach muscles were tender, she could feel those twinges as they pulled again, already anticipating the oncoming rush of more.

Elliott's grunt in her ear turned into a long, drawn-out groan. "You're the only one who's ever gotten me going like this. Nothing comes close. How do you do it, baby? How? I can't think about anything else when I'm this deep. Just getting us off so fucking hard. Feeling your tight pussy milk me and knowing I earned it." His hips grazed the insides of her knees with each thrust; that snapping roll she craved constantly—the brutality and thoroughness of it—was finally hers and better than she remembered. A thousand times better. "Look at me, nailing you to a park bench. God above, you turn me into a pussy fiend. Just for yours, though, you made sure of that, didn't you? Ruined me. You *ruined* me."

"Just returning the favor," she gasped, elation and pleasure and fear throwing a party in her stomach. "Harder, Elliott. Deeper. Like it's the last time."

She whimpered as her legs were thrown up over his shoulders, the cold of the night registering on her bare bottom, but nowhere else. And then, not even there, because he bore down on her so completely, not an inch of her was exposed or left uncovered by his muscular body in some way. His teeth snapped down on the curve of her neck as he drove inside her, reaching places that hadn't been touched since the last time they were together. Peggy's fingers clutched the bench's edge so hard, she could feel cuts forming on her fingers, palms.

"Put your hands on me," he rasped into her ear, the volume of his voice fluctuating with his continued pumps. "You want to grab on to something, get those hands up in my hair, use your nails to open up the scars you left on my back. Touch me. I want you to touch me."

Her climax started to rise like the sun, slower than before, but twice as intense. It wasn't going to simply take the edge off; it was going to create new, jagged ones. It was going to obliterate her, and she could do nothing to stop it. Not with the thick, wet glide of his erection hitting her in that spot—that spot—the base of him giving her sensitized clitoris hell with nonstop rubbing. If she just kept her hands on the bench, rather than him, she could salvage the mission, though. She could keep that one little part of herself from giving over, detaching, and flying away.

As if sensing her resolve, Elliott set out to crush it, his mouth stamping down on her possessively, his tongue sweeping into her mouth and letting her taste his frustration. "Touch me," he urged against her lips. "Skin on skin."

She shook her head, trying to distract him with more kissing, but he pulled away, those eyes drilling into her, his lower body grinding in rhythmic devastation, sending her so close to the point of no return, she lost her ability to think straight.

"Damn you, Peggy," Elliott growled, pressing his face into her shoulder. "I need your hands and eyes. I missed them most of all." Their hearts slammed into each other between them, in perfect time with his rolling hips. But only hers was fracturing, splitting right down the middle, little pieces falling away as he continued. "No one ever touched me like you did. I've needed it, baby. I've been dead without it. Dead inside. Please."

Her hands moved on their own, shoving down the insides of Elliott's jacket, past the waistband of his pants to scrape her nails over the taut flesh of his ass. His guttural groan in response sent her fingers raking up his back, her palms sliding down his spine. "Okay, okay," she whispered, before his mouth took her again.

Elliott was close, so close to the edge. She remembered his signals as if she'd never been gone a day. His thighs began to get restless, shifting and flinching, as if they weren't under his control. He started holding his breath, releasing it in explosive bursts between utterances of her name, in that warning tone. *Peggy, Peggy, I'm going to come.*

He didn't have to say the words—his body spoke for him—but his breath puffed into her ear, along with one final litany that sent her orgasm cresting alongside his own. "Get ready to take it. The only cock that makes your pussy happy...it only comes for you, too, baby. Only between these spread legs of yours." His hand came up to grip her jaw, tilting her head back. "Look at me while I brand you there. Going to pour it in, nice and hot."

Rising on a wave of undiluted ecstasy, she could no sooner have looked away than sever her own limbs. "Elliott," she said, shaking head to toe. "Oh God, Elliott."

His free hand gripped the back of the bench, that giant body pumping one final time, teeth clenching on a moan. His hips gave five unexpected, smacking drives, as if his climax had continued on longer than expected, longer than was possible, and then he dropped down onto her heavily, breath rasping in her ear.

Replete of energy, Peggy barely managed to unwedge her legs from beneath him and rest her ankles on his lower back, staring up at the night sky. Words, touches, sensations were already replaying in her mind, amplified now with renewed perspective.

This walk in the park had been about closure, moving on from the past, away from something she'd come to realize was bad for her. But Elliott hadn't cooperated. Not even close. Now? She couldn't shake the feeling that she'd just made a dangerous miscalculation.

Chapter Fifteen

Nothing looked the same to Elliott as he climbed the steps to his front door. The house itself resembled some foreign object with slopes and edges he'd never noticed before. Had there always been a window there? What was the name of the person who came by once a week to cut the grass? He had none of this knowledge, but honestly, he hadn't given a shit before now. Even the air felt different filtering through his hair, cooling the skin still heated from having Peggy beneath him.

Peggy.

His hands paused in the act of unlocking the door. He could see the way she'd sat up on the bench, looking like a beauty queen who'd been ravaged backstage, just before the talent competition. Shell-shocked, those eyes wider than the end of a cannon. A cannon pointed directly at the center of his chest.

I've been dead inside. I'm dead.

He might have been ready to blow when those words came out, but that didn't make them any less true. He'd walked this same path to his house every day since moving in—right on the heels of Peggy's departure—and yet, he'd never truly looked at it. If he closed his eyes, he wouldn't even be able to describe the color of any surrounding homes or what cars his neighbors drove. Now, details were piling on top of him like falling bricks, battering out of the concussed state he'd been existing in. The smell of someone on the block nursing a fire in their hearth. Oncoming rain carried on the air. None of it went unregistered.

A vision of himself in the hospital bed—instead of Judith—hit Elliott. There was no one in the room with him. Just four empty walls and a single, vacant chair. *How long have I been asleep?* he asked the doctor.

"Fuck," Elliott breathed, twisting the key in the lock and opening the front door. Silence greeted him, which was nothing new, but it was denser than usual. He could feel it parting as he walked through it, down the hallway, like hands traveling over his shoulders and ribs.

Instead of going to the living room and setting down his keys, as his routine usually dictated, Elliott stopped outside of Alice's room and listened, hearing nothing, which seemed to be a running theme among the women in his life. He and Peggy had barely exchanged a word as he walked her back to the hotel. Granted, he hadn't exactly been in the mood for a chat—had he ever been?—after having so many…layers stripped off inside the park. Layers he'd thought were just hardened parts of him that people could either take or leave. He'd never expected to voluntarily shed them all his own.

Or have it feel amazing. Overdue.

Peggy didn't seem to share that sentiment, though, did she? She'd all but given him whiplash bypassing him into the revolving hotel door. And he'd just stood by like a mute referee, refusing to make a call, despite the new... things... slowly but surely making themselves known in his gut. Things that weren't right and hadn't been for a long time, but he'd been sleepwalking past and ignoring them.

When Elliott walked into the living room and tossed his keys into the ceramic bowl whose origin he had no idea about, he was surprised to find Alice sitting on the couch, illuminated by nothing but a low-lit lamp.

He started to ask her if she'd finished eating, if she was still hungry, but suddenly he could recognize those questions exactly for what they were. A way to avoid what had happened over dinner. A way to avoid everything. Even knowing his methods weren't productive, he almost used them anyway, they were so firmly ingrained. But taking a deep breath, he took a seat on the chair opposite Alice instead, and clasped his hands loosely between his knees. "You all right?"

Eyes the same shape as his own widened in shock. "I don't know," she answered tightly, crossing her arms over the pillow sitting on her lap. "Were you with...her?"

"Yes."

Her breath released in a whoosh. "Don't bother softening the blow or anything."

Elliott sighed. "Peggy and I are adults."

"Sure, now you are." Her upper lip curled. "She wasn't, though. Not back then."

"Yes, even back then," he corrected her, hearing the disgust in his voice, leveled right at himself. "I didn't always treat her like one, though."

Alice stared at Elliott for so long across the magazine-littered coffee table, he had to look away. "Is it true what she said? You guys weren't together when Mom was still alive?"

Tears were thick in Alice's voice by the end of her question, but she was clearly attempting to control them, probably for his sake. Something that never would have bothered him before, but now made him wonder why a twelve-year-old felt like she needed to be strong around her father. *You know why. You've been a cold bastard to everyone.* "Yes, she was telling the truth. I—you'll understand when you get older—"

"Oh God. Fuck that." She threw the pillow aside. "Just talk to me for once. We can pretend tomorrow like it never happened."

Elliott shifted on the couch, the desperation in his daughter's tone making something sharpen in his chest. And for the first time, he understood what one of his players felt like when he leaned down and got in their face during halftime. But this had to be worse, right? Because he had no idea how to correct his mistakes in the second half of the game. No damn clue. "What do you want to know?"

Alice didn't quite manage to hide her shock over being given the green light. "Did you love Mom?"

He scraped a hand over his five o'clock shadow and thought back in a way he hadn't in a long time, remembering polite smiles in the kitchen, falling asleep at his home office with game film running only to wake up and find morning had moved in. "My relationship with your mother was more of a friendship, Alice," Elliott said finally. "I don't think either of us were romantic people. We were practical. We had similar goals, but a lot of the time...those goals kept us separated. Love..."

When he trailed off with a head shake, Alice huffed, but her eyes were serious, watching him closely. "Do you even know what love is?"

"You don't ask easy questions, do you?"

"Your players say the same thing about you." She picked at the material of her flannel pajama pants. "But I have to read about it in magazines or see it on television. I don't know firsthand."

"Would you...be interested in something like that?" He gestured in the general direction of the university, then quickly joined his hands together. "Watching me coach up close?"

"No," Alice scoffed. Shrugged. "Maybe."

How many roller coaster loops could he handle in one night? "I promise to have it arranged. For the Temple game." He watched two big blooms of color appear in her cheeks and the tugging in his chest pulled taut. "Is there anything else?"

"Yes," she said quickly, as if she was afraid she might lose her nerve. "You said you're not a romantic person, that you're practical. But...what about Peggy? She's not practical at all."

Elliott couldn't contain a wry laugh. "No, she's not." He raked a hand down his face, picturing her in the doorway of his stadium office, charging in and refusing to take no for an answer about the fund-raiser, seducing him into agreeing to make a speech. Wearing a foursome of engagement rings around her neck, for the love of God. "She's the opposite of practical."

"And yet, you..."

He waited for Alice to elaborate, but she ended the question with a wave of her hand, no longer meeting his eyes. *Sure, leave me without any direction*, he thought. This whole conversation was beyond him already. Trying to simplify the connection he had with Peggy into words was impossible, wasn't it? He'd never even articulated it to himself. "I was at the bottom of the ocean. Everything was dark...and then Peggy showed up. She was the surface. And I finally saw something to kick toward." He cleared his throat. "I know that doesn't make sense—"

"Keep going." Alice shrugged. "Just keep going."

Oddly enough, he wanted to keep going, while at the same time dreading what he might find. There was a tingle at the back of his neck, telling him he was on the verge of something uncharted. A game changer, as he would call it in the locker room. But the game wasn't supposed to change off the field. Not for him. "Peggy. She, uh...looked at me and saw things I didn't know were there. And she didn't judge me for them. That's a rare thing among adults." He swallowed the tennis ball in his throat. "She was selfless while I was selfish. I could say things to her no one else understood. But she already knew what I was going to say."

Alice stared. "Did you have that with Mom?"

"No." He held her gaze. "And I'm sorry about it, Alice."

She nodded and seemed to collect herself. "Did you do the same for Peggy? Could she tell you things?"

Someone might as well have taken a fishing line and pulled it tight around his jugular, the pressure was suddenly so intense. "Some of the time. The thing about Peggy is, she doesn't let you know when she needs you. Not until you've already missed your chance." In hindsight, he could imagine how hard it must have been for a young woman to cope with a widower boyfriend. Yet she'd never shown a hint of jealousy, only compassion. Under the surface, though, she could have been suffering and he'd been too blind to notice. "Mostly I took what she gave me and squandered it."

Alice looked away, but not before he saw horror pass over her features. Horror he was gratified to see, because he damn well deserved it. "Sometimes I say things because I'm upset and I don't mean them, like, two seconds later. Do you have that?"

"Everyone has that. Especially in our bloodline." He leaned forward and snagged a coaster off the coffee table, tapping it against the edge. "You'll apologize to her."

"Yeah," she said loudly, tipping her face toward the ceiling. "What about you? Have you apologized to her for... the squandering?"

"It's too late." A python coiled around his rib cage. "I'd only make it worse."

He could practically hear Alice shuffling through responses in her head. She looked about as hollow as he felt. Nothing like the buoyancy he'd glimpsed in his daughter while she cooked with Peggy in the kitchen. Or when she'd emerged from the auditorium bathroom that afternoon, the sagging quality of her shoulders long gone.

Thinking back on those two recent memories, Elliott acknowledged something important. He'd felt no guilt when looking at Peggy now. No sense of failure within himself, like he had during his darkest period. He'd driven her away because she'd eclipsed the love he'd felt for anyone prior. She'd forced him too close to forgiving himself when he hadn't been ready. But none of that useless resentment lingered inside him now. When he looked at Peggy now, all he saw was the light his soul had been missing. *God*, he missed her.

"You're probably right. It's too late," Alice finally murmured, picking up the remote control and flipping on the television. *Animal Planet* hummed at a low volume while he hoped for her to continue, but she took her sweet time. "She's way out of your league anyway."

Elliott barked a laugh, sending Alice jumping a good few inches into the air. But after his initial amusement faded—and it faded fast—his skin felt raw, stretched out. "Is this reverse psychology you're attempting with me?"

"Nope." His daughter browsed channels without looking at him. "Seriously, the sooner she leaves, the better. You don't have time for some high-maintenance cheerleader type." She made a sour face. "She'd probably want to go on dates. God, can you imagine yourself on a date?"

He really couldn't help it now, could he? The image projected itself before he could stop it. Him and Peggy sitting across from one another in a restaurant, her skin glowing in the candlelight. His hand would rest on her knee beneath the table, holding it still—commanding her attention—when she started to bounce with energy. Walking her to the car afterward tucked into his side. Absurd. The whole idea was absurd.

His stomach churned like a wheel stuck in mud.

"Just lay low for a couple more days and she'll be gone again. She probably won't make it two miles before someone who loves dates asks her on one."

The python squeezed. "Okay, now I know this is reverse psychology."

"Yeah, okay, whatever. Doesn't stop it from being the truth." Alice left the television on an infomercial about some revolutionary shampoo and faced him. "You need to focus on football, right? Peggy would only distract you."

His nod was stilted. "Right."

"So let her go distract someone else who doesn't mind." Sadness passed over Alice's features. "Someone who'll appreciate her."

I appreciate her. I just didn't realize how much.

That same odd sense of vertigo Elliott had experienced while walking to the house hit him again. He was lying there in a hospital bed, listening to someone relate the events that had taken place while he'd been under. *She left you, sir. Don't you remember her getting into the cab? It's been three years since you fell asleep.* Like tree roots gnarling around his organs at warp speed. Being without him had been difficult for Peggy...but until now he hadn't allowed himself to admit he'd been a zombie since she'd gone.

Let her go distract someone else. Someone who'll appreciate her.

I appreciate her now, though. I understand the loss I've been living with. Am I just going to live with this new awareness? Or fucking do something about it?

Peggy could do infinitely better than a man who'd inflicted damage on such a beautiful soul. God. For that alone, he deserved a lifetime of being without her. He could go back to being a member of the living dead, going through the motions, claiming he'd already lost the game. Or he could rally and fight for what he needed. For his woman.

Keeping her in Cincinnati.

Allowing himself to admit what he wanted only brought into perspective what a long shot it was. A hundred-yard field goal. Maybe he should hope for a more realistic outcome, but he wouldn't be satisfied with anything less than having Peggy here. With him. Whether she went to New York and returned. Or never left. Right now, he just needed to focus on earning the right to be a part of that decision *at all*. Then he would take another step, and another, until she saw he'd walk a million miles to keep her.

Ten minutes later when Elliott closed himself in his

office, opening a fresh notepad, it wasn't football that demanded his focus.

No, it was an entirely new set of plays. He'd need to execute every single one of them to perfection if he wanted to win.

CHAPTER SIXTEEN

Peggy stood at the entrance to the room she shared with Sage, squinting into the darkness to find her best friend asleep, buried under a pile of wedding venue brochures. After what she'd done with Elliott, there was no way she could lie down and sleep, but there would be no *Golden Girls* marathon tonight. Her emotions were a pile of shredded cheese, every erogenous zone on her body singing with satisfaction, which she really didn't want to acknowledge.

Moving as quietly as possible, Peggy slipped into the room and snagged her laptop, along with the manila folder resting on top, then ducked back out into the hallway. No sooner had she set up camp in a cross-legged position than Belmont came pacing closer from the opposite end, carrying a green-labeled soda, presumably from the vending machine. Ginger ale?

He tucked it into his jacket pocket before she could confirm, leaning against the wall across from her and watching her with all-knowing blue eyes. Maybe it was the current tangle of her senses or her lack of sleep since arriving in Cincinnati, but a thought flitted through her mind as she regarded her brother, who appeared and disappeared at will.

He's a ghost.

As soon as the brainwave occurred, she hated it. Wished it had never passed through her mind. But it stuck anyway.

As a teenager, she could remember studying for history exams, lying on her bed with an open textbook...and searching the old grainy black-and-white wartime photographs for Belmont's face. It made no sense then and it still didn't. He was standing right there, solid as humanly possible. Maybe it was the way he didn't like to be touched very often, or the way he spoke so differently and with such gravity, that made her wonder if someday, when he wasn't looking, she would lay a hand on his back...and it would pass right through him. And she would trade knowing looks with her other siblings, as if they'd suspected all along.

Belmont's spirit was more substantial than time.

"What are you doing out here?" Peggy asked, staring down at the floral-patterned carpet. "Standing guard over Sage?"

She could sense his abashed expression without glancing up, so his dark rumble surprised her. "Not only Sage."

"But I wasn't even here," she pushed past rubbery lips.

"You're here now." He paused. "Or are you?"

Her laughter was short and humorless. "I was wondering the same thing about you."

Peggy finally looked up at her brother and immediately wanted to take back her words. They'd caused the blue of his eyes to go almost black, but she didn't think making light of what she'd said would help, either. Who was her brother really? If she hadn't wondered the same thing thousands of times, she would accuse herself of using the mystery of Belmont to distract her from Elliott.

Elliott.

Hearing his name echo in her head was enough to make her fists clench. Goddamn him for what he'd done outside. Ruining her chance to escape. To move on without any more struggling. *I need your hands and eyes. I missed them most of all.*

Well the struggle might have just gotten twice as real, but so had her determination to move on. Because whatever she'd felt for Elliott the man? She was declaring it dead. At one time there'd been more than sexual dependency and her need for approval between them, not that Elliott would admit it. But he'd slowly killed the good. She'd be damned before trying to revive it, when he didn't want it back.

I'm over you, Elliott Brooks.

Belmont sat down across from her, although he had a far more difficult time arranging his bulk into a comfortable position. Flicking a glance at Peggy, he removed the ginger ale from his pocket and set it aside carefully.

"Bel," Peggy said on a sigh. "I shouldn't be telling you this, but I don't like to see you worried. Especially when I can save you from it."

He glanced toward the hotel room door to Peggy's left. "Hmm."

Peggy chewed her lip a moment. "Sage just has her period, okay? So if maybe she's acting a little different… that's all it is. Despite what you see in tampon commercials, it doesn't exactly make you want to rappel down the side of a mountain."

For the space of ten breaths, his features were carved in granite. "You must think I'm foolish for not realizing that. Sage, as well."

"No." Peggy reached toward her brother, laying a hand on the carpet. "No one could ever think that about you. Not in a million years."

He didn't believe her. She could see it in the bunching of his shoulders, the way he looked down at the ginger ale, as if willing it to disappear. However, she could tell by Belmont's relative calm that he still wasn't aware that Sage planned to leave. Part of her was desperate to tell her brother, because he would fight like hell to change Sage's mind. He wouldn't rest until he reached her. But Sage's departure wasn't Peggy's plan to reveal. "Are we going to lose you on this trip, too, Peggy?"

"What?" Her heart lurched. Not just at the left field quality of the question, but the reminder that Rita and Aaron were gone, their seats in the Suburban empty. "No. Why would you ask me that?"

No answer. "I don't know how to be alone with Sage anymore. If it were to come to that." He rubbed his thumb along the crease of his chin, then let the hand drop. "I can manage it sometimes, but others..." He avoided her eyes. "The thoughts I have about her are disrespectful."

It hadn't been easy for her introverted brother to make that admission out loud, and Peggy quietly cursed, wishing Aaron were there to pull everything into perspective with a wry one-liner. "You don't have it in you to be disrespectful, Bel. What you're feeling is healthy." She smiled. "There's a damn good chance she's having those same thoughts about you."

Horror took ownership of his expression. "No. Not Sage." They sat in silence for a few long moments, before Belmont spoke again. "Being here is bad for you, Peggy, I can see it. I want to pack you both up and go."

"That sounds like you want to stuff us inside your suitcase." Love clawed at her throat. Love and dread, because he could very well be right. Little parts of her had been chipped away since arriving, only she didn't know which ones. Or if they would fit back into place if she found them. "Don't worry, Bel. We'll go soon enough."

She flattened her palms on the manila folder, before flipping it open to reveal names, phone numbers, and e-mail addresses of Elliott's past players who were now in the NFL. Elliott's secretary—obviously shocked by her boss's agreement—had been very helpful that afternoon in providing contacts. And as Peggy had expected, the generosity of the alumni committee had shone bright as always, showing no hesitation in directing the funds toward the Tate family, instead of the cheerleading program.

"There's just something I want to see done before we go," Peggy said.

"Can I help?" He gestured to the laptop. "I've got one of those in my room. I'm still warming up to the Internet, but—"

"But you've been using it to find your father," Peggy finished, praying he wouldn't shut down on her. "How is it...going?"

He kept his eyes glued on her computer. "Fine. I think I'm close."

She should have been happier, knowing his goal was within reach, but there was a selfish part of her that didn't want some unknown person to have any part of Belmont. He was theirs. "Will you let me know when you find something?"

"Of course." Still, he didn't look at her, nodding once again at the laptop. "Why don't you tell me what I can do to help?"

"You mean get us out of Cincinnati faster?"

The corner of his mouth tugged. "That was somewhere between the lines."

Peggy breathed out a hum of relief that they were back to making eye contact, even if she could still see his secrets lurking. "I met this guy today—a football player—and there was just something good about him." Holding the laptop and folder, she walked on her knees across the hallway, plonking down beside her brother. "He needs help."

Belmont laid a hand on the crown of her head, banishing the remaining chill with which she'd walked back into the hotel. "This is you, Peggy," he said. "This is what the right man will see."

He stood to a height that towered over Peggy, retrieved his own computer from his room, and they worked in silence until the sun came up.

Chapter Seventeen

I told you I make a kick-ass hollandaise sauce," Peggy murmured, drawing the fork back from Elliott's chewing mouth. She was wrapped in a sheet in the center of his bed, his back was propped against the headboard, and the fingertips of morning were just beginning to pick their way through the blinds. "Is there anything she can't do? That's what you're supposed to say next."

His throat worked as he swallowed and, much to Peggy's delight, grunted for more. "I was five minutes late to practice yesterday because I went shopping for eggs and a mixing bowl, just so it would be here when you came over. I'm never late." He snagged a finger in her sheet and tugged. "So yeah, I'd say there's not much you can't do, Miss Clarkson."

Failing to hide her pleasure, Peggy did a sitting victory dance on the bed and forked another bite of eggs Benedict past Elliott's sculpted lips. "Reactions must have ranged *from curious to aghast. The Kingmaker late for practice. Next he'll forget to iron his polo shirt and the earth will forget which direction to spin."*

"You're making my chest hurt."

She dropped the fork onto the plate with a clatter. "What?"

Elliott's gaze cut away, clearly having surprised himself. "The way you're sitting there . . . the sun making your skin glow." He sat up straighter in an abrupt movement that dipped that mattress. "Looking at you makes me want to forget everything else and never stop. Every time I'm with you, I come closer to giving in. Setting aside my responsibilities so I can spend more time looking and listening to each and every damn word out of your mouth. Every time."

Heart running circles around her rib cage, Peggy set the plate of food aside and threw herself at Elliott, laying across him horizontally, her lower half still twisted in the sheet. "You don't have to set anything aside, you can just shift them a little." She smiled into his chest hair. "I'm short. I'll fit."

He didn't speak for a long time after that, but the lighter it got outside, the more tension she could feel creeping into his shoulders. And then it was time to get up.

* * *

Elliott leaned back against the windshield of his truck and closed his eyes, because the feeling of Peggy lounging between his outstretched legs was more satisfying than any sunrise. He needed to snatch up every single second of the paradise she provided, because it couldn't go on forever. Happiness this all-encompassing didn't maintain itself. He could still see his mother and father going through the motions like a residual haunting...and he'd done the same in his own marriage. Through fatherhood. He'd been inflicted with the same DNA and eventually it would poison Peggy. At all costs, he would make sure that didn't happen. He couldn't allow her light to be dimmed by one iota.

She nudged him with an elbow, tipping her head back so he could see her dreamy expression, eyelashes gilded with sunshine. "What are you thinking about so hard, Coach?"

He cleared the debris from his throat. "I'm thinking I've never sat on the hood of a car before."

"No?" She played with the laces of his boots. "It's good to try new things, don't you think?"

No. No, they only set you up for disappointment. "I guess it depends what we're talking about." He slipped his hands into her hair at the back of her head, tugging gently. "Is there something new you want to try?"

Elliott watched her legs grow restless on the hood, her knees pressing together the way they'd done around his head in the backseat a couple hours earlier, before he'd driven them out to East Fork State Park to watch the sun come up over the lake. "Yeah. Everything." She paused. "I want to try everything with you."

It took him a moment to find his voice. "Better be specific while I'm in a good mood."

Her lips curved up into a breath-stealing smile. "Let's go swimming."

He shook his head. "This is the part where I say we don't have our swimsuits—"

"Bingo." She sat up and tugged the T-shirt over her head, sliding off the side of the hood to drop her skirt and crook a finger at him. "Better strip, Coach. Don't want to let me down."

That's what I'm afraid of. *The countdown clock ticking in the back of his mind cranked up the volume as he removed his shirt in one movement and strode after a squealing Peggy.*

Paradise.

* * *

"Every move you make drives my men insane. You should hear how they talk about you," Elliott rasped a breath away from her ear. "One of them plans to ask you out, and I swear to God, Peggy, if you say yes—"

"Why would I do that?" She ran her palms over his heaving pectorals. "I'm here with you, aren't I? I don't want to be anywhere else."

He stooped down and pressed his open mouth to her neck, sucking her skin. Hard. Making his mark? "So fucking jealous. You're going to feel how much."

Peggy caged a whimper as heat ran south inside her. "I can't stop people from looking at me. I'm a cheerleader, that's kind of the point."

"You think I managed to miss that you're a cheerleader?" he growled, settling his hands on her butt, squeezing tight. "I know every time you shake your ass, every time you give some cocksucker in the crowd that smile. You're the reason they're all hiding their laps under balled-up sweatshirts, little girl. I feel everything you're doing, even when my eyes are on the field. So remind me again you're a cheerleader."

She sucked in a winded breath, courtesy of his words knocking the oxygen clear of her lungs. He'd never been like this before...and she loved it. Loved knowing he cared enough to covet her. "Why don't I give you a pri-

vate cheer? None of those sweatshirt douchebags ever gets one of those, you lucky man, you." She reached back and took one of Elliott's kneading hands off her backside, leading him from the kitchen, guiding him into one of the dining room chairs.

Good Lord, the way he filled up the seat, powerful arms crossed, those tree trunk thighs extended and spread. So challenging. But the gray sweatpants he wore did nothing to hide how turned on he was, and that made Peggy confident.

Eyes on Elliott, Peggy grabbed the hem of her dress and slid the material up and over her head, tossing it to the side and leaving herself clad in nothing but panties. By the time Elliott came back into view, his arms had uncrossed, his jaw set in a rigid line as he shifted in the chair, obviously made uncomfortable by that almost cumbersome erection pointing straight up at his waistband.

Peggy turned, giving the coach her back, watching him over her shoulder, raising both arms in the air and clapping her hands together. Once. "We are the Bearcats and we want to win." With a hip roll, she turned, sliding into the V of his thighs, smiling as he sucked in a winded breath. "We did it once before and we can do it again," she continued, holding his knees for balance as she dipped down low and rose slowly, slowly, bumping her hips sharply to one side, and then the other, until Elliott finally gave in, reaching into his sweatpants, his hand moving in vigorous strokes. "Please don't make us mad. 'Cause we'll get nasty and mean," she whispered against his mouth, before licking at the parted seam. "And we just might decide to roll over your team."

Her back landed on the kitchen table a split second later, Elliott grunting above her as he shoved down his sweat-

pants, ripped off her underwear, and rammed home with a shout. "Christ. Christ, what you do to me. It's the devil's work." He mounted her body, dropping his face into the crook of her neck. "When a man loses control of one part of his life, all others follow. All others."

"And I'm the catalyst?" Peggy whispered, her voice shaking. "Guess you better punish me for it."

When his hips gave that first rude pump, she felt it up in her throat, choking her and setting her free, all at once.

* * *

Elliott ground his fist against the concrete pillar of his garage, hoping like hell he would break something. Shatter his knuckles or rip the skin clean off. Anything to distract him from the machete making crisscross marks on his insides. His teeth gnashed inside his head, the sound sickening, but nothing could cause his stomach to rebel more than Peggy's cab pulling up outside. The cab he'd called her five minutes ago. The one that would take her to the airport.

"This is so stupid, Elliott," she half screamed, half sobbed across the garage. "It's just a visit to California to see friends and then I'm coming right back."

"You graduated last week," he ground out, conjuring the coldest of words, knowing they were the only way to make her see reason, make her leave. "There's nothing left for you to return to. No school, no job. Nothing."

Betrayal hung in the air, so thick it clouded his vision of her. "You're really going to do this? Act like we were noth-ing?" She kicked at her overnight bag. "This is like that scene in Harry and the Hendersons *when they shout mean things at Harry so he'll go back and live in the wild with the other Yetis where he belongs."*

He stared at her in probable disbelief, but inside he was fighting a battle not to take the three long strides that would put her in his arms.

"I make jokes when I'm upset." She tucked a group of curls behind her ear. "You should know this about me by now."

"I do," he responded tightly. "I do know that, because I give you plenty of reasons to be sad around me." No. No, he'd given her an opening to protest with that one. His resolve was slipping in the face of the reality of her actually climbing into the cab and never coming back. The only thing that made his blood flow and heat and pulse. His life force. She was leaving and he was the one sending her away. Behind her lay the driveway, the spot where his wife had been found lifeless while he'd been inside his own head, not sparing her a thought. Living with himself would be impossible if Peggy ended up the same way. Miserable, alone...hurt... "I knew going in this was going to be temporary. You were a senior. You weren't going to be sticking around and asking me for more."

Had she ever been so pale? Pale but still his courageous Peggy, through and through. Headstrong and demanding and gorgeous. "I didn't know what this was going to evolve into, either, but you're full of shit if you're telling me it isn't worth keeping."

"You can't put a name to it, either." Elliott's scoff ripped a hole in his throat. "Did you think maybe you'd make a good stepmother?"

She floundered. "I—I hadn't thought that far ahead..."

Yes, she had. He could see it in the sudden pink of her cheeks, the way she couldn't meet his eyes, her defensive posture. God. How fucked up that his love for her should swell to an unbearable degree when he was stamping an end date on their relationship? I can't give you what you need, *he wanted to shout, but she would protest and they would end up back inside, kissing and fucking and making up, just like the last ten times he'd tried to create distance between them. This time it had to be permanent, because the alternative was this beautiful woman building her life around the ruins of his.* "I'm standing here telling you I want it over, Peggy, and it's not because I like the tears and drama. These arguments you insist on making are childish, and they're only delaying the inevitable."

"Childish?" *She reared back like a backhand had caught her across the face.* "You're the one too afraid to admit what's really scaring you."

"Enlighten me."

"You're scared of feeling anything you don't understand," *she whispered.* "I might be childish, but you're a fucking coward."

She was right. God knew she was. But the more his love…yes, love…for Peggy grew, the more tortured he felt about neglecting the one who came before. He hated the constant flux of happiness and self-disgust. It tore at him day and night. It was going to wreck Peggy for the world if he continued to keep her to himself, surrounding her in his misery. "When I look at you, Peggy, I see my guilt." *Her eyes lost their color in degrees, mutilating his insides.* "I see the wrongs in my past. My sins. I can't do it…" *To you.* "I won't do it anymore."

With that final shot hanging between them, Peggy gave him one last devastated look, picked up her bag, and went to meet the cab. Sobs shook her shoulders. A shout for her to come back rose in his throat like an expanding fist, so he pressed and pressed his hand into the concrete pillar, feeling the destruction of flesh at the same time his chest started to collapse. The cab door slammed. He watched it drive away with a scream careening through the landscape of his mind, changing its formation, and as soon as it was out of sight, Elliott got into his truck and drove to church. At least the chanting of the prayers helped drown out the horror.

CHAPTER EIGHTEEN

One would think a sleepless night would have left Peggy lacking energy, but it turned out, setting up an online auction with twelve items valued at over five thousand dollars apiece? Well, it was pretty damn satisfying. E-mails pinged on Peggy's phone every few minutes, letting her know another one of Elliott's—the Kingmaker's—players had pledged an item to be donated. Autographed helmets, jerseys signed by entire Super Bowl–winning teams, game balls.

Until the wee hours of the morning, she and Belmont had reached out via e-mails and phone calls—depending on the player's geographical location—with an explanation of Kyler's plight. Understandably, the professional players had reacted with out-and-out horror at the idea of their revered coach's star receiver being sidelined by his family issues, and generosity had poured out of them. Sage had woken up around six in the morning and stumbled into the hall, demanding that Peggy and Belmont come inside and continue, along with her assistance. True to form, the wedding planner had surpassed them in productivity after merely an hour. But ask Peggy if she was upset.

Hell nope. She was...revitalized.

It had been a long time since she'd felt so useful. Since she'd looked at the fruits of her labor and been proud to be a part of making something extraordinary happen. Had she ever gotten that warm, crowded feeling in her throat as a personal shopper? No. Even when someone looked truly boss in an outfit she'd styled, there was only a passing specter of satisfaction that sailed on as soon as it appeared.

What if she didn't have to be a personal shopper once she reached New York? Sure, that had been the plan, but securing the same job she'd had in San Diego would feel like hopping back into the holding pattern in which she'd lived for three years. Raising funds for good causes wouldn't allow her college degree to collect dust on the shelf anymore. She could finally put it to use.

Peggy took a deep breath and allowed herself to smile as she, Belmont, and Sage exited the hotel, to-go coffees in hand, intending to scavenge up some breakfast. They were all sick to death of hotel food at this point, and Peggy had remembered a little hole-in-the-wall from her college days that made the most insane pancakes—

Elliott's appearance on the sidewalk ground her progress to a halt. Belmont and Sage moved to flank her on either side, as if they were a fearsome trio heading into battle. But apart from the definite flutter of feminine appreciation she experienced over a fresh-from-the-shower Elliott in jeans and a thick, gray, cable-knit sweater, she didn't need reinforcements. She was just fine on her own. There wasn't a woman alive that wouldn't get a down-low tug at the picture he painted. Half distinguished, half rough, all male and very intently focused. On her.

Been there, done that, and stole the T-shirt, babe. This ship has set sail.

"I got this," she murmured to Belmont and Sage, putting a little extra swing in her walk as she approached the coach. "Greetings, Elliott."

"Peggy." His hard gaze swept up her skinny jeans, lingering at her hips, before completing the final journey to her eyes. And okay, the chemical reaction that fired off was just as normal as admitting she found him attractive. Nothing to see here. "How are you this morning?"

"Fine as ever." She heard another ping go off in her jacket pocket and breathed through a smile. "The online auction for Kyler is getting ready to start and we still have donations rolling in. E-mails are going out from the university this morning to major news outlets, letting the public know about the items and—"

"Peggy, it's too late." His face was grave. "I got a call from Kyler early this morning. The foreclosure is this afternoon." He stepped closer, reaching out and letting his hand drop. "I'm sorry, baby. All this work you put in—"

"Don't call me baby...out in the daytime like this." The admonishment sounded incredibly lame, even to her own ears, but she was reeling. No. No way were they too late. They'd worked so fast and it couldn't all be for just nothing. Heat pressed against the inside of her eyelids, the paper cup of hotel coffee all but forgotten in her hand. "What if we drive there and stop it ourselves? Items will have sold by then...we could have enough to hold them off. Once they see the potential to have the debt paid without evicting anyone, they'll postpone."

She felt frozen, standing there waiting for Elliott to make

another placating statement. *It was a good try, Peggy. You did your best, kiddo.* Instead, he nodded and held up his car keys, jerking his head toward the truck idling at the curb. "If you think it's worth a shot, I'll drive."

The world tilted. "You'll what?"

"I'll drive," he repeated, his voice like gravel. "The university e-mails already went out and one of them landed in my in-box. Lord, Peggy, what you managed to do overnight..." He shook his head. "We're not letting that go to waste. Not without trying."

"Oh." At a loss, she twirled a curl around her finger and swore Elliott's eyes went soft. But that couldn't be right. What the hell was going on here? A minute ago, her main focus had been pancakes, and now it felt like she'd stepped into a bizarre dream where nothing made sense.

Before she could address Elliott's odd behavior out loud, the truck's door opened and Alice stepped out, hands shoved into her hoodie pockets. "Hey."

"Hey," Peggy returned, the ground shifting beneath her feet. A voice in the back of her mind told her to flee. She'd just found her way clear of Elliott's grasp and now he was here, looking at her in a new, discerning way and apparently flipping the script.

And she did not want it flipped. She was done.

If it weren't for the project she'd taken on for Kyler, she would have turned on a heel and gone for pancakes. Left them right there in the dust, even if it would bother her to be cold to Alice. But there was something bigger than the rubble of her broken heart at stake. Something much larger. Not only saving someone's dream, someone's family...but finding out if she was capable of a new one as well.

"I'll ride with Bel and Sage," Peggy said finally, stepping away from an Elliott who looked determined to drag her back. So she held up a hand, warding him off. "We'll follow you."

Just before they pulled away from the hotel—Elliott and Alice in the truck, the rest of them in the Suburban—Peggy caught Elliott's eye in the rearview and saw a promise there. One that said they weren't finished just yet.

Peggy made sure he saw how much she disagreed.

CHAPTER NINETEEN

Peggy. What's up?"

The moment Aaron's brisk greeting landed in Peggy's ears, she felt more stable. Something she hadn't been since Elliott's odd behavior back at the hotel. Before the road trip had started out in California, saying Aaron chilled her out would have been laughable, despite them being the closest of any Clarkson siblings. Calling them close, however, would have been pushing it. They'd been comfortable enough to be alone in the same room, which didn't sound like much to normal, functional siblings, but to a Clarkson, it symbolized a rare, unspoken bond.

Since setting out in the Suburban together on this crazy wish-fulfilling journey to New York, the dynamic among the four siblings had shifted. It couldn't be her imagination, could it? Maybe the sense of camaraderie other families felt would never exist for the Clarksons, but if she could feel her stomach settle just hearing Aaron's sharp, all-business tone, maybe when their common mission was over, they would have accomplished more than jumping into the Atlantic and freezing their asses off.

Yes, she was the youngest and, by default, the most naïve of the bunch. But dammit, wanting your family to feel free to look one another in the eye, without the fear they would burst into flames...that wasn't so far-fetched, was it? The day of Miriam's funeral, she'd sensed them splitting apart at the seams and could do nothing to stop it. She'd idolized her siblings during her youth, so losing faith in them had been particularly hurtful. They were slowly gluing the pieces back together, though, restoring her confidence in them—and maybe even herself.

Okay, maybe Aaron's greeting hadn't calmed her as much as she'd originally thought, because she still hadn't answered him, having been thrown for a serious loop back at the hotel. She'd only managed last night to reduce the mountain located in her belly down to a mole hill. No peaks or jagged outcroppings, just smooth and manageable. But one determined look from Elliott had caused an erosion. Not of her willpower. Oh no. But the relief that came with the decision to finally move on didn't feel quite so solid now.

"Hey, Aaron," Peggy pushed out. "How's the camp rebuilding going?"

His voice warmed immediately, even though his characteristic briskness remained. People didn't change one hundred percent overnight, even if a rebellious politician's daughter had caused a transformation in her brother no one had seen coming. "Well. Really well. Grace posted a video on her father's website asking for volunteers and now we're turning people away. She's..." He blew a breath down the line. "She's magnetic. I spend most of the day staring at her, like some kind of thick-skulled Neanderthal." A short pause. "Unfortunately, everyone else does, too, so I spend the rest of my time reminding her she's never getting rid of me."

Peggy had to slap a hand over her mouth to keep a squeak from flying out. Slowly, she let her arm drop. "I'm so happy for you."

"Yeah, yeah. Why are you calling?" He shouted a direction at someone in the background. "I'm surprised it took you three this long to need my invaluable advice."

And it bothered him, didn't it? Just a touch, maybe, but considering she never would have been able to sense that regret in him before the road trip, she decided to chalk it up to progress. "Huh. Well, it's kind of a long story."

"When is it not?"

"Yeah." Through the front windshield, she watched Elliott's truck change lanes on the four-lane highway and wondered—not for the first time—what father and daughter were talking about. And what that glance from Elliott in the rearview had meant. "There's a football player here in Cincinnati—"

"Jesus, Peggy. This is about a road hookup?"

"No! Not a hookup." Belmont sighed in the driver's seat. "And by the way, you'd be one to talk. I seem to remember freezing my ass off in the woods last week to help build Grace's memorial."

"Fair point." There was a smile in his voice. "Continue."

"This player left school because his family farm is being foreclosed on. I've already set up an online auction—"

"Web address?"

She rattled it off.

"Where is the foreclosed property located?"

"Bloomfield, Indiana—"

"Whoa." A door closed on the other end, then all she could hear was Aaron's fingers punching buttons on a computer keyboard. "Please don't tell me you are literally driving back toward California right now."

"It would appear that way, bro." Sage and Belmont must have heard Aaron's question, because they were both shaking their heads. "But not the whole way. Just far enough to reach Indiana and pay the bank."

A low whistle. "Damn. You put this auction together, Peggy?"

She could picture him scrolling, looking at the new items she and Sage had been adding while Belmont sped them toward Indiana. The ticker keeping track of how much money they'd raised, alongside a picture of Kyler in his football jersey. "It was my idea, but I couldn't have done it without Bel and Sage. It was a team effort."

"I'm impressed. Not to mention wishing I'd given you more administrative work while we were pulling everything together in Iowa." A beat passed. "I underestimated you, Peggy. I shouldn't have. This is an accomplishment in itself."

"Thanks." Dammit, she hated being the one crier in the family. The struggle was real not to break into tears over a simple compliment. But a compliment wasn't simple coming from Aaron, was it? More like the Pope blowing you a kiss from the Pope Mobile. "Um. So, we're about an hour away and the foreclosure could be any time. Assuming we make it, I just need a way to stall until the auction closes tonight."

"Can you get the name of the bank?"

"Probably," she said on an exhale, knowing it would mean calling Elliott and having him get in touch with Kyler. "Yeah."

She could sense Aaron's no-nonsense nod. "Text it to me and I'll give them a call." He laughed. "Or maybe I'll have Senator Pendleton do it. He's still trying to lure me back onto his advisory committee."

Excitement was blurred by concern for her brother. "Is that something you want?" She swallowed. "To go back to working on the campaign?"

"Hell no. Grace and I are a team now. We only work for each other." Pride had thickened his voice. Contentment. And maybe a touch of residual fear over having almost lost his chance with the politician's daughter. "But hey. That doesn't mean I can't let him think there's a chance, right?"

Peggy laughed. "Thanks, Aaron."

"Glad I could help."

Sensing he was about to hang up without saying good-bye, the way he always did, Peggy twisted around in her seat, cupping a hand around the cell phone. "Oh, hey. Uh..." She lowered her voice to a murmur. "Could you give Bel a call sometime soon, maybe?"

His pause this time was drawn out. The brothers had made serious headway in a relationship that had been contentious for too long, but neither of them were the heart-to-heart type. Even so, Aaron's sudden worry was a tangible thing, cutting right through the distance separating them. "Is something wrong?"

"I don't know," Peggy said honestly. "Maybe. I just think he needs to speak to another man. About stuff."

"My excitement knows no bounds," Aaron said, voice dry as dust. "I'm going to think twice about answering your next call."

She half gasped, half giggled. "No, you're not."

"No, I'm not." A chair creaked on the other end. "Take care, Peggy. All right? We'll see you soon."

Great. Another blast of heat behind her eyes. "You take care, too, Aaron. Bye."

* * *

There were only a few moments in Elliott's life where he could remember feeling his heart try and rip its way out through his mouth. One had been during his first division championship as head coach, when the victory had come down to his kicker making a field goal. Many games had ridden on those three points since that too-sunny afternoon, but he'd learned to calm his nerves by mentally listing everything he'd done to prepare the team before a game. And he didn't stop until the pigskin sailed through the uprights.

The second time his heart had made that hurtling upward journey, he'd just been informed he would become a father. Parenting had never been in the cards for Elliott, despite his staunch Catholic upbringing. He'd even discussed it with Judith and explained—in a rare moment of total, bald honesty—that he didn't have a paternal gene in his body. She'd agreed. But somewhere along the line, she'd either changed her mind without telling him or there'd been a mistake, because a few years later, he'd stood in the hospital delivery ward, staring down at a tiny, crying little girl. One that would inevitably grow up to resent him someday.

Now, as he heard the popping sound and watched the Suburban swerve on the highway behind him, the usually quiet organ protested inside his rib cage, attempting to tear free from its rightful place.

"Peggy," he shouted. Uselessly. He could do nothing. Nothing. That helplessness was so much worse than the kind he'd been living with all night, because if she were hurt or worse, he wouldn't have a chance to make everything up to her. Wouldn't have a chance to see her smile again or watch as she twirled a curl, worked out a problem, swallowed her pride. Would never have the chance to explain the hurtful words he'd thrown at her three years ago. So many things he'd taken for granted and it occurred to Elliott he deserved to have her taken away. To watch it happen, right there in the front row. Because she was on that highway at his behest, whether or not she denied it. Here she was, trying to solve his problems with kindness and understanding once again, and as the Suburban fishtailed...he was getting his just desserts, wasn't he?

Same way he'd gotten them for ignoring his responsibilities as a husband all those years ago. This was an instant replay...

Only the stakes were through the fucking roof this time around. They weren't just murky and undefined and yes, goddammit, burdensome. His original guilt had stemmed from not feeling enough, but if a single hair on Peggy's head were harmed, that would be the farthest thing from the case.

If he'd thought himself dead inside since she'd left, her light going out would seal the deal.

Elliott released a slow, pent-up breath as the Suburban stabilized behind him. Thank God they were traveling in the middle of a weekday, because Belmont only needed to cross one empty lane, before the car jerked to a stop on the side of the road. Elliott checked his rearview and followed suit, hitting reverse down the shoulder until the vehicles were only separated by a few feet.

"Son of a bitch," Elliott breathed, gripping the steering wheel and willing his pulse back under control. Yeah, not happening. He could hear it thundering in his eardrums, like someone was beating a gong on either side of his head.

"H-hey." Alice was white as a ghost in the passenger seat. "They're fine. We're all fine."

He got the impression her fear came from seeing him unravel, rather than the potential car accident, so he performed a forward and backward mental count to bring himself back down to earth. "Sorry," he offered.

Alice nodded. "Maybe you should go see if they need help."

"Yes." His words were punctuated, leaving his mouth the way they did during a rushed time out. "I'm just trying to get it together first."

"You shouldn't." She turned in her seat. "I mean, if I were a girl—"

"You are a girl, Alice."

"A woman, then. Like Peggy," she clarified, waving off his interjection with a red face. "I wouldn't want a guy to hide it...if he didn't have it together. You should just go. Even if you're sweating and that vein is standing out way more than usual."

He heaved a cut-off laugh. "Thanks." And whether or not his daughter's advice was the culprit, Elliott was out of the car a moment later, needing to get Peggy in his sights. Absently, he noticed the back right tire had blown, but his attention was on Peggy as she hopped out of the backseat. She was the only one to alight, while Belmont sat in the driver's seat, staring straight ahead as Peggy's friend spoke, right up against his ear.

"Dammit." She turned in an outraged circle, delivering a kick to the Suburban. "Not again. I can't believe this is happening again."

Heat rippled in his belly as he watched Peggy, breathtaking even in her state of visible frustration. She'd stripped off her jacket during the ride, leaving her body on display in a white tank top and silver-platter jeans, named for the manner in which they served her cheeks right up. Her blond curls vibrated with annoyance, her forehead was drawn in a sexy pout...and he wanted her like hell in that moment. Wanted to feel her life pulse under his fingertips, a concrete reminder she hadn't been harmed, because he still hadn't recovered. Might never get there.

But he wouldn't allow himself to even try for the privilege of touching Peggy. He wouldn't slide his rough body up against the ripe tautness of her flesh again. Not until he completed the list of tasks he'd designed for himself last night.

Lord help him, Elliott almost reached for an invisible playbook in his back pocket, the way he might during a game, when he needed to make a move. A dramatic one. Thing was, while he desperately needed to stick to the plan he'd designed to make things right with Peggy, looking at what he'd scrawled in a fevered rush last night wasn't necessary. He remembered every word.

1. Apologize for being a sack of shit.

2. Be her friend first (no skipping this step).

3. Repeat Step One.

4. Make her aware, in no uncertain terms, that you find her extraordinary.

5. Beg her not to leave.

So he had a plan, per se. The execution was where he was getting stuck.

Frankly, Step Five was terrifying as all get-out. By the time he reached the final phase of his game plan, his options could very well be whittled down to begging...for forgiveness. Only. That could be where it ended. Begging for a second chance wherein Peggy remained in Cincinnati might be so far-fetched, he would hear her laughing as she drove into the sunset, right out of town.

Peggy fell back against the side of the Suburban and gave him a hollow look, spurring Elliott out of his head and into motion. *Do or die, asshole.*

"Again?" Elliott strode for the Suburban's rear and lowered the rusted back hatch, relieved to find a spare tire beneath the stiff, carpet panel, adjacent to a roadside emergency kit. "This isn't the first time you've had car trouble on this trip, huh?"

Her rich laughter told tales. "No. We lost the better part of a week in New Mexico." She joined him near the deflated tire, dropping down to her haunches beside him as he inspected the blown-out rubber. It took Elliott a moment to focus because she looked like an action movie heroine, big blue sky stretching behind her, hair lifting on the wind. "We were stranded in a little town called Hurley while the local garage waited for the right part to arrive. Only..." Her voice took on a dreamlike quality. "It had been there since the second day. My sister Rita's boyfriend, Jasper, bribed the mechanic to put off the repair so he could woo her."

He was dying to hold those curls back from her face. "And Rita stayed behind with him? In New Mexico."

"Who wouldn't stay with a man who does something like that?" All at once, she seemed to realize whom she was conversing with and started to stand—but Elliott stopped her by grabbing her wrist.

"You deserve that." A wrench turned in his gut. "You deserve a man who'll do that and more."

"Yeah." She breathed the word, life snapping in her eyes. "I think I finally realized that. Right around the time I figured out it would never be you."

He'd prepared himself for the tackle, the verbalization that she'd definitely counted him out of the race, but all the preparation in the world wouldn't have helped. The Elliott who'd allowed himself to live inside numbness for so long might have agreed with Peggy and willed her to move on so he wouldn't have to feel so goddamn much. But this Elliott? He was fighting to the death. He wasn't leaving the battlefield until he could walk away knowing he'd given her every breath in his body.

Before he went into battle for her heart, however, she needed a different kind of hero. One that fixed a flat and made damn sure her hard work didn't go to waste.

Elliott stood and removed his thick sweater, leaving himself bare-chested in the crisp midmorning sunlight, just as Belmont and Sage rounded the Suburban's rear, Alice following behind. Various reactions followed, including Belmont wordlessly covering Sage's eyes and ushering her back around the vehicle and Alice muttering something about being in the truck, listening to the radio.

For Peggy's part, she stared at him like he'd just landed on Earth in a Frisbee-shaped hovercraft, preaching about the end times. "What do you think you're doing?"

CHAPTER TWENTY

Revving her estrogen engine. That's what Elliott was doing by stripping down to nothing but a pair of jeans on the roadside. He even had the audacity to mess up his hair in the process. The wayward strands, peppered with gray, drew an unwanted memory to the surface. Elliott, stubbled, naked, and morning-eyed, his mouth going for broke between her legs, making her late for class in the most delicious way possible.

Great. Fabulous. Now her clit was throbbing.

As if his physique wasn't enough to get her lady juices flowing. Damn him, he'd always kept himself in peak condition—a fact her fellow cheerleaders had never failed to remark on after a few wine coolers—but he must have increased his gym time by double since she'd left. Because…muscles. Muscles everywhere. They almost looked drawn on, they were so defined. Those angular ridges of his abdomen vanished like a tease into his low—

but snug—jeans, a mixture of dark and light hairs curling along the center of his pelvic V, the way her tongue was suddenly aching to do. And there. Now she'd done it. She was looking at his crotch.

That package, hugged in denim, was wrapped up like a present for a birthday girl who'd been extra good all year.

"Why." Oh man. She sounded like a pack-a-day drag queen. No help for it, either. "Why is your shirt off?"

He tossed the garment in question onto the Suburban's roof. "I only have one shirt with me and I figured it for the best if I didn't get it covered in dirt and oil."

"Well, sure. If you want to be practical about it."

One of his eyebrows lifted, completing the picture of ripped, ready, arrogant guy. At least he didn't have mysterious going for him. That's right. She'd solved this whodunit. No mystery whatsoever. Maybe the sex between them was tear-your-hair-out phenomenal, but everything else had gone cold. "I'm always practical, aren't I, Peggy?" he muttered, finding a towel in the backseat and laying it down on the ground, just beside the flat tire. "That's how you remember me, right?"

"Sounds pretty accurate," Peggy hedged, thrown by the questions. Deciding to make herself useful, instead of gawking at his ridiculous body like a goober, she tried to slide past Elliott so she could root through the back storage area first and figure out what she was looking for later. But Elliott moved into her space without warning, taking hold of her elbows and turning their bodies to walk them backward. Her back met the Suburban about the time anger scaled the insides of her throat like ivy. "Stop," she pushed past clenched teeth. "I don't want you touching me—"

"God above, you're fucking gorgeous, Peggy." Her stomach hit the dusty ground. "I know people tell you all the time—which I really don't like to consider too much—but I don't think I've ever said it. Not once. And that's a crime, because you've got the kind of beauty that ties me up in eight different knots." His fingers slipped a lock of hair behind her ear. "It's the way you straighten your spine every time you're presented with a problem. How your eyes go wet and soft over things like people losing their farms. Your stubbornness, your willpower, your sense of humor. It's all of you."

"What is this?" she managed to whisper, feeling like someone who'd just woken up in the middle of a foreign land. "What are you doing?"

"Telling you what I see." He planted a hand to the right of her head, his energy rippling like static over her senses. "Saying the things I should have said the first time you came to me in that locker room."

She barely contained a wheeze. This couldn't be happening. Not now. It was the world's cruelest joke that this Elliott should decide to make an appearance after she'd finally, finally, stopped hoping for him. "I don't want to listen now. I'm not listening."

His nod was grave, but determined. "I'll repeat myself until it sinks in."

Peggy could almost see her hand clinging to the edge of a cliff. "If this is about sex, just say so, Elliott." Cheapen what he said, make light of it. Make it not matter. "You want to get your fill of me before I leave?" She shrugged off the niggling feeling that her words were wrong, out of place between them. "We're both adults."

A flash of misery passed through his eyes and that rare show of emotion made him so there. So live and in person. Grounded and raw. She could smell his sun-warmed skin, the soap wafting off him. He was the one with his shirt off, but she'd never felt more naked in her life. "I'm sorry," he murmured against her forehead. "You hearing me? I'm sorry. This thing between us... it went off course on the first day. The first damn day. And now we're out at sea."

"So now you're going to steer us back? I don't think so." Her voice was too high-pitched and unsteady, so she breathed until it was firm. "Weren't you listening last night? It's not going to happen. You made me..."

"What?" The way his gaze locked on hers, she swore Elliott already knew what she was going to say. Sometime after she'd left him last night, had he figured out what it had taken her three years to realize, too? "Tell me, baby. I want to hear everything you've been keeping in your head, because I was too stupid to ask."

Stop, she wanted to shout at him. *Too much.* "You made me into a sin," she whispered instead, truth jostling free. Maybe it had reached its limit on being kept secret, or perhaps she wanted to see the misery in his eyes again. The kind she'd been feeling forever. "When I look at you, I see the word Alice called me last night," she breathed in a wild gust, realizing for the first time how truly fucked up she'd allowed her self-image to become.

Since they'd arrived on the roadside, Elliott had appeared so robust to Peggy. A man on a quest. But with Peggy's admission, the crackling momentum in him quite simply crumpled. "No. No, don't say that." Wind whistled between them. "Tell me that's not true. I knew it was bad, but Jesus, not... not that."

She just wanted to get back in the Suburban and lay down on the cracked leather seat. To finally read her mother's words in the journal she'd left, something she'd put off far too long for fear of finding out Miriam had been disappointed in her. A wasted college degree, four broken engagements, fewer and fewer friends as time went on. Why wouldn't a mother expect more from her daughter?

Would Miriam be proud of Peggy for finally kicking Elliott to the curb? Or would she encourage her to hear him out? Decisions were too hard to make with their bodies pressed together, but before she even attempted to slide from beneath Elliott's deflated frame, she knew he wasn't going to let her go.

"Peggy, please, just give me a second."

"There's nothing to say." She reached up and clasped the sides of his face. "Nothing to do except change a flat tire and get back on the road."

Strength crept back into his big body in degrees, as if he was recovering from the blow she'd landed. "No." He surged forward, flattening her against the Suburban, causing blood to rush in her ears. "No, there's a lot to say and do between us. There's everything. I'll never make an excuse for myself or the way I've behaved...Christ, for forcing you to leave...but here's the truth." His mouth burrowed into her hair, forcing a whimper from her lips. "When I got your wedding invitation—that deal with the yellow flowers, pink butterflies, and some other son-of-a-bitch's name—the date had already passed. Two weeks earlier."

"You're lying," she whispered, even though he wasn't. They both knew it, so he didn't bother trying to convince her. There was no point in lying after all this time, and he wasn't the type to use something so important to his advantage. As much as she wanted to deny the needle and thread mending something in her chest with that revelation, there it was. Stitching and sewing and repairing.

"I broke my hand punching the hallway wall. I couldn't

feel the pain, though. I couldn't feel or hear anything over the sound of every damn thing inside me dying." He swore under his breath. "And that's how I stayed."

She reached down and traced her fingertips over the back of his hand, reading the bumps and bones like braille, but she couldn't think of what to say. Couldn't formulate a response in the face of her stupid relief. The invitation had gotten there late.

He turned his hand over, allowing her fingers to brush his palm. "There's a metal pin that goes off every time I pass through a metal detector."

Such a stupid time to laugh, but she'd always enjoyed jokes being made at inappropriate moments. "If you liked being frisked at the airport, you probably could have just asked, instead of going to such an extreme."

His breath ruffled her hair on a sad laugh. "You've moved on from me. I acknowledge that—and I'm proud of you for seeing me for the asshole I am. But I'm fighting for my life here. So you're going to tolerate me just a little while longer, understand? I'm not moving. Not until everything is out in the open, all of it, and you can be the one to look me in the eye...and tell me nothing here is worth saving."

Oh God, oh God, oh God. "I'm telling you that now," she whispered, sounding as if she were sitting on top of a washing machine during the spin cycle. And she hated herself for feeling a crack in her resolve. One that seemed to pry wider the longer he impressed his speech upon her with earnest, unrelenting eyes.

"I didn't know what to do with you, Peggy. I couldn't handle the way you made me so happy, when I wanted so badly to feel like garbage. I thought being alone was my due. And you just kept coming and coming, so I fought." He pulled back to impress a meaningful look on her, one that cleared her lungs of oxygen. "I kept on fighting while you were a country away, and I'll regret not going after you for the rest of my pitiful life. But I'll be damned before I let it happen again without telling you."

Peggy's body was paralyzed, except for her knees, which were rattling and knocking together. Run away. Run now. "Telling me what?"

"Before you walked into the locker room that day, before you directed a single fucking word at me, I'd fallen for you. I had wanted you and needed you. And I never stopped. I'll never stop." His eyelids catapulted down, as if he'd been holding those words in forever, just sitting in his lungs like steel harpoons, waiting to impale her.

Was it possible to die from heart failure at twenty-five? It had been beating so hard for such an extended period of time, her chest was sore with the strain. "Can we please change the tire now?"

"Almost." Elliott's lips slid over hers, the warmth of his breath tinged with spearmint and orange juice. And most poignant of all, hope. His hope. "Will you remember something for me?"

"I don't know," she murmured, the need to bolt building.

He pressed their foreheads together, steadying her, despite how hard she wished for the opposite. "I'm the whore, Peggy." When she jerked with a gasp, he caged her in, keeping their gazes locked. "I'm the one that gave my body and nothing else. You gave everything and I wasn't wise enough to accept the best part. Your heart." His voice shook with emotion. "So when you look at me and hear that filthy word, remember who owns the title."

* * *

It was a strange thing, being awake.

Elliott's navigator informed him they were only a mile from their destination, Kyler's family farm, but they'd pretty much already arrived. Green grazing fields stretched along either side of the road, long strands of grass blowing in the breeze. A light rain had started, turning the sky a mottled mixture of gray and white and filling the sound of the truck with the timed squeal of windshield wipers. Cows dotted the hills, a silo in the distance, alongside the outline of three wooden barns. Elliott assumed one of them was the house where his receiver's family lived. A week ago, the idea of walking into the home of a player without the buffer of recruitment to validate his presence would have made him uncomfortable. Hard-assed Elliott Brooks wasn't exactly known for making social calls and for good reason. He hadn't wanted to talk or think about anything but football. That was all. As long as he'd stayed consumed by that bubble, not looking right or left, he wouldn't have to think about Peggy.

Unfortunately, in the process, he'd lost what little affection he'd managed to earn from his daughter or any kind of friendship he might have formed with his players. Now, he didn't believe in being chummy with his men. Having the line blurred between mentor and mentee would never work. But the clear hindsight he'd been living in for a mere twenty-four hours had him wondering if fear was a desirable alternative.

"How did it go with Peggy?"

The way Alice posed the question, Elliott could tell it had taken her until only seconds remained in their journey to work up enough nerve to ask. More fear from people whose respect mattered most. "I don't know," he responded in a flat voice.

He'd left a huge chunk of himself back there on the

road, and nothing would fill the vacated hole but changing Peggy's mind. Especially not the phone call he'd made to his assistant coach to discuss running practice without him, which had caused an annoying amount of stuttering on the other end of the line. Yeah, football had moved down on his list of priorities, well below Peggy, Alice...and helping Kyler's family. He'd never really acknowledged before how much he liked the receiver, and maybe it was crazy, but in addition to lending a hand to someone who desperately needed one, Elliott couldn't help but wonder if this one mutual victory could help shift the course for him and Peggy. Maybe working together would remind her of the good times between them. The times they'd offered one another comfort and happiness, instead of sadness and confusion. It was a lot to hope for, but Elliott would damn well take what he could get.

"You haven't apologized to her yet," Elliott said to Alice as he pulled off the road and began what looked to be a long, bumpy trip up the dirt driveway.

"Yeah, well, you've kind of been hogging her," Alice burst out. "Taking off your shirt and changing tires. I didn't want to steal your weird thunder."

Somehow, even though Elliott was still reeling over Peggy's revelation back on the roadside, he managed a smile over Alice's mini rant. "Do you think she's not going to forgive you?"

A few beats of silence passed. "I don't know. I was kind of waiting to see if she forgave you first." She glanced over at him. "Is she...going to?"

Elliott watched the Suburban bump along behind him in the rearview, reminding himself the new tire was on as tightly as possible. "I'm going to do everything in my power to make that happen."

"And then what?" Alice asked quietly. "Say she does let you off the hook. Are you going to have the new mommy talk with me?"

His knee-jerk reaction was to change the subject, but the question hadn't been posed as a joke. And he didn't want to sweep aside Alice's worries anymore. "Let's not get ahead of ourselves, okay? Right now I'm just lucky she's talking to me." He steered the truck around the semicircle driveway and threw it into Park, both of them considering the three-story farmhouse through the passenger window. Before Alice could climb out, Elliott reached over and caught her arm, sensing there was more to be said, just not sure what. When Alice raised an eyebrow at his staying hand, Elliott removed it and settled back into his seat. "Your advice back there...letting Peggy see that I didn't have it together. It got me into her head, so I know what I'm up against." He rolled his shoulders, thanking God there were no witnesses to this conversation. "What else you got?"

Alice let out a tremulous laugh. "Are you asking me for chick advice?"

"No." He tugged the keys from the ignition, letting them rest on his thigh. "All right, maybe I am."

"Wow." Alice looked down fast, playing with the rubber hairband circling her wrist. "What if I give you bad advice on purpose, because I don't want someone new around?"

The situation snapped into focus, then. Sacrifice was something he'd only ever weighed and executed in terms of religion and football. Sacrificing pleasure and vanity and living a humble life for his church. Sacrificing hours and time at home and sometimes his health for football. Having Peggy back in his life was the ultimate goal here, but that didn't happen if Alice wasn't on board. Cold snapped in his veins, responsibility weighing down on his chest. He hadn't been the kind of parent Alice deserved, and while it would take a long time to learn what exactly went into raising a teenage girl successfully, he had to start now. Tomorrow could be too late. And he'd already been too late for too many people in his life.

"You won't do that, Alice." In the rearview, he watched Peggy alight from the Suburban and inhaled deeply. "But if you tell me you're not ready for someone else in our lives—far off a shot as that is—we'll solve this situation with Kyler...and go home. Just us."

Making that promise burned like a son of a bitch, and he could hear every particle in the air swirling as he waited for Alice to respond. "You would really do that?"

He could feel the incredulity in her expression without even looking, but he turned and nodded once, letting her know he'd meant it. "Yeah."

"Huh," she said finally, sounding as if something were caught in her throat. She stared out the passenger window so long, he thought she'd gone off in her own world until she surprised him. "Well...you know. Yesterday when you left the school, everyone wanted to know, like, stuff about you. Things that aren't in your online bio." She crossed her arms and nestled down into the seat. "Maybe you should tell her something no one else knows. It could make her feel special. Maybe. I don't know."

Elliott frowned, replaying locker room conversations from over the years. "I thought women liked to talk about themselves."

"They do." Alice rolled her eyes. "But you have to give something up, too. And it can't be about football. No football."

"Fair enough." He fought a smile. "Thank you, Alice."

She shrugged and started to collect her headphones,

pushing open the passenger side door...just as another vehicle rumbled into the yard, followed closely by a police car. Before the man in the wrinkled suit and determined expression even climbed out of the late-model Buick, Elliott knew who'd arrived.

The bank.

CHAPTER TWENTY-ONE

If they were playing football, Elliott would have called what happened next a clusterfuck.

The entire Tate clan piled out onto the porch—Kyler at the forefront—looking ready to defend their turf at all costs. Elliott's receiver did a double take when he saw his coach standing there, but kept his game face on in spite of his obvious surprise. He'd phoned Kyler on the drive to procure the bank's name and contact information at Peggy's request, but hadn't let on that he'd be joining the Suburban carrying his family's would-be saviors. Kyler had known better than to attempt to pry too many details out of Elliott, so he'd read off the information and left it at that.

"You need to give us more time now, Officer," a woman, presumably Kyler's mother, called. "We were in diapers together, you and I. It's the least you can do."

The officer scratched the back of his neck, looking like

he wanted to burrow beneath the dirt. "You know this is out of my hands, Jess."

At that, Jess dug her fingers into Kyler's shoulder. "Nothing is out of the law's hands," she responded, almost to herself. "Is it?"

"It's going to be okay, Mom," Kyler said, his voice steady. "Just—"

"Hi! Hi. Okay, hold on."

At the sound of Peggy's muffled voice, Elliott turned his attention from the family to find her upper half buried inside the Suburban, leaving her sweet, bent-over backside presented for two police officers and the banker, all of whom had stopped in their tracks. They exchanged uncomfortable glances with one another and tried not to look. But they failed and they failed hard.

Elliott had already started forward when Peggy straightened and turned, curls in her face, an exhilarating smile decorating her mouth. In one hand, she held a laptop, the opposite one pressing a cell phone to her ear. Even in her state of harried dishevelment, she looked edible. "Mr. O'Leary," she breathed, addressing the banker. "How are you?"

"W-well, I—"

"You haven't been at your office this morning. You've been running around. I understand." Elliott tried to take the laptop off her hands, which started a small tug of war, before Peggy relented. "Okay, just...stay right there and hold it."

Elliott winked at her. "I think I can manage that."

She stared up at him as if they'd never met. "Okay."

Sage and Belmont moved around the back of the Suburban then, looking fully prepared to lend support. Belmont's grunt seemed to shake Peggy out of her stupor.

"Mr. O'Leary—" Peggy started.

"Who are you all?" Kyler's mother yelled from the porch. "I didn't really prepare for company."

Peggy turned and waved. "Just give me a minute and I'll explain."

A beat passed. "Explain what now?"

"Mom," Kyler cut in, still mired in patience. "That there is Coach Brooks."

A chorus of responses came from the porch, but a deep, masculine one stood out above the rest. "We don't get much chance to watch football—the farm takes up our time, you see—but we're glad to meet you, Coach."

Elliott sent a nod over the top of the Suburban, enjoying the fact that he hadn't been recognized for once. "Your son is a hell of a receiver."

Even from thirty yards away, Elliott could see Kyler's eyebrows shoot up to his hairline. "Thank you, Coach."

"Who's everyone else?" Jess wanted to know. "Who's the young one trying to blend into the scenery?"

A familiar groan from Alice. "I'm Coach Brooks's kid." She gave a long-suffering sigh. "I'm not trying to blend...I was just trying to guess your WiFi password."

Kyler shouted down a series of numbers in Alice's direction, before Elliott heard him stage-whisper to the group. "And that pretty blond number over there is Coach's girlfriend, only neither of them seemed too keen on the idea. Seemed to be some animosity floating in the air, so don't say nothing about it."

Highly interested murmurings ensued.

"I'm keen on it now," Elliott called over to Kyler, visibly shocking everyone within a hundred-mile radius. Especially Peggy, who he'd never once witnessed looking dumbfounded since they'd met...and hell if he didn't mind it one bit. No, Elliott decided, he liked surprising Peggy with his behavior quite a damn lot. Better than being the predictable asshole she'd probably been expecting.

"I don't know how I feel about this..." Peggy broke off, wiggling her fingers in his general direction. "Transformation."

Wishing like hell they were alone, Elliott dropped his voice. "We can figure it out together."

"Can we get back to the matter at hand?" O'Leary demanded to know, looking more than a little annoyed that someone had hit the Pause button on his entrance. "This isn't my only appointment today."

"Of course it's not," Peggy said breathily, stepping forward to touch the man's forearm. "You are clearly in demand, so I'm going to make this really easy for you. Would you mind answering your cell phone for me? It'll only take a second."

"My cell phone." O'Leary patted his suit jacket, dislodging Peggy's hand out of necessity and untying the knots in Elliott's neck in the process. With an unimaginative curse, O'Leary trucked back toward the Buick and ducked into the driver's side. From Elliott's vantage point, he could see the banker digging in his glove compartment and finally answering his phone. After a mere hello, the banker jerked back out of the driver's side opening, banging his head off the frame on the way out.

"Aaron came through," Peggy said, deflating against the side of the Suburban. "Let's hope O'Leary is a member of the correct political party."

Elliott checked the urge to tug her closer, make her lean on him instead. "Who's he speaking with?"

Peggy blew out a breath. "Senator Glen Pendleton."

Kyler moved up behind Elliott and took a place on his

right. "The Senator Pendleton that's running for the presidency?"

"The very one." Peggy smiled in Kyler's direction. "Hey. It's the Rose man himself."

Chuckling, the receiver started to move in Peggy's direction and Elliott sidestepped, blocking his progress. "You're fine where you are."

"Yes, Coach."

Elliott didn't miss the wry smile exchanged between Kyler and Peggy, and even though it seemed to be pure friendly appreciation, it made his muscles stiffen.

"Listen, Peggy," Kyler said, shifting on the dirt driveway. "I heard what you did, organizing the fund-raiser. I've been getting calls all morning from my teammates and fellow students. And I...I just don't know what to say." He shook his head, his gaze so full of emotion, Elliott had to look away. "I didn't tell my family about it. Didn't want to get their hopes up, in case the money doesn't come through in time. But no matter what happens, I thank you all for trying."

Peggy squared her shoulders. "It is going to come through. We didn't come this far to be told no." While Elliott struggled to catch his breath at the sight of a beautifully determined Peggy, she inclined her head to indicate Belmont and Sage. She managed to introduce her brother and best friend just in time for O'Leary to stride back into the scene. As if on cue, the Tate family converged, leaving everyone in a massive huddle around O'Leary and Peggy.

The banker blotted his forehead with a hankie he produced from his sleeve. "That was a neat trick..."

"Peggy Clarkson, at your service," she chirped.

"Ms. Clarkson." His tone was grudging. "Can't say I've ever had the pleasure of speaking with a senator before, but as I informed him, he doesn't have any say-so on this matter, and I have a job that needs to be completed to my employer's satisfaction. Or I could find myself in the same situation as the Tates."

"Absolutely," Peggy responded, seemingly undeterred. "No one disputes that you have a hard job. People probably try and stall constantly. But this is a special case, because by this time tomorrow, we'll be able to satisfy the debt in full."

Gasps went up from Kyler's family as Peggy reached for the laptop—but O'Leary halted her progress. "I've heard every story in the book, Ms. Clarkson, and I can't take the chance. I'm sorry. The premises must be vacated immediately."

She gestured to the laptop. "But if you could just—"

"I'm sorry, time has already run short."

All right. A motor roared to life inside Elliott, somewhat familiar but way more personal than the righteous anger he usually experienced after a bad call or a missed opportunity on the field. Enough was enough. Some little piss-ant wasn't going to lose Kyler his family farm over a difference of mere hours. And he sure as shit wasn't going to ruin Peggy's hard work and make her sad.

With the outward appearance of calm, Elliott handed the laptop to Kyler and heard his player give a slow whistle, followed by, "Everyone run for cover."

Elliott approached O'Leary, stopping close enough that the other man had to tilt his head back, just enough to be half resentful, half nervous. "Now you listen up and you listen good," he said in a low growl. "I'm sure your mama is real proud of you for wearing a suit and a Boy Scout haircut to work every day, but she ain't here. It's just you and me. And my growing irritation. Which is something you really don't want to provoke." He moved closer, satisfied when the man fell back a step. "You're not taking away this family's livelihood, just so you have a good story to tell your same-haircut-wearing, jerk-off buddies tonight over mojitos or whatever the fuck the world's biggest assholes are drinking nowadays." Elliott leaned back to size him up. "So here's what you're going to do, unless you intend to go through me." O'Leary pointed over at the cop, his mouth opening on what was sure to be a stammer. "He isn't going to help you. Didn't you hear he went to school with Mrs. Tate? There's loyalty there you'll never understand. But if you don't get back in your pre-midlife crisis of a car and burn rubber back to Mama's house, we'll test that loyalty and see who comes out on top." Elliott gave him a hard smile. "Or you can reschedule for tomorrow and avoid anything unpleasant. And it would get unpleasant. That's the kind of man I am. What about you?"

O'Leary had shrunk about three sizes during Elliott's speech, his anger giving way to self-preservation. Muttering under his breath, the man checked his watch and glanced back at his car, as if weighing Elliott's description of the vehicle. Finally, he turned back to the family with a sour expression. "Fine." Everyone must have been holding their breath, because it was like a gale wind of relief rushing around Elliott. "You have one day."

A cheer went up, which couldn't help but make Elliott smile, but that was before someone launched themselves onto his back, crying thank-yous into his ear. And then Kyler piled on, followed by half a dozen unknown relatives, until Elliott was at the center of a standing dog pile, being embraced from every side.

"All right," he muttered. "That's enough."

Over everyone's head, he caught sight of Peggy, who

still stood by the Suburban, watching him with a stunned smile playing around her mouth. That little hint that she might be pleased with him made the whole damn trip worth it. But when she shook herself and turned around, Elliott reminded himself the battle was only beginning.

Chapter Twenty-Two

The problem with moving on from Elliott was this: She still wanted to climb him like a motherfucking tree. That incessant need had been there before arriving at the Tates' farm, but after the way he'd cowed that pasty banker, backed him down and turned him into a kindergartner on his first day of school? Peggy's underwear might as well have been through a monsoon. As they all piled into the Tates' kitchen, she was grateful for the oversized island, because she was pretty sure the wet spot between her legs was visible, something that had never happened in her life.

Lord. She'd seen Coach Elliott Brooks in action. Goodness knew she'd pined over him, pom-poms in hand, from the sidelines. He was scary as hell when he wanted to be. But she'd never seen it up close. Never watched his back muscles bunch up, heard his voice drop into a pitch so low and dirty, it had strummed cords in her stomach like she'd swallowed a guitar. When he'd been putting O'Leary in his place, he might as well have been thrusting inside her—no exaggeration.

And it was his cause that had made the difference. He'd been fighting for something that mattered. To both of them. For those shining moments, they'd been on the same team...and she'd hated herself for loving it. For feeling proud of what they were accomplishing together.

Across the kitchen island, she watched Elliott accept his third round of smacking cheek kisses from Kyler's grandmother with as much warmth as an ice sculpture, heard him make some modest reply...and dammit if she didn't get wetter. It was a veritable deluge right where it counted, and here she was, hiding any signs of her arousal behind a marble kitchen fixture. Or maybe she wasn't hiding it at all, because Elliott's gaze meandered across the island and caressed her nipples. Of course they were in embarrassing little points. She was an indecent woman. They shouldn't even have let her in the house.

Peggy quickly crossed her arms and searched out Belmont where he hovered by the front door, Sage at his side, looking like she might be pondering the wisdom of holding his hand, but was too afraid to make her move. Something needed to be figured between those two and fast, because Peggy could still sense the nervous energy building in her best friend, and she couldn't decide if it would be better or worse if that turmoil centered on Belmont.

Nearby in the living room, Alice sat on the couch, staring down at her phone. At the opposite end, a girl her same age—probably Kyler's sister—peered down at her own cell, but every once in a while, the girls would trade an interested glance.

Peggy was distracted by Kyler's mother pulling her into a hug, wedging Peggy's crossed arms against her bosom. If she hugged the woman back, there was every chance she would stab the poor lady with her freak show nipples, so she feigned a shiver upon moving back. "Just a little chilly."

"Crank the heat, Lyle!" Kyler's mother called out without interrupting her grin. "Let's not freeze our saviors to death."

Rosy-cheeked Lyle, Kyler's father, looked nothing like his strapping young son. Not classically handsome, he was adorably rotund and possessed the kind of demeanor that made you want to smile, especially now that they'd been issued a short reprieve from the bank. His step was springy as he did his wife's bidding, then returned to the gathering around the island, propping himself on his elbows and nodding at Peggy. "Now, far be it from me to look a gift horse in the mouth, but if you wouldn't mind explaining what you've got cooking on that laptop, I'd love to know what I can do to help."

"Sure," Peggy breathed, nerves bundling up near her throat when she realized she'd have to uncross her arms. But before she could reveal nipples that could probably double as air traffic controller wands, something warm dropped onto her shoulders. Elliott's jacket?

When she turned to give him a grateful look, he passed on a slow wink...and more heat gathered between her legs. This was going to be a long afternoon.

"Now before we go talking business," Jess said, holding up both hands for silence. "Let's get the sleeping and eating arrangements in order."

"Here we go," Lyle said, pinching his wife's waist and earning a yelp. "Now you leave the eating to me. I can throw some steaks on the grill out back and we've got enough corn and potatoes to sustain an army."

"Sleeping arrangements?" Peggy squeaked, noticing the

conversation had turned Belmont's wary expression into a dark frown. "I figured we'd just find the local motel—"

"Won't hear of it! Don't even suggest it!" Jess exclaimed. "This lot will be headed home soon." She gestured to the various family members of unknown origin, all of whom looked content just to watch the proceedings. "We have two guest rooms and a pull-out sofa. I figured we'd put the big feller on the pull-out, Sage and Alice in one room, Elliott and Peggy in the other, since they're a couple—"

"Oh. Whoa." She gave her most sincere smile, noticing in her periphery that Elliott looked pleased beyond words. "We're not a couple. I'll stay with Sage and Alice."

"The car is fine for me," Belmont rumbled.

"And Alice can stay in my room," the phone-obsessed teen said from the couch, before quickly ducking her head back down. "She seems chill or whatever."

Alice's mouth dropped open, then slammed shut, a flush racing up her neck. "Thanks."

As if the teenage breakthrough hadn't just taken place across the room, Jess propped both hands on her hips. "Kyler, you said Coach and Peggy were a couple."

"I also said not to say anything about it," Kyler mumbled, his red face buried in his hands. "Just let them sleep where they want, Mom."

"Fine enough," Jess said, splitting a speculative look between Peggy and Elliott. "They're a mighty interesting pair, is all."

Elliott started to laugh. The sound was so rich and unexpected and made of manliness, the strong muscles of his throat flexing, that every female in the kitchen went visibly loopy-eyed, probably including Peggy. When the rich sound faded, his attention was trained on Peggy. "She's the interesting one. I'm lucky she ever looked twice at me." He turned serious. "Trying to figure out how to make her do it again."

"Stop, Elliott," Peggy whispered, fury clogging her lungs. Who was this man who spoke so freely in front of strangers? She didn't know him. He wasn't her Elliott. He was...everything she'd ever fantasized he could be. Better, though. A million times better. And hope was a terrifying thing when she knew how it felt to have that feeling crushed under someone's foot. The same man who'd inspired it too many times. Straightening her spine, Peggy turned the laptop so it faced the family, who now looked way more interested in her love life than any fund-raiser. "Actually, there is a way you can help..."

CHAPTER TWENTY-THREE

Elliott paced back and forth on the Tates' porch, nodding to no one in particular when he heard a cheer from inside, signaling one of two things. Either a new item had been donated for the auction or one of the offerings had been purchased. After freshening up, Sage had come downstairs twenty minutes ago with her computer and set up camp at the kitchen table—and every Tate relation within a hundred-mile radius had promptly crowded around her to watch the show. Jess had even unearthed a white board from the basement and propped it on the dining room windowsill so they could keep a live running tally. Around the third time the woman had burst into grateful tears, Elliott had made his escape to the porch.

Drifting from the upstairs window, he could hear angst-ridden music and high-pitched teenage girl laughter, signaling Alice was getting on just fine with her new best friend. Belmont had gone off for a walk, appearing anxious over so many people huddled around Sage. Leaving Elliott to wait for Peggy to emerge from the bedroom she'd been assigned. After devising a plan to get the Tates' local businesses involved in the auction, Peggy had politely excused herself, saying she would return to check the progress soon. Although his intuition told him she would stay in the bedroom as long as possible, hoping to avoid him.

Well, screw that. He didn't have much time to work with. While he fully understood that patience was required in this situation he'd created, waiting for her to come to him wasn't going to cut the damn mustard.

Elliott pulled open the screen door and strode past the dining room, no one seeming to notice him heading for the stairs, except for Sage and Kyler's mother, who sent him a thumbs-up. Ridiculous that he should take heart from the simple gesture, wasn't it? But hell, he needed every ally he could get. Before he even reached the door to Peggy's bedroom, his senses picked up on her silent do not enter vibe. It was hanging in the air, clear as crystal.

Hardening his jaw, Elliott pushed past the imaginary barrier and opened the bedroom door. In such an old house, he'd expected the door to creak and signal his entrance, but it didn't make a sound, giving him valuable seconds of looking at an undisturbed Peggy.

Invisible fingers dug into his stomach at the sight of her. There was no flirtatious set to her mouth, no artful posing of her curves. She was lying on her stomach on the bed, her chin propped on a fist, reading through what looked to be a journal. Her lips moved in time with whatever she was reading, and those fingers tightened their hold on his stomach when he realized he hadn't been aware of that habit.

"Peggy," Elliott prompted, regret weighing on his shoulders when she reacted with a gasp, jerking back into a kneeling position. Almost as an afterthought, she reached forward and closed the journal with a decisive snap. "I'm sorry I interrupted you."

She wouldn't look at him. "Do you need something?"

He tried and failed not to notice how soft she looked, her shirt rumpled from being lain on, chin red from where she'd rested it on her hand. There was a far-off look in her eyes that was quickly receding—something was...off— and he wanted to grab that ebbing tide and bring it back to shore.

This was it. His chance to be her friend. He felt it way down deep in his bones.

Elliott entered the room and closed the door behind him, despite the tension that crept into the lines of her body. "What were you reading?"

"Oh, that's..." She scooped back a handful of blond curls away from her face. "That's my mother's journal. She left it behind for us."

He stopped at the foot of the bed, looking between the moleskin journal and Peggy. "Is there something inside it that's bothering you?"

"No. Why would you say that?" she asked too quickly, before deflating into a cross-legged position. "I don't know. I haven't read past the first entry."

Since coming upstairs, she'd changed into a loose skirt, and it took a major effort on Elliott's part not to glance down at her exposed thighs, where the material climbed up toward her— "Why not?"

She quirked a brow over the churned asphalt in his voice, but didn't comment. "Would you want to know the secret thoughts your mother had about you? If you had the option?" Her fingers plucked at the faded yellow bedspread. "Because those thoughts, the way your mother sees you, are always accurate. Whether you like it or not. She knows you better than anyone else."

Elliott thought of his mother. The forced smiles she would send over her shoulder while making dinner, the way she sighed heavily before having to explain things. "That might be true. But don't you think they'd be just as terrified, knowing how we saw them?" His shrug was jerky. These were unknown depths he was plumbing, but he forced himself to keep going. "Kids are perceptive. I'm only just beginning to realize how much. Your mother—our mothers—would probably think twice about reading a journal we'd written, too."

Peggy dropped her attention from him to the object in question. "Damn, Elliott. You're just full of surprises lately, aren't you?"

He resisted the urge to take that statement and press his advantage, tempting as it was. "What exactly are you afraid of reading?"

"Why don't you go first?" Her body jolted a little, as if she'd surprised herself by asking. "What would your mother have written about you?"

Yeah. Definitely some unplumbed depths. "Does it make me a bastard that I haven't thought a lot about it?"

"Think about it now," she returned softly.

All those times in the past when she'd tried to reach him and he'd distracted her with sex? He had to beat back the ingrained impulse to do the same in that moment. To crush her body down into the pillows and test the mattress springs. She'd been turned on by him enough down in the kitchen that she would have a hard time saying no. Especially if he got rough. That was her weakness, and after their conversation this morning, he knew why. Knew she thought punishment was her due. Which was exactly why he would never use it against her again as long as he lived. That silent vow kept Elliott rooted to his spot at the bed's end. "I think she would have looked at me and seen a replica of my father. And been disappointed." It was unexpected, the wind that left his sails after saying those words out loud. "I came to terms with that a long time ago, though. It's not something I worry about anymore."

Peggy's eyes were wide as silver dollars. "Is she still alive?"

"Yes." He gave in to the need to be a little closer to Peggy, sitting down on the edge of the bed to a chorus of creaks. "We don't really speak."

Peggy surged up onto her knees. "Oh, but you have time to change her mind. I wish I had that. I wish I could have shown my mother I was...more."

"More than what, baby? You're a goddamn wonder." He spread his arms wide to encompass the room. "We're all here right now because you had an idea. I was out on the porch and..."

A short pause. "And what?"

There was only one way to find out if he was capable of speaking his thoughts out loud without sounding like some soppy, wannabe poet, and that was to do it. "I was thinking, this thing you're doing—this fund-raiser idea you designed at a moment's notice—it could have a ripple effect across generations for this family." He held her gaze. "And I wondered if you even realize how incredible and selfless you are, Peggy. You give so much of yourself, without asking for anything in return. I wish I could go back in time and make sure you knew I appreciated having you there. I didn't even let myself acknowledge it." The ever-present throbbing in his chest grew more acute. "Hell, I'm part of the reason you don't acknowledge it yourself."

"Elliott—"

"I'm willing to stake everything," he said, pointing down at the journal, "that she saw what I refused to see. Because if she could raise someone as amazing as you, she must have been a wise woman."

When her lower lip trembled, there was no way to stop himself from reaching out and running his thumb over the curve of her cheek. Her eyes closed and she leaned into his touch, swaying a little on her knees. The air around the bed grew heavy with anticipation, as if the house were waiting to see what would happen next. With a will made of steel, he checked his impulse to initiate any more contact with her. Much as he wanted to drag her across the bed and kiss the living hell out of her, patience needed to be employed.

Peggy turned her face into his palm and Elliott's muscles tensed. And when she suctioned her puffy lips around his middle finger, his cock hardened, pushing against the zipper of his jeans. "That feels good, baby."

Her brow wrinkled and she drew away. "This isn't going to work."

His heart rammed into his jugular. "I'll keep apologizing until you change your mind. I'm nowhere near done."

"No, it's—" She tilted her face toward the ceiling. "I accept your apology, okay? I'm not going to hold on to the past anymore. That's why I came to Cincinnati in the first place. But it's more than that. Even if I were willing to try..." Whatever she had to say was difficult for her, and having no skin-to-skin contact while she struggled through was torture, but he forced himself to stay put. "Remember what I told you? How I can't feel...pleasure, unless you're—"

"Unless I'm making you feel like what we're doing is wrong. That you're the wrong one?" He swallowed a handful of nails as the images swam into focus. Words he'd spoken to her in the dark. Harsh words. "I'd die before I treated you that way again."

"I know." She lifted a shoulder and let it drop. "I think maybe that's the problem. I don't know how to accept anything else from you."

"Come over here and try me," he rasped, tensing the air with awareness. Peggy and himself, too. In the space of seconds, they were both panting like they'd sprinted a mile. He'd been resolved not to push, but the situation was painted in a whole new light now, and yeah, that was definitely panic creeping up the back of his neck. She didn't think they could have healthy sex, and animal hunger heated the blood in his veins with the need to prove her wrong. "Come sit on my lap."

The tug-of-war inside her was clear. On one side of the rope, the chemical attraction they shared fought for precedence, but there was doubt on the other side, refusing to give in. Her torn expression hid none of it. When she finally began walking across the bed on her knees, Elliott released the breath he'd been holding.

Smooth as smoke. Fluid. That's how their bodies had always moved together, and now was no exception. She eased her leg over Elliott's lap and sat, the skirt climbing toward her hips the way his hands itched to do. He took hold of her thighs and drew her closer, slowly, slowly, watching her eyelids flutter when she encountered his erect cock. "It's never any other way when you're around," he murmured against her mouth. "But I've got more for you, Peggy. More than sex. More than making you feel like a bad girl."

Her legs jerked around him and she moaned. "Then why do I like hearing you call me that so much?"

"I don't know." He eased his right arm around the small

of her back and rocked her on his dick. "Someday maybe I'll call you that and it'll be okay, because you'll know what I really think. That you're nothing but sweet and right. Every inch of you."

She squeezed her eyes shut, as if trying to block him out.

Elliott wasn't having it. He slipped his left hand up and down her thigh, moving a little higher with each stroke. "Did you have to change your panties when you came up-stairs, baby?" He tucked his thumb just beneath the material of her underwear, dragging it in an arc, stopping just a few inches from her pussy. "When you put on the new ones, I bet you gave your clit a little rub. Just once around with your middle finger. Maybe twice. But you stopped because you felt bad about fingering yourself in someone else's house, sun out and everything. Did I get that right?"

"Yes," she breathed, tilting her head to the side, giving Elliott an opening to scrape his teeth up the side of her neck. "How did you know that?"

"I know, because even though you were damp and horny in someone else's kitchen, you're a good girl deep down." He sensed her withdraw at that, just a touch. But he wasn't finished. "And I know because when your pussy gets wet, that real, aching, slick type of wet, you want to hold out for my cock. Don't you?"

Their mouths just sort of found each other at that point. Neither one of them initiated the kiss; it was merely a temp-tation that refused to be put off any longer. When their lips slid together and opened, tongues flicking against each other in teasing licks, he felt an answering grip in his groin. The kind only Peggy ever made him feel, the kind that would normally have him pinning her to the bed and yank-ing down the zipper of his jeans.

"This feels like something that can't be fucking great, no

matter how we do it?" He groaned as her warm pussy gave a rough writhe on top of his erection. "It doesn't matter what I call you or if I spank your ass first. You hearing me, baby? Nothing is going to stop it from feeling like heaven when you open your legs and I slide inside. Right into that tight spot you're keeping warm just for me."

He shot forward to consume her mouth with enough ferocity that her head fell back, back until she was bent over his forearm, legs clinging to his hips, body arched. With the temptation of her tits pressing into his chest, Elliott could no more resist releasing her mouth and feasting on her perky nipples than he could stop the world from spinning. His tongue bathed, his teeth nipped, right through the cotton of her shirt, dampening the material.

"Elliott, oh please...please just..." She shot back up into a sitting position, slanting her delicious mouth across his, delivering hot, hurried strokes of her tongue until the need to fuck her mounted, his breaking point approaching faster than a fired bullet. "Just do it. Tell me what I need to hear. Say the prayer."

Denial and regret delivered a one-two punch right to his skull. "No, baby. We don't need that."

"Y-yes." She took his earlobe between her teeth and tugged, hurtling a bolt of lust straight to his lap. "I do."

He took her face in his hands and waded through the conflict in her eyes. God, he wanted to take it away from her, ease her load so damn bad. "Peggy—"

"No. Stop telling me I'm good and beautiful. I don't want that from you."

"Why?"

"Because then I'll never let go." Her mouth snapped shut, but it fell open a moment later, and even though her voice was softer this time, it was still a fastball that shattered his rib cage. "And I need to, Elliott. I can't get caught up in the fantasy of this, like I'm that twenty-two-year-old girl again. You have football and church and there's no room for anything else. You've said it a million times. We would end up back at the beginning in no time."

"Look at me. Look at me." He rubbed his thumbs in circles on her cheeks. "I won't let that happen."

She just sat there, suspended in time and animation. Waiting for something more? What else could he...

"Come out with me tonight."

A single blond eyebrow lifted. "Huh now?"

Jesus. He hadn't asked a woman out on a date in...had he ever asked a woman out on a date? He'd met his wife at church and the majority of their meetings had taken place within those very walls. The time he'd spent with Peggy had been inside his house, his car, her dorm room. Anywhere they wouldn't be seen. Dates were not his forte. No time to question himself, though. He was losing Peggy. This was literally his Hail Mary pass to get to the end zone. "We're here for the night. Let me take you somewhere."

"Like a date," she said slowly. "Where?"

"Anywhere I can be with you, Peggy."

A strange—clearly reluctant—light entered her eyes, but he never heard her response, because the door opened behind them, followed by an "Oh shit," delivered by none other than Alice.

Everyone moved at once, Peggy diving off his lap, Elliott turning his upper body to face the door, just in time to catch Alice's stricken expression and her black-clad figure streaking off down the hall. With a sigh, Elliott turned his attention back to Peggy. Her hands were clapped over her mouth, shoulder up somewhere near her eyes. "Oh shit is right," she said, the words muffled.

Elliott stood. "I'll go after her."

Peggy dropped her hands and attempted to smooth her skirt. "Can I? Go after her, I mean." She seemed to be searching for the right words. "I'll just assure her that nothing is going to—"

"You will not." His command came out a little too harshly for either of them, Peggy slapping both hands onto her hips in response. "Or you can say whatever you want and I'll work even harder to make it a lie."

A flush woke up on her skin. "You're working hard enough already."

"Good of you to notice." Elliott eliminated the distance in between them, plucked up one of the hands on her hips, and kissed the back, the palm, the fingers. "I want to be alone with you tonight. Just agree to that and I'll let you go."

She shifted, her eyes trained on his mouth's movements. "Oh, you won't otherwise?"

Elliott brought their joined hands to the small of her back, urging her forward and up against his chest. "No." He leaned down and licked the seam of her lips, one way, then the other. "I won't."

She expelled a shaky breath. "Fine. But no cornfields. There are killer turkeys lurking in them this time of year."

"Is that so?" They shared a searching smile. "You have a lot to tell me about this trip you're on, don't you? I want to hear all of it. I want to know every thought in your head."

"So you can strategize, Coach?"

"Maybe." He gave in to the primal need to kiss her until she ran out of air. "But afterward, baby, we're going to find a place where I can show you how good girls get off better than anyone." He laid a kiss on each corner of her mouth. "See you tonight."

CHAPTER TWENTY-FOUR

Another cornfield. Beautiful.

Peggy wove her way through what remained of the corn crops, the stalks standing at half-mast thanks to cooler December weather. She could see Alice sitting cross-legged up ahead in the sparse shade of a bare poplar tree, staring out at the flat farmland. Just like that afternoon in the school auditorium, she had no idea what she would say once she reached Alice. And this time, she didn't have an audience to charm or a door to hide her face. It was just them, stripped down in this barren, unfamiliar place. Even the crisp breeze seemed to go still as she neared the younger girl, giving her even less of a cloak.

Without turning, she could feel Elliott watching her from the upstairs bedroom. Could feel him wanting to join them out in the field, if for no other reason than to make sure Peggy didn't make any good-bye promises to Alice. Ones that he would try like hell to make her break.

Too bad. She couldn't think clearly around Elliott, but outside, without his hard body pressed up against her, his words trying to tear down her resolve, her decision was a no brainer. She needed to run as fast and as far as she could. This hope kindling in her chest was bad news because the fall would be brutal. One more night. Just one more night with Elliott, and she would participate in the fund-raiser tomorrow and then hit the bricks. Maybe it wouldn't be easy to leave knowing Elliott finally wanted to make them work, but she had the advantage of knowing what was best for herself now. That knowledge had to count for more than the only touch she'd ever craved, the only man who could make her heart go wild with a single look. Yeah, self-preservation had to rate higher.

Didn't it?

The wind kicked up with such force, it shoved Peggy back a step, her foot crunching in a combination of grass and hay. Alice's head whipped around in Peggy's direction at the sound, her hunched-over figure tensing, an audible grumble leaving her mouth.

Steeling herself, Peggy wandered the final few yards and sat a safe distance away from Alice, both of them avoiding eye contact by playing with field debris, smashing the brittle pieces between their fingers.

"So listen," Peggy started, anxious nerves sending her into a fidget spell. "I'm sorry you walked in on me smooching your dad. You can never unsee that."

She could feel the resentment rolling off Alice like downhill skiers. "You and my dad use the same strategy when you talk to me. Like maybe if you treat me like an adult, I'll just magically start acting like one."

"And that bothers you?"

A derisive snort. "Oh, now we're in school counselor mode."

"Hey, you know what?" Peggy laughed without humor. "Here's some advice. Lower your expectations for adults. We don't know what the hell we're doing, either. We might look older, but we're still thinking and agonizing over our own version of locking ourselves in the school bathroom." She pulled her jacket tighter around her body to brace against the cold. "I shouldn't have been kissing your dad. I should never have kissed him in the first place. And there's a chance it'll happen again."

"Why?"

"Because none of us are perfect? Because sometimes your heart gets the drop on your head? I don't know, Alice. Take your pick."

A full minute of silence passed. "I was supposed to be the angry one. You kind of stole my thunder."

"Yeah, huh?" This time Peggy's laugh was genuine, tumbling unexpectedly from her belly. "Sorry. It's your turn now."

Alice changed positions, drawing her knees up to her chest, wrapping both arms around her bent legs. "Are you staying or leaving?" Serious eyes landed on Peggy. "Cincinnati, I mean."

"Leaving." Dammit, she'd answered way too fast. "I don't know if your father mentioned it, but we're on our way to New York to fulfill my mother's dying wish. And Bel...he needs me. He's looking for his real father—he has a different one than the rest of us—and he'll need a push sooner or later." Trying to ignore the horrible coldness permeating her sternum, Peggy pulled off an easy shrug. "So you'll be seeing the back of me soon enough."

"You don't have to put it like that," Alice muttered.

Peggy had enough self-awareness to realize she was being flippant for her own sake, as well as Alice's, but she also didn't want to leave on the final leg of the road trip with Alice thinking she didn't care. Or didn't find the decision to never see her again difficult. "What I'm trying to say is, I understand. My mother dated after her divorce from our father. We hated every single one of them before they walked in the door. And you know what? She probably should have been more sensitive about that... and talked to us about it."

She thought about what Elliott had said up in the bedroom, about seeing faults in parents, same as they saw the faults in their children. Loving them in spite of it. At the earliest opportunity, she was going to read the journal. She had nothing to lose. For once, seeing her mother's final words on the pages didn't inspire an army of termites to start nibbling at her stomach lining.

"My father talked to me about you," Alice said slowly, breaking into her thoughts. "That's how I knew he was serious. He never talks to me about anything."

"Sounds like he's trying to change that."

"Yeah." Alice scrutinized Peggy for long moments, her mouth screwing up tight, until she released an exodus of breath. "I'm really sorry for the name I called you," she said with a tremor in her voice. "Even when I was saying it, I didn't mean it. I was just surprised. My dad isn't supposed to... date. And then you had to look like that, you know? Like he just became every guy in my school who wants to date the pretty cheerleader and I couldn't stand it. My own father." She swiped the sleeve of her coat beneath her eyes. "God, he must think I'm so underwhelming in every way."

Peggy's throat started to ache. Not only because of this young girl who didn't realize her father's love was unconditional, but also because her decision to leave had never seemed wiser. She'd wedged herself between the two of them, and she needed to wiggle her way free as soon as possible, before it caused lasting damage. "Well, I think you're way off. Remember what I said about adults? We're all dealing with our own shit. He's probably just as worried you find him underwhelming."

Alice scoffed. "The Kingmaker? Underwhelming?"

"Yeah." Peggy gave a decisive nod, sympathy for Elliott like a rock in her stomach. "But try and have a little faith in him. He's trying."

The younger girl murmured something that Peggy couldn't hear, but it sounded like *only since you showed up*. But before she could comment, footsteps approached them from behind. Peggy didn't have to turn around to know it was Sage, each of her steps poetic and thoughtful. She entered Peggy's line of vision and arranged herself with fluid movements on the ground. "The Tate family is lovely," she said in her melodic voice. "But they're giving me a rash."

Alice shifted and regarded the third member of their pity party warily, the way she'd looked at Peggy when she'd shown up on her porch. "How did you two become friends? You look and act like total opposites."

Peggy swiped a discreet hand across her neck. "That's a story for a different day."

"What do you mean by 'total opposites'?" Sage said, tilting her head.

Alice shrugged. "In my school, you would be eating at different tables in the cafeteria."

Sage's curiosity still wasn't satisfied. "Which table would I sit at?"

The younger girl's mouth twitched at one end, reminding Peggy of Elliott in a good mood. "Probably the yearbook committee."

Sage pursed her lips and slumped a little. "I was on the yearbook staff. It meant I could stay longer at school and avoid going home." She jerked, as if the telling words had slipped out without permission, her eyes widening on Peggy. "You know. Because we had...a terrible Internet connection. The school's was much better." Her spine straightened, her lips curling into a smile, but Peggy wasn't fooled for a moment and wanted nothing more than to launch herself at Sage, hold her close, and never let go. "I'll have you know," Sage continued, "that yearbook committee is the best-kept secret. Do you know how willing students are to trade favors for having the more flattering pictures of them included in the book?" She arched an eyebrow. "Very willing, indeed."

Peggy couldn't keep herself from laughing, but the joy didn't reach her chest. "Sage, you secret con artist." She laid a hand on Alice's knee, feigning outage. "I had no idea who I was traveling with, Alice, you have to believe me. I was in the dark."

"What's another secret about you?" Alice asked, a smile threatening to bloom on her face. "Something else Peggy doesn't know."

A cold hand swept through Peggy's bones at the way Sage's features seemed to turn to stone as she stared out into space a moment. "I plan weddings because...when I was a child, I snuck into a wedding back home in...back home in the South." The wind blew a strand of hair across her face. "And it was the first beautiful thing I'd ever seen before that day. And it was the last beautiful thing I saw for a really long time."

Peggy reached a hand out toward Sage, but she moved lithely to her feet and clapped her hands, her serene expression back in place. "I have to get back. There could be more items selling."

There was no choice but to watch her best friend leave,

her petite figure dwarfed by the massive Indiana sky. The moment felt like a crossroads. Their journeys had intersected in California, but if Sage stayed true to her word, she would be heading off in a different direction soon. After her accidental slip about not wanting to go home as a child, Peggy wondered if Sage could be facing something bad. Something she would need Peggy's help contending with.

Just as Peggy came to her feet, ready to go after Sage, Belmont stepped out from the Tate house's shadows, pulling Sage into an embrace. It stopped Peggy from moving. Stopped time from moving.

Sage's journey would always lead back to Belmont, wouldn't it?

Where would hers lead?

CHAPTER TWENTY-FIVE

Elliott wasn't the hovering type. He went from point A to point B with purpose, and he didn't make pit stops along the way. Unfortunately, he was at point A, and in order to reach point B—his date with Peggy—he needed...advice. Which was what had him pacing back and forth in front of the Tate family room, attempting to get the attention of his erstwhile receiver without drawing any unwanted eyes.

Lord, the word *advice* sat in his mouth like acid. But his only hope of pulling off a successful evening would mean asking one of his players to steer him in the right direction. Asking his players questions without already knowing the damn answer was unheard of, but hell, he'd never been desperate before. Or at least, he'd never been aware of his own desperation.

Kyler was occupied wading through bills with his parents, deciding which ones needed to be paid first, come the morning. The sheer amount of overdue notices on the table was enough to turn anyone green, but the prospect of paying those balances had lightened the mood in the house. Music poured from an old stereo beneath the television, on which a game show played on mute. The family members who were supposed to hit the road hours earlier were still in attendance, already making sandwiches out of the dinner leftovers, their lively conversation filtering through the swinging kitchen door.

All the damn noise made it impossible to catch his receiver's attention, however, and only a few minutes remained until Peggy met him downstairs.

He could all but smell her perfume drifting from the second floor and it made his skin tight, made his belt feel like it rested too low on his groin. After their make-out session in the bedroom earlier, he'd been tempted to find somewhere private to give himself a hand job in order to remain halfway decent on their date. But the walls were thin in the packed house, and after having Alice walk in on Peggy straddling his lap, forgive him for being a little spooked.

Above his head, footsteps moved across the ancient floor and he envisioned Peggy topless and barefoot, preparing for their date. Their *date*.

Elliott rapped his fist on the arched wall leading to the family room, everyone's attention snapping to him and staying there.

"Front and center, Tate," Elliott barked, nodding with satisfaction when muscle memory had Kyler on his feet, jogging out to meet Elliott in the foyer before he'd even finished making the command.

"What's up, Coach?"

Elliott jerked his chin toward the porch, both men exiting the house a moment later, right into the thick of the black evening. After the crowded warmth of the house, walking into the brittle cold was a shock, and as the crickets made lazy notes around them, Elliott wondered absently if Peggy would be warm enough. Realizing that Kyler was watching him pace, amusement ticking up one corner of his mouth, Elliott clasped his hands behind his back and forced himself to stop. "Where are we at on the fund-raiser?"

"Another twenty-three thousand will put us in the clear." Kyler scratched his chin. "This morning I would have called that a long shot, but Peggy's idea from earlier is making all the difference. Word is out about the fund-raiser and now local clubs and committees are pooling their money, buying the memorabilia. Not just here, but back in Cincy." He fought a smile and lost. "There's a bidding war taking place for drinks with Peggy—"

"Excuse me?"

Kyler held up his hands. "Her idea, Coach. Not mine. Someone suggested it on the message boards after Peggy posted a video to thank everyone for paying promptly... and she said as long as the date took place tomorrow, before they all leave for New York, it'd be fine."

Had Elliott actually thought it cold outside? It felt like one hundred piping hot degrees inside his coat all of a sudden, a painful twinge in his jaw telling him he was grinding his teeth. "No one ran it by me."

"Feminism says they didn't have to."

Elliott narrowed his eyes. "You're kind of a smart-ass, aren't you, Tate? How come it took me four years to notice?"

The younger man's smile thinned. "We never talked off the field or outside the locker room until now, 'cept that one time in your office."

"Well." Elliott tried to clear the jealousy over Peggy from his throat, but it didn't work. He'd be wondering the

entire damn evening who was going to take her out for
drinks. "We're talking now and you're just pissing me off."

Not even Elliott's downhill mood seemed enough to
dim Kyler's. "Did you bring me out here to ask me something?"

"Yeah," Elliott said, crossing his arms over his chest.
"You grew up around here. Is there somewhere you'd rec-
ommend taking a woman?"

Kyler rocked back on his heels, disbelief passing over
his features. "If we filmed this conversation and auctioned
it off, do you reckon it would fetch the highest price of all?"

"Answer the damn question, Tate."

"Gotcha." Watching as his receiver sauntered to the
porch rail to prop both hands on the worn wood, it occurred
to Elliott once again how much he liked the kid. But even
having a fond respect for Kyler, he would've just let him
leave, allowed the Tate family to lose the farm without lifting a single damn finger.

What if he was kidding himself here? Trying to turn
himself around, to make a fresh start when he barely knew
where to begin? The mad dash to make things right with
Peggy hadn't given him much time to think, but looking
across the porch at one of the most loyal players he'd had
the opportunity to work with…and realizing he'd known
exactly zero about him until a couple days ago, well, it was
a fucking gut punch. A man didn't just go from a stone
statue to a warm-blooded ally overnight. What if he only
managed to screw things up worse than the man who'd lived
inside the same gray routine for years?

Tell me something good you did today. Once upon a time,
Peggy had thought him capable of performing noble deeds.
Did she still believe that?

Kyler turned with a finger in the air. "I got it, Coach.

Now, you're going to be tempted to shoot me down, but give me a chance."

His throat still feeling somewhat constricted with doubt, Elliott only grunted, a signal his receiver interpreted as you may continue.

"Marengo Cave." Kyler shoved his hands into his pockets. "I took my..."

When Kyler left his words hanging in the air, Elliott frowned. "You took your what?"

The young man had turned white as a ghost. "I was going to say I took my girlfriend there once, but she ain't my girlfriend anymore."

Both men shifted, not exactly thrilled to be having a conversation with a definite romantic theme. "Seems like you're not very happy about that," Elliott said with a sniff and sudden fascination with the porch light.

"No, can't say I am. We were together since we were kids. Until I left for school and she wouldn't come along," Kyler all but choked out. "Let's focus on your date with Peggy, though, all right?"

"Hmm."

Kyler gave a grateful nod. "They do walking tours of this cave, but if you slip the manager a twenty, they'll hook you up with a couple of lanterns and send you down there alone. Women..." The younger man seemed to be replaying a past memory, red creeping up the sides of his neck. "God bless them, but they do get scared in the cave, you see? It has been known to lead to...comforting. Of a sort."

Good Lord. "The Bible refers to that as deception."

"Here in Indiana, we refer to it as good business."

Elliott laughed. An honest-to-goodness laugh that just about sent Kyler jumping a few yards from the moon.

"Write down the directions," he said to a stunned Kyler. "And Tate?"

"Yes, Coach?"

"You breathe a word about this to any of your teammates and I'll have you running bleachers until you vomit breakfast you ate back in middle school. Do we have an understanding?"

Chest puffed out, Kyler saluted. "Secret is safe with me, Coach."

Elliott glanced toward the door, anxious for Peggy to walk through, but his stomach didn't feel quite settled. Not yet. "And Tate..." He coughed into his fist. "If you miss this old girlfriend, take it from me. You go get her and you don't wait."

The younger man shook his head, his eyes haunted. "I don't know if she'll come. Short of me hog-tying her and loading her into my trunk."

There was no way Elliott could leave without impressing a lesson on Kyler. The one he'd wished someone had taught him. "Imagine you have one more day to fix everything... before she never thinks about you again. Once that happens, it could be hopeless forever. Trust me on that."

If possible, even more color drained from Kyler's face, and Peggy chose that moment to exit the house. Perceptive as always, she stopped short as if she'd been stonewalled by the gravity of the conversation, even though she didn't know what it was about. Elliott couldn't deny a sudden rush of nerves, as though he were some kid taking a girl to the prom, which was far from the case. He was bringing an amazing woman to a cave—and apparently attempting to terrify the hell out of her.

Her legs should have been illegal. At least a mile long each, they were hugged by dark blue leggings, and some kind of flowy top peeked out from beneath the bottom of her coat. She'd worn her hair up, twisted in the back in some way he'd never seen it before. A way that made his fingers anxious to mess it up, set it loose again.

"Is everything okay?" she asked, splitting a look between him and Kyler.

"Peachy as pie," Kyler answered, moving between them for the door. Before he walked inside, he leaned over and spoke to Elliott out of the side of his mouth. "Do I have to write you instructions for this date? Tell her she looks good."

"You should start dreading your first practice back." Elliott hesitated a moment, before yanking out his wallet with a curse and removing one of his credit cards. Lowering his voice, he handed the plastic to Kyler. "I don't care how much you have to spend, the date with Peggy is mine."

Kyler's laughter followed him into the house, leaving Elliott alone with Peggy on the porch. Exactly where he wanted to be. "I like your hair like that." He went toward her, noticing the way her lips opened on a puff of air, her fingers tightening around the strap of her purse. "If you let me kiss you, getting at your neck is going to be easy."

Her face transformed with a knockout grin. "Seduction is usually reserved for the end of the date."

Elliott narrowed his eyes, pretty sure she'd heard Kyler's offer to give instructions on the way into the house. "I don't need a couple of smug twenty-somethings telling me how to go on a date."

"Are you sure about that? We're a long way from the nineties." She batted her eyelashes at him. "Maybe you'll make me a mix tape afterward."

He reached down and took her hand, holding tighter when her smile wobbled. "If you're still around afterward, I'll make you a million of them."

CHAPTER TWENTY-SIX

It shouldn't have felt so easy. Sitting in the passenger seat, her head lolling on the headrest while Elliott's capable hands steered them down the rocky pathway. He hadn't told Peggy where they were going, keeping his new, mysterious streak alive. After checking the business hours of their destination on his phone and finding out it was closing within the hour, they'd decided to head straight there, instead of having something to eat first.

That was just fine with Peggy. While both of them had skipped dinner at the Tates' in deference to their date, Jess had insisted on Peggy eating a biscuit. Which had turned into two biscuits, because damn, they'd been delicious. So she was in no rush to sit down for a meal. She was, however, curious as all get-out over where Elliott was taking her. It was the opposite of his personality to be mysterious...and she had to admit, the way he'd winked in lieu of spilling the beans? Her tummy had been in a heavy knot ever since.

After returning from the field with Sage and Alice—and trying unsuccessfully to get her best friend alone to talk—she'd decided tonight would be about saying good-bye. Tonight, she wouldn't think about leaving tomorrow and the healing process that would have to begin immediately. She would enjoy herself—enjoy Elliott—without worrying if she were making the right call. She *was*...now she had to believe in that decision, despite the awful cramping feeling in her stomach that wouldn't relent. She needed to trust herself.

But for the next few hours, she would live in the moment.

When they passed a sign that said, *Marengo Cave Walking Tours*, Peggy sat up a little straighter in her seat. "Are you taking me to a cave?" The passing foliage had gotten progressively...dense. "Like with bats?"

Elliott drummed his fingers on the steering wheel. "Hadn't thought of the bats. Maybe that's why women get scared."

"What women?"

"This is a bad idea, isn't it?" He looked like he wanted to beat his head on the dashboard. "This is the last time I ask a kid for advice."

Something tickled the insides of her rib cage. "You asked Kyler where to take me?"

"Yes," he admitted, sending her a sidelong glance. "To be honest, though...you're adventurous. You're the kind of person who drives cross-country just to jump into the ocean. The kind of person who impersonates an acting coach." His lips twitched at the same time as Peggy's. "I kind of thought you'd be into it, but we can just go to dinner—"

"You were right." Those brushing wings near her heart were most definitely made of surprise. Since that morning, he'd managed to cause that same reaction half a dozen times. Agreeing to drive to Indiana at the drop of a hat, his speeches on the roadside and the bedroom...not to mention the way he'd stood up to the banker. Elliott couldn't seem to stop flipping her expectations of him onto their ass. "You were right. I love stuff like this." She turned to watch the truck's progress eat up the path. "Everyone in the world right now is eating dinner. But I bet only a tiny little percentage are going exploring in a cave."

"Bats and all?"

She put up her dukes. "Bring 'em on."

Elliott seemed to be having a difficult time keeping his eyes on the road. But in order for her to know that, she would have to be staring right back at him. Which she was. Hearing Elliott's hands creaking on the steering wheel, Peggy forced herself to look away, but every inch of her felt...alive. Excited.

They pulled into the small parking area, located on a slanted dirt hill, and Elliott crossed behind the truck and opened her door before she got the chance. He held out his hand and she took it, sparks racing up her palm and wrist. God, she could feel his energy, feel his thought crackling. His hunger was familiar as his gaze landed on her mouth, his hand braced on her hip to ease her descent. But that was where familiarity ended. There wasn't a hint of stoicism in his expression, none of the usual tightness around his eyes. He was zeroed in on her, cataloging everything she said and did. His intentness told Peggy he wouldn't be shifting that attention anytime soon.

"I can't think when you're looking at me like that," she murmured.

"Can't help it." He splayed his hands above her on the truck, and his aftershave caused a rushing in her senses. "I never could. But I'm seeing so fucking much now, I'm just trying to take in as much as I can."

Everything registered in the space of a breath. The slight brushing of his belt buckle against her stomach, their height difference. His jacket was open and those impressively honed muscles were outlined beneath his shirt, tempting her fingers to slide under and play. "Again, I have to insist you're doing the date all backward," she breathed, her pulse racing under his scrutiny. So intense. So hot.

"Yeah?" He eased forward, slowly crushing her body between him and the truck, pushing, pushing until she gasped. "I've done a lot of things backward," he said against her ear. "But licking your pussy isn't one of them."

"Whuuu?"

His lips traced the sensitive skin of Peggy's neck and her damn legs actually started to shake. "It occurred to me earlier when you were kneeling on the bed in that skirt..." A long, growling suck of her flesh. "That I haven't had my tongue in your cunt since you were a cheerleader."

"Oh huh." For the umpteenth time that day, she grew slippery between her thighs. Her head fell back, hitting the truck with a bomp. "I remember."

"So do I." His fingertips slid down the car's exterior, landing on her hips. She held her breath at the feel of those blunt digits curling in the waistband of her leggings, tugging her up onto her toes, sending her tummy into a somersault. "Your roommate was studying and wouldn't leave. I couldn't bring you to my house." His cock fit into the notch of her thighs and both of them groaned. "Licked you for an hour in the stadium parking lot, didn't I, baby? With your pristine, white cheerleader shoes dangling over my shoulders."

"Yes." She could still remember the way he'd dragged

her out the driver's side of her car the second she arrived
and pushed her down on the backseat, his head disappearing
beneath her skirt. While devouring the sight of her wet
panties like a starved animal, he'd confided that Peggy was
the first woman he'd ever given head to. He'd been fan-
tasizing about doing it with her. Only her. And once he'd
gotten started, he'd *loved* it. God, after she'd lost count of
her orgasms, it had taken pleading to make him stop, his
tongue and lips having tested every angle, every speed, every*where* until he'd perfected the skill. A skill he'd honed
constantly afterward until Peggy could get wet just looking
at his mouth.

"You were wearing your game clothes. That polo shirt
with…with the team name on it. I loved it…because you
looked just the same, but no one knew how you could be.
Not like I did."

"No one."

His mouth claimed hers with voracious ownership, his
tongue moving with such purpose, sliding over hers, his
arousal pressed between her legs like an invitation. The
rough maleness of his jaw and cheeks rasped over her
smooth skin as he worked her mouth, slanting his head and
taking, offering, giving, savoring. She had no need to hold
herself up because his crushing body did it for her, elevat-
ing her just off the ground so her toes brushed the dirt.

"Uh…excuse me, folks."

Elliott broke away from Peggy's mouth with a frustrated
sound, pegging the flashlight-holding newcomer with a
look designed to kill. "Yes?"

The beam of light lowered and Peggy saw their
interrupter—who wore a bright orange Day-Glo vest and a
hat—couldn't have been more than seventeen. She tapped
frantically on Elliott's shoulder until he let her down from

her perch on his erection as the newcomer shifted with obvious discomfort.

"Is, um..." Peggy smoothed the sides of her pulled-up hair. "Is there still time for a tour of the cave?"

"Well, the guided tours are over..."

With a rumbling curse, Elliott reached into his pocket and approached the employee, the words they exchanged too muffled to hear. Then he reached a hand out to Peggy, winking at her when she took it. "He's going to give us helmets and let us take a look on our own."

Heart still pounding in her head, panties now clinging far too much for comfort, Peggy fell into step behind Elliott, casting a suspicious look in his direction. "Not going to lie, this feels a little orchestrated."

The tension in his jaw loosened in degrees, his gaze sliding down Peggy's front, proving that both of them had not recovered from the kiss. "I might have had some inside information about the effectiveness of a bribe."

Peggy clucked her tongue. "Elliott Brooks. You're going to have one doozy of a confession this week."

His voice was ripe with meaning when he responded, "Right now, you're the only one I care about confessing to."

They were brought to an office and given hard hats by Orange Vest, as well as a map of the cave and a quick tutorial on how to stay safe and operate the lights on their helmets. Before they'd even walked back out, the kid had already planted himself in front of the computer, probably to alert every single one of his friends he'd just caught two old people making out. "We're totally going to be town gossip."

Elliott tugged her into his side. "A few more minutes and we'd have been using some of that fund-raiser money for bail."

A laugh tripped out of Peggy. "*Kingmaker Jailed.* I can see the headlines now." She gave in to the urge to turn her face into his shoulder, catch some of his scent. "It would have been good for your street cred."

"You don't need street cred when you have championships."

Peggy's mouth fell open. "Oh my God. Such a Kanye thing to say." She hip-bumped him. "Aren't you going to ask me who Kanye is?"

"I live my life inside weight rooms, locker rooms, and a football stadium, and you don't think I know who Kanye is?" He cleared his throat... and rapped a few lines from a popular song about no one man having all the power.

Oh God, it felt good to laugh. With Elliott. Stolen moments from the past reminded her this wasn't the first time they'd laughed together. But tonight was the first time she didn't fear him shutting down afterward. In fact, he didn't even seem to realize he was laughing himself, he was so busy staring at her mouth.

They stopped at the cave entrance and Elliott reached over to switch on her light, his fingers lingering at her neck a moment, before he turned on his own.

"If we're attacked by cave people, don't suggest we split up to find the exit, okay?" she murmured. "That's when people start to die."

"I'll agree to that if you pretend to be just a little scared." Elliott smiled and tucked a piece of hair beneath her helmet. "I have to get to second base tonight to make up for the street cred I'm not earning."

"Oh, there's a whole manly point system in play? I had no idea."

"Now you do."

"Now I do." The easy way they were bouncing off each

other was making her thighs clench. "Quick tour of the cave, Elliott," she breathed. "Then you take me somewhere and hit a grand slam."

A low growl from the depths of his throat. "Football coaches usually hate baseball metaphors." He took her hand, bringing it to his mouth to French-kiss her palm. "But I'm getting over it."

Her laugh was unsteady. "So selfless."

Elliott's fingers trailed down from her hair, over her collarbone and hip. Lower. Until he cupped his warm hand against the juncture of her thighs. "You have no idea how selfless I need to be tonight," he rasped, bending down to swirl his tongue in the hollow of her neck. "You're going to have to tap out when you've had enough of me eating you."

"Elliott."

"Good girl. Practice my name now."

Before she could respond to those arrogant instructions, Elliott took her hand and guided her down the sloping pathway into the cave. It was pitch black, damp, and smelled faintly of moss, stagnant water, and mold, but it wasn't in the least unpleasant. Apart from their headlamps sending beams down side to side, there was no light until they turned a corner and saw an illuminated entrance on the left.

Peggy stopped short when the massive cavern came into view. It was nothing short of extraordinary, with slabs of rock forming the nature-made structure. There was a huge spotlight set up in the corner of the cave, casting shadows in every direction. From the ceiling all the way down to the rocky floor, it seemed as if at some point in the past, the cave had started melting, dripping its earthy substance down, down...and then it had frozen halfway through. There was a sense of active movement all around, even though the walls were totally still.

"Wow. This isn't what I was picturing," Peggy whispered.

"What were you—" He broke off when Peggy shushed him. "What?"

"You're not commanding a football team. Try and keep it under a dull roar."

"Or I'll wake the cave people?"

"Exactly."

Peggy let go of Elliott's hand so she could circle around one of the giant suspended drips angling down from the ceiling, examining all the crevices and mazes of rock decorating the sides.

When she looked back to Elliott to say something, his easy smile was gone.

CHAPTER TWENTY-SEVEN

Elliott rarely went for two-point conversions, unless it was the only option. But every once in a while, a white zap of lightning singed his nerve endings. Maybe it was the energy of his players or the crowd, maybe some chink in the defense's armor that no one had seen yet. When he got that down-deep gut roll and went for two points, he could never explain the reason behind the decision, so it was a good thing his assistant coaches and the post-game reporters rarely asked him for an explanation of any maneuver. They wrote down what he had to offer—and that was it.

For all that evening's lightness and the way Peggy had seemed—thank the Lord—comfortable with him, there he stood with his nerve endings on fire. This moment was urgent. The same sixth sense that encouraged Elliott to attempt two-point conversions was blaring a high-pitched whistle in the farthest regions of his mind, far more powerful than anything he'd ever encountered on the sidelines of a football game. *Make an impact. Make it count. Don't wait.*

As if some divine providence—or maybe the man upstairs—heard his mental gears grinding, the spotlight in the cave's corner landed on the rings Peggy wore back around her neck on a defiant, makeshift chain of string, making them glint, sparkle. Across the distance separating them, he could hear the silver objects clang together, as if his hearing ability had been cranked up to ten.

Elliott realized Peggy had stopped her journey around the cave's interior and was watching him, somehow curious and...knowing at the same time. Which didn't surprise him. Hadn't she spoken to him in total silence, long before they'd ever exchanged so much as a syllable? Time fell away, leaving their connection locked and enduring, much like the very structure in which they stood.

"What is it?" Peggy murmured, her gaze cutting down to where she toed the edge of a small pool. "Is this where you tell me a cave person is standing right behind me wearing someone else's skin?"

Fuck, he loved her. Loved her with the kind of intensity that he would never be able to describe in a million years. If someone else claimed to feel what was shifting and growing inside his chest, Elliott himself might have considered them insane. But not now. Now he understood.

"I want you to tell me about the men you were engaged to." Neither one of them moved or spoke for long, heavy beats. "Trust me, no one is more surprised than me that I just said that."

She curled her fingers around the edges of her jacket. "Why did you?"

Elliott's step was purposeful as he crossed to Peggy, skirting the pool's edge to stop right in front of her. His pulse sounded like the rapid ticking of a wooden roller coaster as it dropped a car full of screaming people down a giant hill. Did he want to hear about Peggy's ex-boyfriends? Hell fucking no. Already his skin was crawling with the idea. But that was the point, wasn't it? "You wear the rings because you feel guilty," he explained. "I know what that feels like. And I don't want you to experience it anymore."

Peggy breathed a laugh, but her eyes were haunted. "Easier said than done."

"I know." He stepped closed. "That's why you're going to give me the guilt. Right here, right now. You're going to hand it over to me and I'm going to carry it for you."

"That's not going to work." She backed away, then stopped. "There won't be an even balance unless you give me yours in exchange." Waiting for her to continue, Elliott was wired, attuned to every emotion flitting across her face. "You still carry the rosary beads."

"Yes."

She set her chin. "When we broke up, you said when you looked at me, you saw your own guilt. Your sins." Her gaze cut to the ceiling. "Are you sure you don't feel that way now?"

Remembering the shocked horror on her face when he'd said those words, he wanted to roar his anguish. "What I said that day was the wrong half of the truth, Peggy. I was guilty, yes. I'd been absent when my family needed me. I *still* haven't been good enough for Alice." He took a step forward. "If you'd come along later, the shit in my head might not have dragged you down with it. We'll never know. But after feeling...less for the person I failed, then falling straight into crazy for you right afterward, I couldn't accept what you made me feel without the guilt. So I fought it. It's no excuse for driving you away. Jesus, I'll want to take back that day for the rest of my life. But I need you to understand, the failure was mine. You didn't deserve any part of it."

She pressed her knuckles to her mouth a moment, clearly processing everything he'd said. "When I came back, though, you were still angry with me."

"No." His voice was two knives sharpening. "I was terrified. I spent the years without you playing defense against feeling a goddamn thing. And you walk in and find every hole in my resistance, just like you always did."

"Brought it right back to football metaphors, didn't you?"

When she let out a shaky laugh, Elliott's relief almost knocked him over. He wasted no time reaching into his pocket, removing the rosary beads, and handing them to Peggy. "You've always had every single part of me. Good and bad. From here on out, I'm going to make sure it's so much damn good, Peggy. Try and trust me." Not quite ready to give her a breath to say no, Elliott moved closer. "Your turn."

She tried to slide past him, but he halted her progress by gripping her arms. He hated the trapped vibe she was giving off. But he was learning that progress never came without some kind of sacrifice. Some kind of work. Hoping she didn't try to make a dash for the exit, Elliott slid his hands up to Peggy's nape and untied the haphazardly repaired necklace. Truthfully, there was a huge part of Elliott that wanted to take those rings and throw them far as he could, listen to them clatter and roll, never to be seen again. Someone besides him had put those symbols of commitment on her finger—something he'd been too stupid to do himself—and he hated the sight of them. Instead, though, he placed the jewelry in her palm and closed her hand around it.

She blew out a long, stuttered breath and removed the first ring from the string. A plain silver band with a modest diamond that winked at Elliott, as if to mock him, but he squeezed Peggy's shoulder and waited, despite the pain burrowing into his stomach. "This one is from Peter the accountant. Small in stature, but...huge on his dedication to the Padres." Her swallow was audible. "He wore his Padres jersey everywhere, even restaurants. And he ran up and high-fived anyone else wearing their gear. Really nice guy."

Elliott focused on the words instead of the unwanted images. With Peggy standing right in front of him, breathing and smelling like the highest point of heaven, he absolutely could not picture her on a date and maintain his composure, be the support she needed.

"What do I do with the ring now?" Peggy whispered.

"What do you want to do with it?"

Her luminous golden brown eyes wrecked him. "Never see it again."

Elliott nodded and took the ring, dropping it into his pocket. "Done. It's mine now, Peggy. I made us go without one another for three years and these failures are mine. They were mine when they happened. And they're mine now."

Her brow wrinkled as she ducked her head again, sliding all three rings off the string and holding them out, a fistful of diamonds. "Morris the bass player was next. He never woke up before noon a day in his life. But it was eleven fifteen in the morning when he proposed, so I think he was trying to change." She used her free hand to give Elliott the ring. "Then there was Carlos, the attorney and total adrenaline junkie. Took too many selfies. This one...this was the hardest engagement to break, because I could tell he knew. He saw it coming." Elliott accepted the third ring,

praying like hell this was helping Peggy so his absolute, unbearable suffering wouldn't be for nothing. He'd earned the
suffering. He knew that. Didn't make it any less of a mind
fuck. "Last one is from Samson, a bicycle shop owner." She
looked up at Elliott. "This one I can't really be blamed for.
He proposed to me in front of his mom on our third date.
She was videotaping the whole thing. I couldn't say no."

"No," Elliott agreed through stiff lips. "That would have
been too hard for someone with a good heart like you."

She breathed a shaky laugh. "The way this little ceremony is hard for you?"

"I've just listened to the woman who rules me—mind
and body—list her ex-fiancés," Elliott gritted out. "Nothing
is this hard."

Clearly stunned by his vehemence, she searched his face
for long moments, before reaching over and pushing the final ring into his pocket, letting it join the others. Then she
tucked the string into her pocket and dropped both hands to
her sides as if she didn't know what to do with them anymore. "Will you mail them back?"

"Yes," he forced out. "Whatever we need to do."

Peggy's gaze traced away, landing on the water. "I didn't
expect to feel better, but I do." Her mouth twitched. "Maybe
because you feel worse."

Unbelievable that he should want to laugh and smash the
entire cave to pieces with a sledgehammer at the same time.
"You ready to get out of here?"

The look she sent him from beneath her eyelashes was
seduction without most of the darkness that had been there
before. "Couldn't be more ready."

Elliott bit back a groan as his cock reacted to the rasp of
silk in her voice. He reached out to grab her hand, prepared
to drag her out of the cave fast as humanly possible—

A bat dropped down from above them, landing in the water with a splash. If they could bottle the jumping ability Peggy exhibited while launching herself at him with a high-pitched scream, he would stock it in the locker room. She left the ground and drew her legs up at the same time, giving Elliott no choice but to think fast, catching her in midair against his chest. She burrowed her face into his neck and slapped at his shoulders. "Jesus Christ. Go. Go go fucking go."

Lord, there was nothing better than holding Peggy. Nothing in the damn world. And he owed his receiver big time. "What happened to 'bring 'em on'?"

"I lied."

His laugher echoed off the cave walls.

CHAPTER TWENTY-EIGHT

Oh wow. There was something about a man who could carry you up a steep incline and set you down in the passenger seat of his truck without breaking a sweat. He seemed to relish the task, even, holding her like he'd growl at anyone who came close. His chest was an unmovable object, his arms like iron bands. With every step he took, the weight in her tummy sank a little lower, tickling down into her thighs.

Peggy couldn't pinpoint a time when she'd been more desperate to get laid. And it needed to be Elliott. Needed to be now. As the truck bumped back up the path toward the road, she swiped her palms down her legs, trying to get rid of the sweat. She could barely control her breathing, either, and if they didn't stop soon and get naked, she was going to fog up the windows.

This is bad. So bad. So bad.

Because tonight was supposed to be about easy. About

that final tick toward closure. She definitely hadn't expected to walk down into the cave and hand over her guilt, taking away Elliott's in return. Hadn't expected to say words out loud to Elliott she hadn't known were dying to break free. But they had been. They'd been stretching her diaphragm with the need to release, and now she felt like a springtime breeze.

"You all right over there?"

Her nod was jerky. "Where are you taking me?"

His hands flexed on the steering wheel, probably in response to the breathlessness in her tone. "You don't want dinner."

"No."

As if he sensed she needed an anchor, he reached across the seat and laid a warm hand high on her thigh, which just about sent her into an orgasm spiral. This was unreal. She'd been feeling so shitty for so long and now it was all gone. Gone. And she couldn't even get her pulse under control. In order to maintain the high, she needed Elliott now. Immediately.

"Our options are limited around here," he said in a low voice.

"Anywhere." She threw her head back against the seat. "I don't care."

The truck picked up speed. When they hit the road, Elliott fishtailed, before righting the vehicle. Then they were speeding in the opposite direction from which they'd come. "There's a turnpike up ahead, which usually means a motel." He bashed his fist into the steering wheel. "I hate bringing you to a place like that."

Not sure where she ached worse—her chest or between her legs—Peggy dragged his hand higher, cupping it around her center. "I won't be paying attention to the décor."

"Fuck, baby," he groaned. "You're soaked."

The goddess of sexual frustration must have heard her cries, because a neon sign flickered on the horizon and Elliott put the pedal to the metal, bringing them into the parking lot in under a minute.

"Wait here," he ordered, climbing from the truck, slamming and locking the doors. As if she'd needed to be told to stay put. The clerk would take one look at Peggy and ask where she'd gotten the good ecstasy pills. She watched Elliott disappear into the front office, nearly wrenching the door off its hinges in the process. And once she was ensconced in the dark truck alone, she ripped off her jacket in an attempt to lower her body temperature and closed her eyes, counting to one hundred, trying to focus on something other than the slick flesh between her legs. *Hurry, hurry, hurry.*

When the passenger side door was flung open, the blast of cold that sailed over her damp flesh did nothing to cool her down. Elliott wrapped an arm around her waist and pulled her out of the car, closing the door with a bash and shoving her up against it, much like he'd done back in the cave parking lot. Only this time, she wasn't even attempting to play coy, her legs tangling around his waist, hands tearing into his hair to bring him down for a kiss. The first encounter between their tongues was accompanied by an aggressive hip pump from Elliott and Peggy broke away with a half cry, half gasp. "Keep going. Oh God, I'm one more of those away from coming. Please."

"No." His stubble rasped against her neck, her ear. "No, I'm getting you inside. It's happening on my tongue."

Elliott turned, Peggy all but suctioned onto his front, and walked them down the row of doors, the key in his hand jangling. They almost descended into another round of kissing, mouths hovering so close, breath racing out in heated gusts as Elliott unlocked the door, but they made it inside. Elliott kicked the door shut behind them, took two steps, and laid Peggy down on the closest available surface. She curled her fingers into the cold, hard...bureau? Yes, she registered vaguely, her fingertips encountering the coarse finish of the drawers. Elliott perused her as he drew off his shirt...and splayed her thighs with one desperate outward push.

The glow of the flickering motel sign outside filtered in through the cheap curtains, teasing light into the otherwise pitch-black room. But that was all Peggy could process once Elliott was bare chested...and that chest was heaving as he unclothed her from the waist down, leggings and panties both, then trailed his tongue up the inside of her right thigh. His fingers reached her center before his mouth, parting her, exposing the bundle of nerves that so desperately needed tending.

"Yes," she wailed as Elliott did just that. Tended to her like they had only one minute until the Apocalypse. His stiff tongue raked over her clit, lapping at it, while his middle finger slipped through moisture into her entrance. "Yes."

"You don't need to tell me yes when you're this wet," he groaned, stabbing his tongue as far inside her as it could go and drawing it out slowly, until his stubble met her sensitized flesh and scraped, before repeating the move several quick, mind-spinning times, all while his thumb strummed over her clit. "Keyed up in my passenger seat, wiggling around like I was already tongue deep in this soaked pussy of yours. Were you remembering how much I love licking it?"

Elliott pushed two fingers inside Peggy and her hips jerked off the bureau, her bare ass slapping back down into the surface as she cried out, "Oh God. Yes, I remember."

Through a fog, she made eye contact with Elliott as he began his stiff-tongued torture of her clit once again, moving up and back, in circles, fast, slow, sideways, until a scream battered the inside of her throat. The arches of her feet curved around the slope of his shoulders, smoothing, rubbing, until she no longer had the strength to keep her legs up and they fell open once again.

"My favorite part was afterward. After you'd come enough to be fucking delirious..." A prolonged suck of her swollen nub that had her legs shaking, one knee bashing off the wall. "Then I'd slide you toward me or flip you over, whatever you were begging for, and your cunt would be so shiny for me. Ready for a pounding from my cock. Gorgeous."

"Ohhh." Her fingers plowed into his hair and gripped tight. "Do that again. Don't stop. I need to. I need to—" Her pleas ended with a scream when Elliott pushed his fingers deep, jiggling them rapidly, while his mouth applied the sweetest amount of suction to her clit and sensation exploded below her waist. "Elliott. Jesus Christ."

Elliott must have inherited some priestly traits through osmosis during all those hours spent at mass, because the way her back arched, her eyes rolling back in her head, he could have been performing an exorcism on her. And maybe she *was* being rid of demons because she'd never experienced that brand of all-encompassing pleasure before with Elliott. There's always been a barrier between them. Ghosts. Regrets. But no more. No more.

Through half-blind eyes, she saw the room for the first time swimming in some kind of upside-down, dreamlike quality as the muscles between her thighs clenched, milking Elliott's fingers. Words poured from her mouth, sounding as if they were spoken from some other dimension. Another orgasm wracked her body and she moaned, sweat rolling down her sides and making her slide backward on the bureau, but Elliott yanked her closer for more torture. And it was endless, the movements of his mouth working in a rhythm lost in the racing of her heart, the contracting of her private flesh, the deep down shudders in the pit of her belly.

Pinpricks of pain dotted along her skull and Peggy realized she was pulling her own hair, her throat gone raw from screaming Elliott's name. How long had he been using his mouth on her? How many times had she climaxed?

Urgency washed over Peggy and she sat up, knocking Elliott's hands away when he attempted to lay her back down, his mouth opening and closing as it French-kissed her between the legs.

"Elliott—" He looked up as he flickered his tongue against her nub, causing her to moan and sway on the bureau. "Elliott."

He pushed her legs wider with a sound of protest, but she struggled against his hold until he relented and straightened, his chest hair curled with sweat, his eyes glittering in that lust way she remembered... but there was a difference. There was unfathomable depth to them as he perused her naked lower half, trailing his gaze up to her face. The beating of her pulse grew noisy, rattling in her ears, the organ in her chest simultaneously rebelling and rejoicing over what she encountered as he watched her.

Ten thousand watts of emotion radiated from Elliott like a beacon. Peggy's instinct was still to avoid the meaning there, so she grabbed the hem of her shirt, lifting it over her head and tossing it away. Elliott made a harsh noise in response, adjusting the bulge in his jeans when her breasts were exposed. "You're a fucking work of art, Peggy. Head to toe." He reached out, but instead of touching her breast as expected, he laid his palm flat over her heart. "And this is the best damn part right here. I need you to let me in."

Were her knees still shaking against the furniture's wooden edge from the orgasm or his gesture? She didn't know. Didn't know. But she couldn't seem to form words, pressure expanding inside her ribs until she worried she might pop like a balloon. She opened her mouth and nothing but a hum emerged.

Elliott lunged forward, obliterating the space between them. His lips interlocked with hers, but didn't kiss. "Not ready yet? Okay. Okay," he murmured, his voice ripe with...everything. Lust. Intensity. She heard his pants unzip and her anxious wheeze, brought on by the metallic reminder that he hadn't even been inside her yet. The tearing of the condom wrapper. "I'll fuck you until you're too weak to fight what we both know is here between us. Still. Here. Never left. Never lost strength."

Peggy's self-preservation screamed from under the dense blanket of need in her head...and she heard the warning to run. She did. But when Elliott's hips fit between the notch of her legs with a low growl, and she felt his erection slip through her folds and press against her entrance, there wasn't an alarm in the world that could keep her thighs from blossoming open. That could stop her from wrapping her arms around the back of Elliott's neck and receiving that first savage thrust.

"Ohhhh," she cried into his shoulder, trying to absorb the incredible sensation of being full. Full to the point that she hovered on the brink of discomfort for a few seconds, before it abated and she saw her fingernails digging into his shoulders, felt his heaved breaths pelting her neck. They were locked together as they'd been so many times before, only there was static between them now, an electrified connection due to the lack of mystery. Every card had been played and they all lay face up on the table. She and Elliott were so very there in the moment that it was stark and unquestionable how they'd ended up in that motel room. There'd never, not for a second, been another outcome. But did she control the ultimate one?

"Hey," Elliott rasped in her ear. "You get back here to me right now, Peggy. I'm going to drown without you, and you know it. You can feel that if you're not right here with me, I'm going to slide under the surface. Can't you?" He crushed their bodies together until she could feel his heart, could feel the brutal speed of it, how it matched her own. "Don't leave me."

Three words with two meanings, and they made her want to sob, but her body's demands were fast becoming the sole focus of her existence. At the place where they joined together, a hot throbbing had begun, and every time she scooted her legs higher around Elliott's waist, the urgency kicked higher. The low, continuous rumble in his chest told her how ready he was to spin-cycle her senses again, his erection solid as steel inside her.

"Elliott." Her own words surprised her so much, she barely realized she'd spoken. "Tell me..."

"Tell you what?" He breathed into her ear, kissing the lobe, drawing it between his teeth. "Let's hear it, baby. I want to know everything that goes through your head when you've got me inside your tight pussy."

The words came out in a rush, as if they'd been hiding from her all along and needed to escape before she reeled them back in. "Tell me you missed me."

Elliott's head snapped up, his gaze homing in on her, disbelief crackling like a fireplace fire in his expression. Before Peggy could draw a bracing breath, Elliott jerked her off the bureau and walked her toward the bed, laying her in the center and coming down on top of her, muscle pressing softness, without ever withdrawing from her body. The gravity of his weight on top of her was divine, and although she could tell he was poised to say something, she could also sense his inability to keep from pumping deep into her body and staying there, stretching her as she gasped.

"Miss you?" He grated the incredulous question, dropping his mouth to her temple. "You left me without a soul. I can barely remember the days since you left. They passed without me feeling a single thing. Because you are feeling for me. You're the only thing that keeps me from being numb. Twice in my life you've turned me back into a living, breathing man, and missing you…missing you, Peggy, doesn't even begin to cover it. You revive me."

His lips traced down the side of her face and meshed with hers. Vocalizing the tumult of reactions colliding in her chest was impossible. There was no way to match the beauty of his words, so she showed him with her mouth. She opened for him the way he liked and allowed him to devour. Exulted in her destruction.

Elliott went from savoring to aggressive, hungry, in the time it took to blink. His hips started to move with turmoil, his kiss pausing to accommodate the groan that roared out from somewhere only he knew about. "Baby…I'm going to fucking break you like this. You've got me so awake. I can hear your heartbeat, all your little gasps…the slap of my dick sinking in. Cut me off."

He fell onto her, his thrusts so powerful she couldn't get breath into her lungs. The desperation in him kindled her understanding, her intuition, though, and she moved before her brain made the command, pushing with all her strength until Elliott rolled onto his back. His muscles were strained in the muted neon light, his jaw clenched, chest heaving. She'd never seen him so lacking in control and an answering wildness rose up, wrapping around her like a second skin. "Worried you're going to break me?" she whispered, leaning down and kissing his chest as she seated herself with a moan. "Aren't you worried I'll break you?"

"You could," Elliott said, voice vibrating, his hands rasping up her thighs. "You might."

There were two sides of the storm that built inside her. Power. Power because she was finally on top of this man, when it had been the reverse for so long. But that side of the storm lacked any real satisfaction now, so she focused on the opposite half. The driving need to lose herself. It had started back in the cave, this flinging flight into recovery, this return to herself. And she wanted—needed—to revel in it. In Elliott, whose intent expression told her he could read every thought in her head.

With Elliott buried as deep as possible between her legs, she was anchored, centered, and her hands lifted in celebration, threading into the strands of her hair, moving in slow circles that her hips began to mimic. Her eyelids grew heavy, doing their best to obscure her vision of a rapt Elliott as she started a slick up and back grind. "You like the way that feels?" she whispered, confidence building and strengthening inside her. "You like me sliding up and down on your cock?"

"Fuck," Elliott groaned through his teeth. "Break me a little faster, baby. Please. You remember...you remember how hard up I get after licking your pussy."

"That's the best part," she said, one corner of her mouth lifting. "Seeing how much you need it over, but you're trying to hold on because it feels so nice."

"Nice?" Elliott's laughter was full of pain, his lower

body lifting beneath Peggy to push her higher, pumping his hips and bouncing her until she had to hold his shoulders for balance. "Nice is no way to describe the way you wring me out with a smile. Ask me again if I missed you."

A quaking had started a couple inches below her belly button, spreading to her thighs and calves...everywhere. She rubbed her clitoris, the epicenter of her lust, against him mindlessly, writhing and undulating, racing toward something that she knew would shatter her. And she needed it, needed it so bad, masochist that she was. "Did you m-miss me?" she asked through chattering teeth.

Elliott flipped their positions, using one hand to support his weight, the other to reach between their moisture-slickened bodies and pet her right where she required touch. His open mouth dragged up the side of her neck, into her hair, down the side of her face, before ravaging her lips. Peggy heard herself whimpering, and no wonder, because the man looming above her was extraordinary in that moment, his body a machine, his chiseled face a mask of determination, blistering heat...and adoration. For her. It was there in the tenderness blazing from his eyes, the measured strokes of his hips, every move designed to drive her toward release.

His middle finger picked up the pace where their bodies joined, dampness making her slippery, so slippery. "Peggy..." He trailed off with a groan, his eyes closing tight, and she knew he was fighting to last, giving himself no other option but to turn her inside out one last time, even though he'd already wrung her out with his mouth. "If you never left again, I would still spend the rest of my life missing you," he panted. "The missing of you over three years...it overflowed and I'll be wading through it forever."

A sound left Peggy's mouth, halfway between a cry and

a sob. She didn't think, just threw her arms around the breadth of his back and pulled him down on top of her, their bodies locked in the tightest of embraces, Elliott's face buried in her neck as he rocked with increasing force in the cradle of her thighs. His labored breaths in her ear, the growls of her name were what blew Peggy out of the water. Her legs flew up around his waist and clenched, her back bowing off the bed. "Elliott," she screamed, the inner walls of her womanhood seizing around his hard, driving flesh.

"Yes," he ground out, slamming into her with brutality that signaled his peak, his face burrowing into the comforter to the right of her neck and roaring, roaring, loud enough that she felt the vibration ripple down her spine. She tried to keep her legs up, but her energy deserted her, both lower limbs falling heavily to the bed. Elliott gripped her right knee, though, holding it out wide while he flooded her, his big body wracked by tremors. "Christ, Peggy."

She tightened her hold on him, laying kisses on his shoulders until he stopped shaking and released her knee, the tension ebbing from his frame. But he didn't stop moving completely for a second, his hands soothing up the sides of her thighs, his lips whispering words into her hair that made her throat close up.

"Beautiful. So beautiful. Took me so good, baby. God, you were sweet. Sweet everywhere just for me, weren't you? Sweet and tight. Hot. Just for me."

When she'd walked out on the porch tonight, there'd been no question in her mind that she was leaving Cincinnati and never looking back, but panic crept into her chest like a crew of burglars, robbing things she'd kept safe, spinning her lock combinations and landing on the correct numbers. The moment was so honest between them. In the light of day tomorrow, she might regret murmuring back to Elliott in the dark, but she plowed her fingers into his hair anyway. Lifted his head to find eyes gone liquid and ... loving. "Elliott?"

He kissed her lips softly. "Yeah, Peggy."

"I, um—"

Across the room, Elliott's cell phone went off.

CHAPTER TWENTY-NINE

Y ou have to go," Peggy said from across the console of Elliott's truck. "You have no choice."

Elliott ground his teeth together. Not only because she was right and his presence was needed immediately back in Cincinnati, but because her guard was up again. Somehow, someway, he'd managed to reach Peggy tonight. Managed to make her smile, put that sparkle back in her eyes when she looked at him, instead of doubt and distrust. And with one phone call from his assistant coach, he'd had a front row seat to watch her shield click back into place.

It had been unbearable, watching her lift the pillow to cover herself as his assistant coach explained loud enough for everyone in the whole damn motel to hear, that there had been a last-minute injury with Temple's quarterback. There might not have been a cause for panic, but the second string QB was left-handed and favored the corresponding side of the field, meaning Elliott's staff needed to meet about a new defensive strategy before the team convened tomorrow morning. If the Bearcats crew was scrambling, he could only imagine the Temple coach's stress, but frankly, he didn't give two flying shits about anything right now, save the girl sitting still as death in the passenger seat of his truck.

"I don't want to leave, Peggy. You know that, right?" He took his eyes off the road long enough to glance over. "I've got a responsibility to the team, the school, to give them the best chance of winning."

The words rang hollow. Pressure had been a welcome distraction from being without Peggy. It had enabled him to cope by exerting all his energy on the sidelines. But now that he could feel his chance with her slipping out of his hands, it was hard to reconcile the need to win at all costs. Maybe the *ultimate* cost. Winning had pushed his daughter away, too, hadn't it?

Now he was going to lose Peggy over it—when he'd only just started earning her back. He could feel the loss of her happening in real time, like watching a slow motion corrosion of a mountain, rocks rolling into the sea.

I could leave this in my assistant coaches' hands. I could stay and prove right here, right now, that she's more important to me than any goddamn game or championship. Because she is. She's the rest of my life, and she's sitting right there where tomorrow only smoke and a memory will exist.

And Elliott would have done it. Would have pulled the truck over, dragged her into his lap, and confessed every last unpoetic word pushing to get free of his heart. Would have done it without hesitation, if it weren't for the promise he'd made to Alice.

I promise I'll have it arranged. For the Temple game.

He'd made that promise with the intent to keep it, come hell or high water. And Alice hadn't yet told him she was ready for someone else in their lives. After checking out on her for...God, as long as he could remember, he couldn't continue without his daughter's blessing. Not only could it damage his relationship with his daughter beyond repairing, but it would douse the spark Peggy had lit with her presence in their lives. He couldn't allow it. Couldn't allow either of those things to happen.

Fuck. His chest was being pried apart. As he turned onto the driveway leading to the Tates' farm, the pain intensified until it was excruciating. He'd called Alice after hanging up with his assistant coach and told her to be ready with her things when he pulled up. Ahead, he could see the porch light on, people gathered on the other side of the screen door. This was it. He would drop off Peggy, drive away, spend tomorrow occupied with the game...and then she'd be leaving. It would happen faster than fingers snapping.

When they'd almost reached the house and Peggy still hadn't answered him, Elliott's panic made his mouth dry as dust. "Did you hear me? In a perfect world, I'd walk into that house holding your hand and it would be understood that we're sharing a room." Even when her lips popped open on a breath and she gave him her attention, he felt no satisfaction. "I don't want to leave, baby. But—"

"Elliott. Look at me." Peggy pointed to her face. "I'm not playing head games with you. You really don't have to explain. Do you think I'm going to bitch and stomp my foot because you have a job to do? A nationally televised, big-ass deal of a job? Well, I'm not. I wouldn't."

"You could." His voice was low as he cut off the engine. "I want you to feel like you have that right. I want you to know you do."

She didn't quite pull off her incredulous expression, because he could see the flash of hope, fleeting though it was. He never had a chance to find out what she would have said, because excited voices cut into the stillness of the truck's interior. A lot of excited voices. The sound of footsteps banging on the wooden steps joined the chorus and both of their doors were flung open. On Peggy's side stood Sage and Mrs. Tate, while Kyler and Alice appeared on his left.

"We did it," Elliott's receiver whooped, reaching out his hand for a shake. "We hit the goal. Happened about two minutes before you pulled up. Can't believe it. Someone is going to have to pick my father up off the living room floor." His hands came up to pull at his mess of hair. "Wow. Just wow."

"We had a last-minute donation." That was Sage speaking, and Elliott had to strain to hear her soft-spoken voice. "The game-winning football from last year's Super Bowl." She folded her hands and tucked them beneath her chin. "We'll have enough to settle the debts and give a sizable chunk to the cheerleading program, Peggy."

"That's…" Peggy sucked in a breath and dove out of the truck, wrapping her friend and Mrs. Tate in one enthusiastic hug. "That's amazing. Amazing."

Elliott was so focused on Peggy's transformation, it took him a moment to realize Kyler was still holding his hand out for a shake. He took the younger man's hand, and was taken by surprise when Kyler hauled him out of the truck and into a back-slapping hug. "Jesus, Tate," Elliott grumbled. "Control yourself."

"Ah, come on. It's a celebration." He pulled back and gave a conspiratorial wink. "Did the cave trick work for you?"

"I don't know yet," Elliott answered honestly, too wrecked

in the head to do anything else besides tell the truth. "Listen, I know everything is happening at once…" A throb started in the dead center of his forehead. "But there's been a last-minute—"

"Who's having ribs?" Lyle shouted from the top of the porch. And just like that, the entire Tate clan cheered loud enough to rival the college stadium on game day. No one wasted any time stampeding up the porch and into the house, except for Elliott, Alice, Kyler, Jess, Peggy, and Sage, all of whom seemed to sense there was more than a celebration taking place.

"What's up, Coach?" Kyler prompted.

Elliott swallowed the boulder in his throat. "Need you to get your gear and come back to Cincinnati with me, Tate. We're calling in the team early tomorrow." His attention strayed to Peggy on the other side of the truck. "I'll fill you in on the road."

His respect for Kyler went up another notch when the younger man gave a single nod and moved past him toward the house. "Give me five minutes, Coach."

That left Alice standing there in front of him, shifting side to side in her sneakers. "I guess I'll go grab my jacket. I don't want to miss standing on the sidelines with you to-morrow."

"I don't want you to miss it, either."

Her shoulders lowered, her relief that he hadn't changed his mind evident. Which only made his decision that much more crucial. His own daughter didn't expect him to follow through. She cast a glance over his shoulder to where Peggy, Sage, and Jess had begun talking excitedly about the news. "Is she…are they coming with us?"

Elliott kept his features schooled. "I expect they'll follow in the morning."

Alice was silent for long moments. "Okay."

When his daughter passed him and jogged up the steps into the house, Elliott gathered oxygen into his lungs and turned. Sage and Jess had gone back inside, and Peggy, after retrieving her coat from the truck, was preparing to follow them. "Wait," he ordered, harsher than intended. "Just wait."

She was the picture of serenity, waiting for him to round the truck. Except for the white-knuckled grip on her jacket. Did that give him a sliver of a chance?

Elliott had every intention of speaking to Peggy, although he had no idea what the hell he could say in the eleventh hour to repair the remaining hurt and make a future seem possible. Maybe those words didn't even exist. Turned out, none of that mattered, because as soon as he got close, his heart took control of his hands. They curled around her shoulders and pulled her close, his mouth landing on her surprised lips and taking. He took for every second he'd lived without her in the past. For every second he could very likely live without her in the future. She fell back a step under his assault, but he didn't allow her the room, following and devouring, gathering her closer and closer, until she was flattened against his chest.

He would remember the second Peggy stopped being resistant and gave herself over as one of the most exultant of his life. The hands that had been unsure whether to push or pull on his shoulders tugged him closer, her head tipping back to give him better access to her open mouth. He couldn't get enough of her taste. As if they hadn't just blown each other's minds less than an hour earlier, his need reared its head back and roared like a living thing.

This time, when Peggy pushed at his shoulders, he released her mouth so they could both get a breath. "Elliott, what—"

"Don't fucking count me out, Peggy." He took her face in his hands and leaned in close, the condensation from their panting breaths mingling in the air. No matter how many times he swallowed, he couldn't seem to get his heart back to where it belonged in his chest. "Time is against us. Maybe it always has been. But I'm asking for you to just beat it with me."

"How?" Her eyelids dropped to half-mast. "We don't have any left. I can't make more out of thin air."

"You?" That single word was rife with disbelief. "You, Peggy, can do anything. I—"

Behind her, the stairs creaked. Elliott looked up to see Alice paused on the stairs, watching him and Peggy with… fascination. And he couldn't have this conversation with an audience, especially when he didn't know the ending, didn't know what to ask for.

"Tomorrow night is the fund-raiser. Promise me you won't leave before then. I don't have the right to ask you for anything. But can you give me that?"

Her nod was vigorous. Thank God. "Yes."

"Okay." The relief was mild and fleeting, because he was getting ready to climb inside his truck and leave the woman he loved to get smaller and smaller in the rearview. It was a knife in his gut, twisting and mangling him. With a final inhale of her scent, he pressed his lips to her forehead, lingering, before walking away.

Peggy was inside the house before he even started the engine.

CHAPTER THIRTY

Peggy sat on the top porch step and listened to the rushing of wind, the crickets calling to one another. Behind her, the house was finally silent, the Tates probably sleeping with clear heads for the first time in months, secure in the knowledge they would still have a home come tomorrow. Before coming outside to get some much-needed air, Peggy had arranged the transfer of funds from the fund-raising website into a checking account and had been assured it would show up as available in the morning. Although having that worry ironed out in her mind didn't leave her relaxed by any measure. Oh no.

In her lap sat Miriam's journal, made heavier by the prospect of what she might find inside. She closed her eyes and conjured up her mother's voice, the soothing but fiery sarcasm, the way she spoke out of the side of her mouth when she was imparting a secret or some kind of advice.

And right now, Peggy needed advice more than anything in the world. Unless Miriam had been some kind of psychic, she wouldn't have had a clue about the pickle Peggy found herself in right then, but maybe, just maybe, her mother would have written down the words to nudge Peggy in the right direction.

She could go to New York with what remained of her family. Not to mention Sage, who she suspected would sorely need her soon. After her attempt to gain Sage's confidence back in Cincinnati, there had been no progress. Every time she tried to get her best friend alone, Sage smoothly made excuses to be somewhere else. It wasn't a brush-off—it was just Sage's way of saying, *I'm not ready*. If Peggy remained on the road to New York, would she eventually solve the wedding planner's mystery?

Her other option was to stay behind and take a leap. To believe in the connection between her and Elliott. A connection her soul had continued to believe in far longer than her mind knew was reasonable. Something in her gut hadn't let her give up the fight, even though she'd walked away from it three years ago. Maybe she'd been lying to herself that she'd come to Cincinnati to get closure. Maybe she'd come because her love for Elliott had refused to die, and she'd known—known—she just needed to come back here and shake him up. He'd always been a stubborn mother-fucker. She'd matched him at one time, but being stubborn now—walking away even though the notion made her hurt head to toe—could break them both.

Alice didn't want her around. Peggy tried to swallow the jab of sadness but didn't manage it. Elliott's daughter was only beginning to reconnect with her father and she didn't need an interloper messing with their new flow. That needed to be the biggest factor of her decision. Because she'd fallen a little for Alice, too, and wouldn't hurt her for anything. Not even a closet full of Chanel.

Realizing her throat ached from missing Elliott already and how much worse it would be when she took off tomorrow for New York, Peggy blew out the breath she was holding and flipped open the journal.

Yes, my Peggy is a Rubik's Cube with many sides, all bright and colorful. But the color block that always clicks into place at just the right time is her strength. There are people who would count Peggy out in the clutch, or expect her to call in one of her big brothers to fight battles on her behalf. And they would, by the way. Those two would walk onto any battlefield for their sisters, even in the middle of a squabble (when are they not in the middle of a squabble?).

But Peggy is like the Earth. The outer crust might look sweet, but it's bolstered by a hundred thousand miles of rock hard will and an inner core that could rival that of an Army general. Does using that lovely outer layer to get what she wants once in a while make her weak? No, it means she has studied her arsenal and knows when to brandish her country's flag and when to pull out a bazooka.

When the time comes to face whatever put a dark spot on Peggy's heart, sure as the one on her index finger, I hope Peggy realizes that new weaponry arrives all the time during a battle. Reinforcements show up and the tide changes. It takes time to accustom oneself to new roles, new experiences, and sometimes it means flying a helicopter when you're more comfortable in a tank. But there's no one more adaptable than my Peggy. She's my Rubix Cube, and she'll twist herself into the right pattern when the battle call sounds.

Peggy closed the journal with trembling hands, a cool,

calming presence coming to rest on her shoulders. "Thanks, Mom," she whispered into the Indiana night.

* * *

They were losing by three points. One minute remained on the clock and the Bearcats had just recovered a fumble at Temple's forty-yard line. When everything should have been a tunnel of screams and frantic decisions, Elliott centered himself and breathed.

Winning had always meant he'd earned his salary. That he hadn't let down the players who'd picked his program over several others. And more recently, winning had been validation that choosing the sport over his personal responsibilities hadn't been for nothing, however hollow the proof made him feel. But as he stood on the sidelines, his throat raw from shouting over the chanting crowd, the whistles, the stomping feet, the cheerleaders, the sideline reporters, the trash talkers, the cannon that fired every time someone scored a touchdown...winning meant something different.

Because his daughter was standing ten feet behind him, listening to every word that came out of his mouth. She was swamped inside a giant Bearcats sweatshirt, the sleeves too long for her arms. He'd asked two of the medical trainers to keep an eye on her, and when the pair had cowered in response, Elliott realized he'd never spoken to either of them before. So he'd shaken their hands and asked their names. Simple as that. Now he couldn't turn around without them sending him enthusiastic thumbs-up where they flanked Alice.

He kind of liked not being the boogeyman.

How long would he have gone on alienating everyone if Peggy hadn't shown up in Cincinnati? Forever?

Yes. Elliott was positive of that. For his daughter's sake—and the sake of other players like Kyler Tate—he wouldn't go back to being that hard man. No matter what happened, he would live to honor the way Peggy had shaken up their lives. Would he live hollow or whole, though? As much as he wanted to be the good man Peggy deserved, he knew he'd be living with bleeding insides once she left.

Winning wasn't only important because he wanted to make Alice proud, but that sixth sense in the back of his mind was firing again. He and his daughter needed this victory together. They needed this to happen today. Right now. Sure as there was only one minute left on the scoreboard clock. Sure as Peggy was on the line. He'd felt the conflict in Alice on the drive back to Cincinnati, and he sensed it now, even as he spoke into his headset and held up the right amount of fingers to signal the play to his quarterback.

Elliott hadn't been in the position to lose a game in a good while, but a calm settled over him as he made the call and watched his team move into formation. Tension strapped in the players on the sideline like a seatbelt, their gloved hands reaching out for one another, prayers being whispered. His offensive coordinator clapped a hand down on his shoulder and said something Elliott didn't hear, because his thoughts were on Peggy. Was she watching? God, he would have given his final days on this earth to have her there at that moment, standing beside him and mixing baseball and football references, pulling everything into perspective with a wink.

The snap took place on the field, the ball went up...but instead of Elliott watching to see if Kyler made the reception, he turned and looked at Alice. Her face was buried in the sleeves of her sweatshirt, her eyes peeking out over the top. But at the last second, she met her father's gaze...and that's how they stayed as the crowd essentially lost their minds. The roar was deafening but something in his head muffled it, made it almost silent as chaos erupted around him. He opened his arms and Alice rushed in, throwing her arms around his neck, hugging him in a way he couldn't remember her doing since she was in elementary school.

"I'm sorry," Elliott said. "I'm going to do better, okay?"

"Okay, me too. Me too."

The crowd's initial explosion had died down and their chants of "Tate, Tate, Tate" had kicked off, loud enough to be heard ten miles away. But even with the pride simmering in his chest for Kyler and the family he knew must be ecstatic in their living room back in Indiana, his daughter's tears plopping on his neck pulled all of Elliott's focus.

Alice tugged out of his embrace, her face and eyes red. "God, of course I look like crap in front of a bunch of football players," she sobbed, swiping at her tears with the sleeve of her sweatshirt.

"You look great," Elliott forced through stiff lips. "Great."

For long moments, both of them observed the mayhem. His players were still on the field, dog piled on top of Kyler, and for once, he didn't order them into the locker room with a reminder to act like grown men. He just let them have the moment. His coaching staff were recapping every single second of the game, gesticulating wildly. As usual, everyone steered clear of him, except for the two trainers who stopped by to give him awkward back pats and more of their signature thumbs-up move. That was good enough for now. He'd work on the rest of them later.

"Dad," Alice said, drawing his attention back. She shook her head, knocking loose a handful of tears. "Peggy should be here, too."

He couldn't swallow, couldn't get a good breath around

the hope that rushed into his lungs, so all he managed was a hoarse, "Yeah."

Alice rolled her eyes, but he caught her lower lip trembling. "Well, go get her."

* * *

A man didn't just wing a proposal to a woman like Peggy. Especially when you were a planner to the bone. After the game ended and he gave his customary locker room speech and made a statement in the media room, Elliott took Alice home. Without him having to ask, she called her aunt and asked to spend the night, since Elliott was going to be busy. After sharing a fair bit of uncomfortable eye contact over that assumption—which he prayed to God came true— Alice closed herself in her room to pack.

The fact that Elliott had a speech to make tonight at the fund-raiser had gotten lost in the chaos of driving to Indiana and the football game, so in addition to finding the right words for Peggy, he was jotting down some talking points. Although both speeches were beginning to blur together because he couldn't concentrate on football coach talk while his head was filled with Peggy.

When Elliott's hand cramped, he leaned back in his chair and checked the clock, as if he hadn't done that enough for today. One hour. He needed to be there in one hour. The game had nothing on tonight in terms of importance. But he was ready. Adrenaline moved through his veins like gasoline in the fuel line of a race car—and it sped up at the mere thought of seeing Peggy. Finding her face in the audience or across the room and just existing in the knowledge that such a gorgeous, dynamic woman had wanted him at all at one time. That she'd been beneath him in the dark and handed him her burdens in the cave. Taken his in return. He wanted to look at her and remember those moments, because who knew if he'd ever get the chance again?

The doorbell rang and Elliott pushed to his feet, glad Alice's aunt, Tabitha, had shown up a little early, so he would have time to change into something decent. Lord, he was still in his game gear. Peggy liked him in his game clothes, though, didn't she? A smile ticked up one end of his mouth as he answered the door, revealing Alice's aunt on the other side. When she stepped into the foyer, her smile was somewhat pinched, as it always was when they crossed paths, which didn't happen too often since Alice communicated with her and made plans independently.

Elliott called for Alice down the hallway, who replied in a singsong voice that she'd be out in a minute. Tabitha faced him, hanging on to her purse strap, and that movement reminded Elliott of Judith. Maybe it was the mission to bring home his woman—a new woman, to Alice and Tabitha, at least—that spurred a sense of duty in Elliott, but he found himself speaking, before he could sort out his thoughts. "Thank you for…continuing to be a part of Alice's life." He blew out a breath. "I know you're not my biggest fan and I understand why. But I wanted you to know that I appreciate what you do for my daughter."

If Tabitha was surprised, none of it registered on her face. She ran her fingers down the strap of her purse in a fluid movement, a smile playing on her mouth, and Elliott got the impression she was gearing up for something.

"You're welcome," she said finally. "But I do it for my sister. Someone has to keep her memory alive."

Elliott took that hit on the chin without flinching. "I'll own that. I haven't done near enough to help Alice remember her mother. That's going to change."

"Yes, Alice mentioned over the phone there were going to be some changes around here." Tabitha's expression grew even more pinched. "Something about a woman who's been in town all of three days. That's pretty impulsive, wouldn't you say? I'm not sure this change in you is for the better."

Elliott could see the path they were walking down, and he could do nothing to turn them back. He didn't want to. If turning a new corner meant owning up to his shortcomings, so be it. He would take it like a man. "She's been back in town three days, but she's been with me longer. Am I moving fast? Yes. But I can't let her leave again."

A flash of resentment. "Where was this enthusiasm when my sister was alive?"

He would never say out loud to Tabitha what was carved on his heart. The feelings that burned in his soul for Peggy simply hadn't existed for Judith. In those early days of marriage and fatherhood, he hadn't even believed in the possibility of what Peggy inspired inside him. The kind of love that made you ache to prove it any way you could. The kind of love that could put you to sleep for three years in the absence of its potency. Or make you a lunatic at the idea of her ending up with someone else. "All I can say is I'm sorry. I know that'll never be enough."

Her laughter was void of humor. "How long do you think you can keep this up before you start skipping dinners again, Elliott? Before you're late coming home and quick to leave. Before you start forgetting her birthday, too?" He could feel himself going pale, could hear the demons cackling down deep in the hell of his stomach. "People don't just change overnight. You'll fall back into the same pattern soon enough and she'll be as miserable. I give it a year. Hopefully—"

"Hopefully what?" he pushed through numb lips.

Tabitha sighed. "I would never wish ill on another person, but if this woman actually sees fit to stay here…I hope she knows what she's getting herself into." She hiked the purse higher on her shoulder and slapped a hand down on the door handle. "The last three phone calls my sister made the day she died were to your office, Elliott. And all the messages went unanswered." He didn't have time to recover from the blow of that damning reminder, before she hammered the final nail into his coffin. "I often wonder if she'd still be alive if she called me—or anyone else—instead."

The sound of Alice's bedroom door opening and slamming shut snapped Elliott out of his dark trance. Both adults managed to glue frozen smiles to their faces as she trudged down the hallway, juggling her backpack and cell phone. "Ready."

Elliott gave a stiff nod, everything seeming to move in disjointed starts and stops around him. "Okay. I'll pick you up in the morning."

"I'll drop her off. Have a good night," Tabitha said before walking out the front door, leaving it open for Alice to follow.

Alice stared after her aunt a moment, before turning to Elliott. She slipped her cell into the back pocket of her jeans and leaned in to give him a hug, which he returned, grateful she hadn't deserted him, even though his equilibrium had. "I would wish you luck, but that makes it sound like there's a chance you could screw up."

"Thanks," he managed as they both stepped back. "But I'll take the luck anyway."

She suddenly looked so wise beyond her twelve years. "Do you think maybe…I should go with you? You seem weirder than usual."

He forced himself to smile. "I'm fine. I'll let you know . . . how it goes."

When the door closed, Elliott moved through the hallway like a ghost, finding himself in the living room without any memory of how he'd gotten there. Had he really expected to transform overnight into the man Peggy deserved? To change from the man who'd delayed returning his wife's phone calls so he could watch recruitment videos into a devoted husband to Peggy?

No. Truth was, a man didn't change. Not without time and effort. Not without work and sweat . . . surrendering part of himself.

Inside his pocket, the speech he'd written weighed twenty pounds, words that would now ring hollow. Because he hadn't proven that he could shift his course and be a different man. He hadn't made enough of a sacrifice. And sacrifice meant change.

Was he ready to do what it took?

CHAPTER THIRTY-ONE

Elliott wasn't coming.

That fact had become obvious ten minutes ago, but her stupid heart had maintained its steady beat. The way he'd kissed her last night...people didn't just give kisses like that willy-nilly, did they? Not men like Elliott. That moment outside the Tates' house had been a force of nature, but it was eroding under the landslide of minutes that continued to tick past, the podium empty at the front of the massive auditorium.

Usually, the event was only alumni and their guests, but since Elliott had signed on to make a speech, not to mention the buzz created by the online fund-raiser, ticket sales had gone sky high. Bodies were packed in like sardines against the wall, camera phones at the ready. One of Peggy's fellow ex-cheerleaders was happily acting the host and stalling like a champ, razzing the dean, who sat in the front row absorbing the attention like a sponge. But there was a definite impatience sweeping the room, murmurings beginning to float on the air, and suddenly it seemed as though every member of the alumni committee was staring at Peggy and tapping their wrists.

Last time Elliott had shattered her heart, she'd screamed and broken things and generally launched the fight of the century. This time, it was a very pronounced, but very quiet, shattering. Like someone had laid a towel over her heart and slowly ground their heel down on it, so no one would hear the cracks forming.

As if Belmont and Sage had some kind of Peggy Alarm, they caught her eye as they entered through the back of the auditorium. And they just looked at her. Waiting. Not showing her any sympathy, because they knew her well enough. Knew any kind of coddling would be equivalent to throwing her out of a moving vehicle. But she could see that Belmont was holding the Suburban keys, even if he wasn't being obvious about it. They were inside his curled hand, resting against his thigh.

Peggy glanced back at the podium one more time, wishing she were twenty-two again, so she could storm up there and kick it over onto its side. Scream epithets into the microphone and walk out with her chin up. But she could see those actions now for what they would be—what they had been those years ago—fear. But she wasn't scared anymore. Elliott had deserted her again and she stood there, whole and confident. A Clarkson. Her mother's daughter. The mediator, the bombshell, the liar. And she was fucking good with that.

But that didn't mean there wasn't a smoking crater in the dead center of her chest that would take a long time to repair. Maybe longer than last time.

After whispering a sorry to the alumni organizer to her

right, Peggy began to skirt her way through the packed house, apologizing as she stepped on people's toes—grief was making her clumsy. She kept her attention focused on Belmont and Sage, because really, there was no more comforting sight on the planet, and she was almost there... almost there...

"Good evening."

Elliott's voice halted Peggy in her tracks. Gooseflesh rose on every inch of her skin, her mouth falling open in shock. But she didn't turn around. Couldn't turn to look at him and still keep walking toward the door. It had to be one or the other, didn't it? How could she see him standing there and walk out? How?

You could hear a pin drop in the auditorium as Elliott adjusted the microphone, creating a squeal of feedback. "Sorry," he said, his voice gravel-like. "I don't use these things too often. Usually I just yell."

"And we listen!" one of his players called from a table. The rippling of laughter in the crowd moved through Peggy's middle. Amazing that she could be proud of him for opening with a joke when her heart was hanging in limbo.

Peggy couldn't help but look back over her shoulder as Elliott tweaked his collar and removed a piece of paper from his pocket. The silence grew thick as he stared down at whatever was written in his notes, eventually shoving them back where they came from. "I love a woman," Elliott leaned forward and said into the microphone. "I...love a woman."

A tingling started in the top of her head and rioted down, making her nerve endings pulse. If there had been a free chair nearby, she would have fallen into it, but there was nothing but her trembling legs to hold her up. So she just stood there, like a newborn deer, while the crowd whispered, their heads swiveling around to find the unknown woman the Kingmaker referred to.

"These lights are so damn bright, I can't tell if she's here. Or if she left me again." Elliott narrowed his eyes, his frustration that he couldn't find her in the audience evident, but her hand wouldn't lift to wave, her vocal cords wouldn't do their job. Maybe she didn't want to let him know at all, because he might stop talking and she desperately needed to hear every word.

"I earned this uncertainty, though," Elliott continued. "So I'm going to live with it and hope she's somewhere out there hearing me." Peggy rotated to face the stage fully, not daring to take a breath. "I wrote a speech about seizing the moment and making sure you let your loved ones know how you feel, but all that just makes me sound like a hypocrite. And I won't be a hypocrite on top of a fool." He tapped a fist on the podium, appearing deep in thought. "A fool is the kind of man who pushes away someone who makes him laugh. Makes him think. Makes him want to try harder and love harder and live harder. Live at all. That's what Peggy Clarkson did for me. Twice in my life. Twice more than I earned. And this heart she woke up inside me loves her. It'll beat for her until it stops altogether."

An object shoved at the back of her knees. She prayed it was a chair as she fell into it, encountering the familiar, elusive squeeze of Belmont's hand on her shoulder before it was gone. Emotion gathered in her throat and refused to be swallowed or cleared away. Through the shimmering cloak of tears in her eyes, she absently registered the looks in her direction, coming from several ex-cheerleaders...and Kyler. Kyler was right there, smiling knowingly at a nearby table, but the time it took to notice those things was too long. She needed Elliott.

"I've made some mistakes. With my family. With my Peggy." His possessive way of referring to her earned an ocean of sighs from the women in the room. And an inner one from her, too. "They say the definition of insanity is doing the same thing repeatedly and expecting a different result. So I'm not going to continue as I have been. I'm not going to ask the woman I need in my life to make changes without giving her anything in return. I need her to know I'm real. That I know what's important, and I'm going to fight to make her happy. Harder than I've ever fought to win a football game. Harder than I fought to push her away."

Peggy knew Elliott better than anyone in the room, so she saw the next part coming. Felt it quaking in her stomach as she rose to her feet, shaking her head, unable to allow it. But he barreled right through her silent pleas.

"I'll be taking a leave of absence next season." Elliott's expression didn't change as the room's energy skyrocketed from merely captivated to total shock...and in some cases horrified panic. Cell phones were yanked out of purses, fingers moving in a blur over their keypads, people shouted questions from their tables, and the dean looked like he was going to get sick right there on the floor. "I have a daughter I don't know well enough, and someday, she'll stop caring one way or another. Then there's the matter of the woman I love." He made a gruff sound. "I need to build her happiness into my life and keep it there permanently. I'd trade away every game, every championship, to make that happen. So if she's here—"

"I'm here."

The words tore through her restraint and burst out of her mouth on a shout, earning her the attention of every eye in the auditorium. Except for Elliott, because he clearly couldn't find her through the damn spotlight. Although the confirmation that she hadn't left had him staggering backward, away from the podium, before he lunged forward again. "Baby, I can't see you," he rasped into the microphone. "Let me see you."

Peggy took two steps toward the stage, her heart somewhere up in the clouds, but there was a click in time, audible only to her. A changing from before to after that had her turning around to find Belmont and Sage. But they were no longer standing at the entrance. They were gone. And there was a huge part of her that wanted to run after them, climb into the Suburban, and live in their comfort forever. A much larger portion of her needed Elliott. Beyond words or reason. She'd needed him for so long, and he finally realized he needed her, too. "You'll be all right," she whispered to Belmont and Sage, wherever they were. "You have each other."

And then Peggy turned and weaved her way through the now-standing crowd toward Elliott. A slow clapping started, gaining speed the closer she got to the stage until it sounded like a thunderstorm, bursting in the air around her. Peggy knew the moment she became visible to Elliott because his big chest heaved, the tension in his shoulders falling away. She'd only made it halfway up the stairs when Elliott reached down and hauled her up the remaining way, right into his arms.

"I still loved you when I got here," Peggy breathed into his neck. "I love you now. Forever."

His hold tightened, and this time, when he started reciting a prayer, his heart was in the right place. Knocking against hers in double time. "Enough to marry me, Peggy?" He stepped back and searched her face with eyes full of relief, adoration, and the remnants of possible loss. Then he fell to his knees and removed a ring box from his pants pocket, offering it up to her as the audience whistled and applauded, cell phones flashing.

"Is that why you were late?" She half laughed, half sobbed.

His nod was solemn. "I wasn't showing up here without every single thing you deserve. Marry me, Peggy. Marry...us."

Alice. He meant Alice, too. She wouldn't be marrying just the man. She would be joining a family. She'd be a stepmother. Before Cincinnati, the idea of it might have terrified her, but now she wanted the chance so bad, she couldn't imagine ever having driven away. From either of them. "Does she want me?"

Elliott's face was carved with gravity. "Yes."

Peggy's legs turned to jelly and she went down to the ground, kneeling in front of Elliott...and holding out her finger. "A year off, huh?" she whispered. "What are we going to do?"

He slid the ring onto her finger and crushed her into his embrace, laying a kiss full of promise on her mouth. "We're going to make up for the last three and plan the next thirty."

"Sounds good to me, Coach," she breathed. "That was one amazing speech."

Elliott lifted her into his arms and carried her off the stage. "Get used to them."

EPILOGUE

If Elliott turned around one more time to check for Peggy, his neck was going to get a crick. He'd walked into the middle school auditorium, prepared to find an empty seat without any fanfare, but he'd been ushered to the front row by a student with a cowlick and a blazer. Now the seat beside him was the only empty one in the whole damn house, and Alice's performance was set to begin any minute. Already the lights were dimming in preparation for the curtain to go up, and there was no sign of Peggy.

A fine time for her to be late when he still couldn't believe his own fortune. Maybe he'd imagined carrying her off the stage and the two nights she'd spent sleeping in his bed, having breakfast in his kitchen, riding along with him to drop Alice off at school that very morning. An elaborate dream created as a coping mechanism by his brain because in reality she'd never agreed to stay in Cincinnati and become his wife. That had to be it, right? He couldn't possibly deserve to have the most extraordinary woman on the planet sit beside him in the front row.

"Sorry, excuse me, sorry."

Elliott shot to his feet as Peggy scooted past the other parents in the row, using the sleeve of his dress shirt to dry the sweat on his upper lip. "You're here," Elliott said gruffly, glancing down at the giant bouquet of flowers Peggy was cradling in her arms, but unable to keep his attention off her face for too long. "Lord, you don't stop getting prettier, do you?"

When a scattering of sighs went off around them, Elliott realized he'd spoken out loud. But it was worth the slip when Peggy eyes softened and she did a little twirl, fanning out the edges of her bright green dress. "I knew you'd like this dress because it's the color of a football field. You're too easy, Coach."

"I didn't even notice." A smile twitched his lips as he reached out, sliding a hand around her waist and tugging her close for a kiss. "But now that you mention it..."

She laughed against his mouth. "You're crushing the flowers."

"If buying flowers is why you were late, they better have magical powers." He allowed his nerves to show, because there was no more hiding between them. "I was about to send out a search party."

Sympathy flitted across her expression. "Let's say they do have magical powers. What would you wish for?"

"A thousand years of you," Elliott murmured, rubbing his forehead side to side against Peggy's. "I wouldn't even have to think about it."

"Wish granted," she whispered, sounding a little breathless. "Except for the whole thousand years part."

Elliott dropped into his seat and pulled Peggy down onto

his lap, already knowing they wouldn't be needing the second seat because he wasn't letting go of her for a single damn second. And he didn't give a damn who was watching. When you were granted the love of a woman you, by all rights, should have lost, you didn't pause to worry about any other perception of yourself save hers. "Oh, I don't know," he said into her hair. "If I can get lucky enough to put a ring on your finger, I have to believe anything is possible. Even a thousand years together."

She looked up at him, contentment making her eyes shine. "There's nothing to stop us from trying. Maybe if you want something hard enough, it comes true."

His heartbeat went wilder than any crowd he'd ever heard at his back. "Then consider it done."

A moment later, the curtain went up and Alice took the stage with her cast mates. After delivering the opening line, her voice only shaking a little, she found Peggy and Elliott in the audience and smiled.

* * *

In all forms, change was the enemy. When things changed, there was a domino effect. Belmont could hear the clacking of the tiles now as they tumbled on their newfound course and the earth took a new shape, a new perspective. So he did what he'd grown far too accustomed to doing when a new situation presented itself and gave him no choice but to get on board or lose... something, because there was always something or someone to be lost, wasn't there?

He focused on Sage.

And the clacking ceased and his blood stopped raging to get out of his veins and her scent kicked him in the back of the throat and coasted down, down, down, until it coated his heart and made his bones feel less brittle. He couldn't allow them to be brittle around her because she might have need of them. To lift or carry or fight on her behalf.

Belmont opened his eyes—when did he close them?— and realized he was holding Sage two feet off the ground, her slip of a body wedged between him and the Suburban. His mouth was open on her shoulder, the way it had been doing too often lately, trying to steal a small taste. Anything of her or from her. But even when the catastrophe of change showed up on his doorstep, his mouth didn't dare take that sample. No, even when his brain grew fevered and the dominoes began to fall in their twisting paths, he remembered to keep his goddamn tongue inside his mouth and off the glowing perfection of her skin.

Perfection. What was he doing holding her so close? He could snap her like a twig if he didn't get a grip on himself. Problem was, he couldn't seem to accomplish calm unless they went through this ritual. This ritual of trying to meld their bodies together without crossing the line he'd drawn in the sand for himself. Hold. Cherish. Benefit just enough from her grace to retain normalcy, but not enough to use her or take advantage. God forbid. God forbid anything ever happened to her.

That was just it, though. *He'd* happened to her. His family had tried to downplay the fact that they'd sent for Sage back in New Mexico when he'd started to get a little too restless, making them nervous. And now it was just the two of them. Just him and the woman he alternated between wanting to carry around on a plush pillow and...wanting to use one hand to tear her dress down the center, while the opposite one climbed up her thighs. What did she look and smell and feel like between her legs? Would she smile if he kissed her there? Or be angry?

Stop. Stop. Never happening. Look at him. He was a fucking disaster. Couldn't handle the slightest change to his schedule or the prospect of new, untraveled roads ahead for him and Sage. All the unknowns that could touch her while she was in his keeping. So he rocked her side to side on the Suburban and listened to her summer wind of a voice counting one to ten, one to ten, until he joined her. Their heartbeats began to slow down, like the wing beats of bees that had flown straight into a jar of honey. He'd done heroin a few times trying to cope with the anxiety, and this was what the come down had felt like. Lethargic and awful and beautiful and fleeting and forever. But there had never been Sage on the other side of heroin, the slow motion butterfly of her, dancing on the breeze and beckoning him toward sanity. Sage, Sage, Sage.

"We're okay now," she whispered against his neck, almost collapsing him with the soothing nature of her voice. "We're okay, Belmont."

"Not we," he slurred. "Me. There's nothing not okay about you."

He was grateful for the evening wind hiding his slow, rasping inhales of her scent. "There's a lot of things not okay with me," she murmured, hazel eyes trapping him in their depths. "You just don't want to see them."

"I can't see what isn't there," he insisted.

Her gaze took on a sheen that had premonition prickling the back of his neck. "I have to tell you something you won't like, Belmont. I need you to try and understand."

A circular saw started spinning in the back of his skull, sharpening his denial. She was going to cut him off and he would prolong that forever. Forever. "The way I am might be...wrong in a lot of ways. But the part of me that's right? It would demolish whatever is making you not okay, Sage.

That part of me knows exactly what it's doing. It's just waiting for you to ask. Or signal. Or just..." Dammit, he looked at her mouth, that double-arched upper lip that got chapped faster that her lower one. That one she was always licking when she concentrated. "Tell me what I can give you."

His world suspended itself when she squeezed her eyes shut. There was something. Something was coming. His heart slowed under the anticipation. When the hazel was focused back on him, he almost begged her to put him out of his misery, but his cell phone rang. His cell phone? Couldn't be. He'd recorded an outgoing message letting anyone with salvage business know that he'd be gone until further notice and turned the damn thing off back in California.

No, wait. He'd turned it back on to search local hospitals when he'd thought Sage was sick. "Answer it," Sage said now. "I'll be here when you're done."

"No. Talk to me now."

Sage shook her head. "It could be important. It could be Peggy asking us to wait, or..." She trailed off, both of them knowing his sister was staying put in Cincinnati for good. They'd both seen it in her backbone when she started walking away. "It could be about your father."

Not as important as you. Nothing is important as you. But when Sage tapped his shoulders and wiggled, he had no choice but to set her down or embarrass himself. Sage...wiggling. He distracted himself from the memory of the feeling by taking out his phone. Aaron? His brother? "I'll just..." He answered the phone with a curt "Hold on," before unlocking the Suburban for Sage and locking her inside. Keeping her within sight, he backed up a few paces and pressed the phone to his ear. "Yeah."

"I miss you, too," came Aaron's dry response.

This was when Belmont would usually make an excuse to get out of the conversation as fast as possible. He kept too many secrets from his siblings, withheld so much that when he was around them for any extended period of time, the pressure of those lies by omission pushed at his insides. But there'd been rare moments of ease between him and Aaron back in Iowa, and he wasn't ready to let go of it just yet. He sensed Aaron... needed that ease. And there was a need inside Belmont to provide for his siblings. It just was. "How is everything going?"

He could sense Aaron's surprise on the other end over such a casual question. "Great. Really great. But..." A pencil tapping on wood. "I was calling to see how you're doing."

Belmont narrowed his eyes, and inside the car, Sage's head whipped around, as if she sensed his suspicion through the glass. *What does she need from me?* "Why?"

"Because you're my brother, Bel. I don't need a reason." He didn't answer, just listened to Aaron's energy shift around on the line. "How are things with Sage?"

Back in Iowa, he'd talked to Aaron about Sage because there'd been a sense of urgency building in him since she'd joined them in New Mexico. As if they were heading somewhere other than just New York, and there was a deadline to figure out where and why. And how she could make him feel so much. So damn much. "I don't know," Belmont said slowly, distracted by Sage's distraction, watching her brow furrow in the passenger seat. "I'm just trying to keep from touching her the wrong way."

Aaron was silent a moment. "What's the wrong way, Bel?"

There was no putting the images in his head into words. Not for him. He didn't know how to articulate wanting to make a woman one with his body so bad, he'd barely slept in two weeks. Painfully aware that even if he was allowed that entrance to heaven, he didn't have the experience to know how to please her. Or if he would just throw himself down on her like a beast and forget how delicate she was. "Any way I touch her would be wrong. I'm wrong."

"This. You're wrong about this." Aaron's voice was more patient than he'd ever heard it. An effect of his girlfriend, Grace? Belmont liked Grace. She was just on the other side of normal, but still nowhere near him. "Don't you see the way we all fucking orbit around you? You don't, do you?" A beat passed. "You don't see where this road trip is headed. I've had time. I see it now."

"No, I think there's going to be a detour," Belmont said tonelessly, his gut tightening when Sage once again cast him a sidelong glance. "She's finally going to need me." The wind kicked up around the Suburban and a gentle drizzle started. He'd have to be cautious driving. "Peggy is staying in Cincinnati."

"What?"

Belmont hung up the phone and cut through the dark to the Suburban, climbing into the driver's side. He didn't start the engine right away, and the only sound to be heard was their slow inhales, slower exhales, and the pattering of raindrops. "What was it you needed to tell me?"

"Nothing." Sage laid her palm alongside his cheek. "I was just a mixture of sad and happy over Peggy. It was nothing."

That was the first time she'd ever lied to him.

Embracing the twist in his stomach, Belmont started the engine.

He'd have to be ready to find out why.

Sage Alexander has been in love with Belmont Clarkson since the day they met. But as much as she wants to join him for the rest of his cross-country trip, she's needed at home. She just never expected Belmont to follow her, or to volunteer to face his biggest fears to save her.

Please see the next page for a preview of *Too Beautiful to Break*.

CHAPTER ONE

Shaking Belmont Clarkson wasn't going to be easy for Sage Alexander.

For several reasons.

One, she didn't want to.

To an outsider, the dependency Belmont had on Sage appeared to be one-sided. Over the course of the road trip from San Diego to New York, she had fielded several sympathetic looks lobbed in her direction. To the other Clarkson siblings, none of whom were left in the rattling Suburban as it lumbered down the highway, it probably seemed as if Belmont merely used Sage as a crutch for his anxiety. Every time he teetered a little too close to the edge of his comfort zone, Sage would get bundled up in Belmont's big arms and rocked until he relaxed. They didn't see Sage's need for reassurance, too. They didn't realize she stockpiled those moments in Belmont's arms like a hoarder, memorizing the sensation of being anchored, the feel of his hard chest beneath her cheek, his heart laboring in her ear.

When she was growing up, those moments of solace had been nonexistent, so she'd allowed herself to accept Belmont's. Until now. Now she had to stop. Unfortunately, cutting off the growing dependency they had on each other meant welding shut Belmont's escape hatch...in order to escape herself. And this particular Band-Aid that required ripping off would take ten layers of skin along with it. Right down to the bones he'd invaded.

They were only five miles from the train station now. Five miles to convince Belmont to pull over and leave her there. Continue driving to New York alone.

Sage closed her eyes and went to her happy place. Long, white satin aisle runners, covered in pink and red rose petals. Proud fathers walking their daughters toward the altar, faces freshly shaven. The joyous strains of organ music altering the congregation to stand and marvel over the bride. If she squinted, Sage could see herself in the back hall, clipboard in hand, marking off her checklist.

No more, though. No more fairy tales and flower arrangements and flowing gowns. She had a responsibility to attend to back home. In order to do that, she needed Belmont gone. Panic lifted like an elevator in her sternum, lodging against the base of her throat. Would he be all right? Would *she*? Even since that first wedding she'd planned for Peggy, Sage and Belmont had fed each other's need for contact. Severing it would be like choking off a mighty oak's water supply. There was no other way, though.

If Belmont knew where she was headed...and why...he would go berserk. There would be no calming him down to explain. There would be no talking him out of helping. And she knew Belmont more than anyone. She knew the kind of help she required would kill him.

"Belmont," Sage whispered. "Can you take the next exit, please?"

As always, he'd gone on high alert the second she spoke, hands tightening on the wheel, back straightening. So intense. So much. His energy spun like spiked boomerangs around the Suburban, all of them careful to avoid her. "You're hungry," Belmont said, slowing the vehicle.

"No." She twisted handfuls of her dress in her hands, even though Belmont's eyes were sharp to catch the movement and remain there. "No, I need you to take me to the train station."

Back in Cincinnati, right before they'd left Peggy behind, she'd almost confessed everything. Almost exposed all her skeletons. But the two of them maintained a balance. He'd been too off-kilter after losing his third sibling in a matter of weeks. Hesitating to confess had bought Sage enough time to come to her senses. Thank God. But she couldn't shake the feeling Belmont had been watching, waiting, for this moment. The man saw everything.

Sage just hoped she'd prepared better than him.

Belmont's eye twitched as he pulled off the highway. "What are you doing, Sage?"

She couldn't help but take a moment to appreciate him once more, his brutally powerful silhouette outlined in the sunny driver's side window. If this was the last time she'd see Belmont, she needed an image to bring along. A perfect vision to tuck into her memory and keep safe, where no one could touch or tarnish it. The place she was headed could muddy up almost anything, but it couldn't reach into her mind. She wouldn't allow it. She never had.

Belmont was attractive. Yes. That much was made obvious by the way women got a certain look in their eye as he passed. He evoked a chemical reaction. It started in your stomach, as if he'd tucked his coarse index finger into your belly button and twisted. His height might have made him rangy, if it weren't for all the muscle, honed from hours working on his salvage boat. His skin had an all-weather texture, bashed with salt water and sunshine, but his inner glow kept it from dulling in the slightest. Dark hair skirmished around his face and collar, no style to speak of, but thick and inviting and gorgeous in its disarray. The first time she'd set eyes on Belmont, she'd thought of far-off places. Grassy moors and mist and trench coats. Things she'd never witnessed, but read about in books. He was the only one of his kind. For some reason, he'd chosen her to crowd into corners, to worry about, to beg for eye contact. And now she had to destroy their connection to keep him alive.

"I'm going home," Sage said, forcing her fingers to stop fidgeting. "There's nothing for me in New York. I want to see my family."

"I'll come with you." His voice was calm, but she knew if he turned his head, she'd get burned by the sparks coming from his eyes. "I'll find a place out of your way. You don't have to introduce me to them. I'll just be there if you need me."

Sage shook her head, cursing the red light where they were forced to stop and wait. The longer this took, the more impossible it would become to keep up a front. Already the foundation was cracking. What she wouldn't give to have Belmont come with her when she faced the upcoming test of courage. *God*, what she wouldn't give. "I..." She barricaded herself against the rushing river of guilt. "I need some time away from you, Belmont."

The Suburban rolled forward a few inches, as if he'd lost the power to keep it braked. "I won't ask you why. I already know I've been...needing you so much lately." He said the next part to himself. "I could see it was too much."

It *wasn't* too much. It was exactly what she craved. Which was part of the major issue. "It is. It's too much, the way you rely on me." She rolled her lips inward and tasted the bitterness of her memories, the self-hatred at hurting the man she'd fallen deeply in love with. "My father...he does the same thing to my mother. And vice versa. Depending on one another for support until they have no energy left to worry about themselves. Or desire to accomplish anything. There's no encouragement, only excuses for what *is*." She shook her head. "And I don't want to be like that. I'm not the stuffed animal you can pull off the shelf whenever necessary."

His face was stricken as he turned. "Sage..."

"You don't treat me like a woman." She blurted that genuine insecurity, heaping as much fuel as she could on the fire. "When men hold women, it's usually because they have romantic inclinations. But you drop me and walk away so fast, I feel like a freak sometimes."

Behind them, a car beeped and Belmont applied the gas too hard, jerking the car forward. She'd visibly shocked him, bringing up their physical relationship. Or lack thereof, rather. They must be the only two people on the planet to log hundreds of hours in each other's arms, without kissing even once. She cared about Belmont. She didn't know where his pain originated, but she respected and sympathized with it. Sometimes, she swore they shared a fractured pulse. But she was a red-blooded female and the man treated her like a fellow monk. Intentional or not, it hurt.

Stop. Stop trying to solve problems that won't exist five

minutes from now. The ache in the middle of her chest intensified. "What matters is...it's wearing me out. Not knowing when you'll demand I drop everything to...be held by you. Or calm you down." She resisted the impulse to cover her face. To hide the lies. "I can't do it anymore. You're suffocating me."

By the time she finished speaking, Belmont's hands were shaking on the wheel. Sage turned away so he wouldn't see her misery. So she wouldn't be tempted to demand he stop driving so she could crawl into his lap and beg his forgiveness. "Once we get back to California, I'll get myself back under control. It's just all the change happening." His throat muscles shifted. "I don't do well with change."

"I'm not going back to California."

It was a good thing she'd braced herself, because Belmont slammed on the breaks, skidding the Suburban to a stop mid-avenue. Just a few blocks ahead, she could see the train station. A three-minute walk at best. She just needed to get out of this car and make sure Belmont didn't follow her. Was it even possible? "Sage," Belmont began, his impatience beginning to bleed through. She could almost see his rope fraying through the window of his eyes. "You've been scrapbooking. There's glue all over your fingers. And paper cuts. I *hate* the paper cuts. But I knew I was crowding you, so I didn't pull over and bandage them. Even though that's all I've wanted to do for the last two hundred miles."

Would she ever breathe again without experiencing the sharp pain in her side? "What does this have to do with anything?"

"Because you only scrapbook when something isn't right." He ignored the cars honking as they were forced to pass in the opposite lane. She barely registered them, too, because Belmont was hypnotic, his every feature imploring her, his voice resonating deep inside her mind. "Just come over here and whisper it in my ear. I'll stand between you and whatever it is. I'll make up for being so greedy with your time. I will. Nothing touches Sage while I'm around."

Don't break. Don't break yet. "There is nothing *wrong*. Except for your...reliance on me. I need to go somewhere I won't be smothered every minute of the day." She touched the door handle and he jolted, blue eyes fixating on that signal she'd be leaving. "Go to New York, Belmont. Meet your sisters and Aaron on the beach for New Year's Day, like your mother wanted. I'm not your worry. I never was."

"You can take yourself away from me, but you can't take away the worry." His tone was concrete, unbreakable. "Don't try. I covet my right to fear for every hair on your head."

"I never asked you to," she half sobbed, half whispered.

"You *did*." He reached across the console, his fingers hovering just above her thigh, branding the skin beneath her dress. "Your heart asked mine. And mine was already begging."

"Stop," Sage pushed through clenched teeth. "Just stop. Can't you see how...how *confusing* and forward every word out of your mouth sounds?" Acid rose in the back of her throat as she laid the final nail in the coffin. The one that would keep him sitting in the Suburban while she fled and saved his soul. "Whatever you feel, Belmont, it's not the same for me. I've tried to help you because Peggy is my best friend, and she loves you. But you're not good for me. You're stopping me from living a normal, happy life."

The color drained right out of his face. "I'm sorry, Sage." Slowly, he took back his hand, stealing back the blessed warmth along with it. "Go. You have to go."

Now, of course, she couldn't manage so much as a blink,

fear over being parted from Belmont stabbing her in the back. "Okay. I'm going."

"Will you..." His voice had gone from robust to deadened. "Check in with Peggy, please. At least check in with Peggy. And bandage those cuts."

"Yes," Sage breathed, scrambling to get out of the car. She saw nothing, heard only the wind rushing in her ears as she staggered to the back door. Retrieving her luggage was the easy part. It was passing the front window again without glancing inside that presented the challenge. In the end, she couldn't manage it.

So the final time she saw Belmont, a war took place behind his eyes. And both sides were losing.

"You're doing the right thing." Her breath hitched, suitcase wheels catching on a sidewalk crack. "You're doing the right thing."

Sometimes the right thing was the most painful. Sometimes it gutted you and ruined you forever, so that not a single second would pass without a reminder.

Sage knew that lesson all too well.

© Nisha Ver Helen

New York Times bestselling author **Tessa Bailey** can solve all problems except for her own, so she focuses those efforts on stubborn, fictional blue-collar men and loyal, lovable heroines. She lives on Long Island avoiding the sun and social interactions, then wonders why no one has called. Dubbed the "Michelangelo of dirty talk" by *Entertainment Weekly*, Tessa writes with spice, spirit, swoon, and a guaranteed happily ever after. Catch her on TikTok at @authortessabailey or check out tessabailey.com for a complete list of books.

You can learn more at:
 TessaBailey.com
 Facebook.com/TessaBaileyAuthor
 Instagram @TessaBaileyIsanAuthor
 TikTok @AuthorTessaBailey